Melissa's Daughters

Also by Terry Leeder

The Iron People

A Fighting Lady

The Long Sault

The Great River

The Soldier's Son

Pioneer Among the Mountains

White Forehead of the Cypress Hills

Daughter of the Old Pioneer

Brand 9999

Canadians in a Far Country

Melissa's Daughters

by

Terry Leeder

iUniverse, Inc.
Bloomington

Melissa's Daughters

iUniverse books may be ordered through booksellers or by contacting:

iUniverse
1663 Liberty Drive
Bloomington, IN 47403
www.iuniverse.com
1-800-Authors (1-800-288-4677)

ISBN: 978-1-4620-0777-6 (sc)
ISBN: 978-1-4620-0778-3 (ebook)

Printed in the United States of America

iUniverse rev. date: 4/26/2011

Contents

Melissa's Version

1

He's sitting on a big oblong rock by the side of the trail and his bike is lying sideways with its front wheel turned up and the handlebar hooked on the edge of the rock, like it's a dead dog or something.

He's leaning forward with his feet apart and rubbing the calf muscle of his right leg. It must be thirty one Celsius. Sweat is dripping from his chin and falls off on the white gravel beside the rock. I brake and put my feet down, lean the bike a bit, take out my water bottle, tilt it up, take a long drink – and look down at him. He's stopped massaging his calf muscle, but he's still panting. How long has he been here?

"Do you want some water?" He shakes his head and leans forward with his arms resting on his upper thighs. "Do you feel sick?" I ask. I don't feel sorry, I told him not to push it. He kept lagging behind and when I turned around, he wasn't following. I came back and here he is. He won't admit he's getting old. Fifty and he doesn't think he's getting old.

He's still leaning forward on his rock and shakes his head like a damn marathon runner at the end of the race, disappointed with his results.

"Take a bit of water," I suggest and lean on my handlebars and push the bottle in his right hand. He sits holding it, leaning on his arms, panting.

"You'll give yourself a heart attack."

He shakes his head again. It's hot and he shouldn't be sitting in the sun like this. Highway Fourteen is right behind him, over an artificial hill they've built all the way along the side of the bicycle trail. There are half-built houses along the trail, nobody's working, it's Sunday. The houses are one room wide, houses for thin people, really thin people. At the back of each one is an ugly little building that's supposed to be a garage. There's tire tracks in mud on the bicycle path, they'll have to put down more gravel. A little curved footbridge behind me, wood along the railings, the steel parts are rusted already. Three big chunky rocks with flat tops, just this side of the bridge, and Stan is sitting on one of them. The ridiculous thing is, the bridge leads to nothing, there's dried brown clay all rutted on the other side, and unfinished houses. The path I took turns right and runs away from the bridge beside the berm beside the highway. He tried to make the turn and went over.

The top of a large white transport trailer goes sliding by on the highway. Hardly any traffic today. It's quiet. Across the highway up a slope is a field with yellow-brown rolls of hay as high as a man, and a farm lane with a wire fence on each side and a diseased tree half way along the drive and an old pink-colored brick house at the end with an inverted V above its front door and white cream brick in a line just below the roofline and down along both sides of the facade.

At one time, Stan seriously considered buying that place. At least, I assume that's the one. He told me he'd take me on some dumb path where you could see an old house and a farm he had thought of buying. Right now he can't talk, so I don't know if this is the thing he was talking about or not. He's always talking. It looks like what he'd do, though. Like the latest place he bought and that one doesn't even have a house, just some weeds and a big hole in the ground and a ratty little barn, I can't believe the price he paid.

I walk my bike up the bridge and lean it carefully on the steel railing, and come back and pick up Stan's dead dog, and lean it on the other rail. Then I go back and sit beside him. "Take some water."

He doesn't move.

"Take some water or give me back my bottle."

He leans back, puts the nipple of the bottle opposite his mouth and squirts.

"Not too much," I tell him.

I shouldn't be sharing my water. He's got a bottle of his own. I wipe his forehead and his face and he hands me back the bottle and says thanks.

There's no shade anywhere. We'll have to turn back. The trail was packed down and finished until just before we reached the bridge, here it's loose and rutted. The developer has leveled fields and taken out big trees and packed in houses and planted little sticks that will be trees in twenty five years and not much good until then. The trail we came up went through a dry marsh or a sort of grassy area, no trees there.

"You can't push yourself, Stan." I go to the rack on my bike, release a blue towel I usually carry, pour some water on it, come back and sit down beside him again. He puts his hand on my upper thigh. His palm is clammy, but he likes to feel my leg so I let him leave it there. He lifts his face so I can wipe it with the towel.

"Good," he says.

"You'll give yourself a heart attack."

Yesterday he went running for two hours and came back limping. He should be resting at home today, but no, he had to take me for a bike ride.

I wet the towel again, wipe his neck, squeeze the cloth and let the water run down underneath his shirt.

"Better?" He nods. "I told you not to do this." I wring the towel, fold it and put it back on the carrier, above the back wheel of my bike.

"We can coast back," he says. "The way we came."

"That's good." I sit beside him.

I'm rested. We could go across the berm, there's a wide shoulder along the highway heading west, we could go toward those hills over there, the escarpment. Me, I'm ready to go again, I'm good for another three hours, I love this, it makes me feel good, it clears all the poisons.

And Stan, Stan is red-faced and bagged out. He takes his hand from my leg and leans forward on his arms.

"We need to make a deal, Stan." He stares at the gravel. "Stan?"

He grunts.

"No showing off. I won't be your nursemaid."

He nods.

"If you want a nursemaid, find someone else. I am not going to be your nursemaid."

He nods, still staring at the gravel.

I have to start think about the house, seriously. The carpet in the den is really nice, it's deep pile, it's real good to walk on, and it's pretty new. But the carpet in the living room has to go, I hate the color, a sick off-green that makes me feel like throwing up. The chandelier in the dining room is gone. We could use a new stove and fridge, they don't cost all that much, and for sure we'd save on electricity, and that'll more than pay for replacement. White is okay, but why not something matching, and while we're at it, repaint the kitchen and maybe tear up the congoleum and put in some tile. Tile isn't all that expensive, maybe there's something reasonable in marble, it's easier to take care of and looks good.

We'll have to have some parties, Stan and me, to show the place off, once we've fixed things up. Stan won't like it much, he's all into saving, pretending he's poor, talking like he's starving himself to death. As far as I'm concerned, what's the point, if you don't fix it up, pretty soon you won't have it to show. So we're fixing it up.

I love the den, that I won't change, the windows, the backyard, the bar, the built-in TV, all that dark wood. Except for one thing, the war collection, that has to go. Guns and medals and a sword and a live grenade for godsake and a wicked looking saw-edge knife that you clamp on the end of a gun barrel, it can rip a man apart, Stan says like he'd love to see it happen, a long wide wicked looking blade, black tempered-steel with that saw edge, something dark and evil that reminds me of Marshall, that look on his face, god what he'd do if he got that thing. That whole thing has to go, guns swords glass case everything. It's sick. No wonder Stan's wife left him.

And now he sits here, a tired old man, staring at the gravel. There's bits of white stone partly imbedded on his right knee. I brush them off.

"We could go somewhere," he says. Right now he doesn't look like he's ready to go anywhere, if anything he's worse than he was five minutes ago. "Hawaii. Something," he takes a breath, "like that."

"We can afford it?"

He smiles at the "we," he likes the idea I'm talking "we." "Got some mutual funds," he says. I thought I knew his investments. What else is there?

"Hawaii would be nice," I'm trying to be positive here, snap him out of it. He doesn't offer any more information, I'll find out later, after sex or something.

Neither of us moves. He's much more tired than he admits, I don't think he's ready to go yet.

He scared me, I saw him sitting here slumped over like he'd had a heart attack or something and I thought, oh my god, how will I get an ambulance out here? I put my hand on his chest. His breathing is still too fast and his chest feels spongy or something, not like Marshall's.

"I told you what the doctor said," I tell him, making conversation, and slide my hand inside his shirt.

He grunts.

"When I went in?"

"You didn't tell me anything." A complete sentence. What's he got to be resentful for? I don't have to tell him this.

"I told you, Stan. Don't you remember, I told you I'm okay, he wants to see me back in a month or so. Don't you remember?" He says nothing. "I'm not pregnant."

He slumps over a bit more, the old fool thinks I meant him.

"From that guy," I explain.

"Oh." Now he sounds disappointed, it's kind of touching, in a dumb kind of way, he really thinks there's a chance, like I'm too stupid to take precautions.

"One thing you have to admit, though," I keep rubbing his chest, he loves the feel of my hand on his chest, "There's one thing you have to admit, Stan."

"What's that?" He straightens up a bit, he sounds better now, his voice is stronger, when I stop rubbing I can feel his heartbeat, it seems to be getting slow and regular, gradually, his breathing is evening out.

"I haven't mentioned Noreen once -- have I?" He doesn't answer. "Not once." He still doesn't answer. "Have I?"

He shakes his head.

"Should I have?" Rubbing his chest, rubbing his chest, he's getting better, this seems to be doing some good.

No answer.

"Should I have?" I lean forward, turn my head and gaze up at him. "Should I have mentioned Noreen?"

He looks down at me, not sure how to figure me out.

"I haven't mentioned Noreen once."

I wish she'd paddle out on that lake of hers and disappear.
And bob up three weeks later, bloated and stinking.

2

She's back. I've had two weeks of peace. As much as I'm entitled to, I guess.

Morning.

I don't feel like going.

I'm tired, trying to satisfy an old man, if it wasn't for this house. I'm even getting tired of that.

How do I get myself into these things?

I turn the TV up high and he goes to his desk upstairs. He doesn't care, it's more important than I am.

When he comes back he takes the channel changer. "I'd like to go through this," he says.

And hands me a list, and explains who the people are he wants me to meet downtown and the searches I have to make, and I go to the kitchen and get a notepad he keeps there and come back and make notes as he goes through the things, and by the end, he's relaxed, and I put my notes in the file folder with his list and he sets it on the floor and puts his right arm around me.

"This is important to me," he says.

"I know."

"I mean my investments. My lot." I turn on the TV, he takes the channel changer and turns it off. "I want you to understand that, okay, it's nothing personal."

"I understand. You want me to go downtown so you're free to meet Noreen."

He shakes my shoulder. "You're like a board. Holding you is like holding a two by four." He's smirking. He wants me to think it's all a joke. "All rigid."

"I don't mean anything. I understand that."

"You mean a lot to me. A hell of a lot."

It's quiet, there's no wind out, sometimes when there's wind you can hear the trees blowing and it sounds so lonely, it's quiet in here now. I scratch his shirt and the sound is funny.

"I almost lost it," he says. "When I think about it."

"Yeah."

"I owed everybody. This was just after I got fired. They didn't say that, of course. Early retirement. Stan's tired of the rat race, he's retiring early. Lucky Stan." He pushes me over and undoes my jeans and puts his middle finger inside me. I don't smile, I stare at him like a serious little child. "I can't believe what I've got," he says. "It's too damn perfect."

"I don't want to," I say, but I let him work me and I don't feel a thing, I imagine I'm on the ceiling looking down, watching this like it isn't happening to me, like it's happening to someone else, someone I don't like too much.

"It's nothing personal," he says, "I want you to understand that, she's just a partner, I'm with the person I want to be with right now, it's no contest." He puts himself inside me and I stare at him I don't smile I just stare it's quiet no wind totally quiet the drapes are open he hasn't thought about the drapes. "I sort of went bankrupt, you know that," he breathes, I don't answer. "I thought I was right down the tubes," he keeps running his hands up and down my body and he gets excited and I let him go on, so he's satisfied, and I watch like I'm seven feet above us, looking down from the ceiling, watching everything, seeing him go crazy, hearing him saying all the humping bumping thumping words that get him all excited, it gets him so damn excited all those stupid words, he is so pathetic, I look to my right, lying here, the man in the house behind us is staring at us, and I stare back, and Stan keeps saying, "I don't care, I don't care," as if he's trying to convince himself, and when he's done, he won't look at me, and he says, "Are you okay? I didn't hurt you, did I? Is your cut okay?"

He looks at my bandage, where I tried to cut Marshall's name from my tattoo, gets up and closes the drapes. The man has gone and I don't know if Stan knows he was watching us, but he's acting so stupid, like he does know.

"I used to make jokes about guys like me," he says, and comes back and lies down beside me and puts his arms around me again. "Old guys with young girls."

He hopes I'll deny it. Why should I, I'm nineteen, he's over fifty, he thinks I can't count or something.

He won't look at me.

He backs out the driveway with his right arm over the seat and his neck stuck out, and his left hand manipulating the steering wheel and whirling it at the end of the driveway and when he brakes,

he turns and looks ahead and our eyes cross for a split second but he won't meet my stare, and he knows I'm still staring at him

but he says nothing and looks ahead,

I watch him and when he reaches the corner he flashes a glance to his right, right at me and won't stay there and looks the other way and almost hits a car

the other driver blares his horn but Stan doesn't say anything

we stop at the traffic lights,

I remember this place and the bus stop down there, the night I walked out and he didn't come and get me and I had to ride all the way home and I was scared, he drums his fingers on the steering wheel, I turn away and look ahead

if he's ignoring me, well

me too.

"Do what you can today," he says. "If you don't get it all done..."

He drums. I stare.

"As long as you meet some people."

The light is still red, he leans forward and looks up as if it will turn green because he's looking at it, as if he can figure out why it's taking so long, as if he can see something up there that will tell him when the light's changing.

"Do you think they're stuck?"

He's trying to get me to say something, so he can convince himself it's okay.

The light turns.

"God!"

He shouts.

He turns left and we go down Warwick.

The traffic is heavy and a jointed bus pulls out from the stop. He's got the air conditioning on, I roll the window down, it's tepid out, clammy, he doesn't say anything and I leave it down. The bus roars beside us and we stop in the passing lane and the right lane goes on and the bus passes and sticky diesel fumes up the car. I roll the window up.

"God that's awful," he says.

He checks the side mirrors and pulls into the right lane and we stop and the left lane goes by us.

"Come on, come on," he says to the bus up front, stopped to let on passengers.

He turns right at the next light and we go along a two lane street and turn left on Jefferson, it's faster.

Instead of letting me off in front of the doors of the GO train station he pulls into a taxi stand. "I've got something for you," he says. He takes my right hand and holds the second last finger and gets a ring out of his shirt pocket. It has a tiny sort of basket openwork and three green stones.

"This is some kind of family heirloom, I've been told," he says.

I pull my hand back.

"It's a gift, you can have it, no strings attached. Me to you. A gift."

I fold my arms and hide my hands inside my elbows.

"No strings."

I shake my head and turn toward the window and a freight train with three big red and black engines in front grumbles by on the track half way up above us and I stare at the big steel boxes as they pass by, and then black open frameworks with cars inside and more big boxes with peepholes stuck through the sides, a car somewhere behind us blows its horn.

"I wish you'd take it," he says, and the wheels of the freight cars squeal and I shake my head. A car horn blows again and he leans over and opens my door and I get out and he hands me my briefcase with the shoulder strap and zips open a side pocket and drops the ring in.

"You can give it back tonight if you don't change your mind," he says.

I stare at him and then start to walk away.

"Melissa!" he calls and I turn and come back and look down at him like a child being called before its teacher. "We could drive each other crazy if we're not careful," he says.

"Is that all?"

He nods.

I walk away and drop the ticket he gave me in the turnstile box and walk under the rumble of the freight train it sounds like a steel avalanche above me and come up the stairs to the platform, I can see his car going off up the road that leads away from the station and he waits at the light and three buses make a left turn in front of him and come up the road towards the station, he sits there in the right hand lane and the red in the light looks bland and dim in the sunlight, and I can make out his head above the neck rest and he stays sitting there, though he could turn right and the three cars behind him are all wondering, probably, why he doesn't, and then the light turns and he does.

I unzip the pocket and take out the ring.

It looks old.

The stones are small.

Emeralds.

I don't know if that's my birthstone, I've never bothered, I doubt if it means anything anyway, just some stupid ring his wife left.

It's quieter and I look to my right and the back end of the last freight car goes away with a light below on the coupler flashing at me.

I don't know why I'm going.

He must have thought I'd just agree to it and not say anything and now he's trying to make it up, when it's too late, I put my hand with the ring in the briefcase pocket and reach down to the bottom and drop the ring in a corner where it's safe, I have to remember it's there.

It's really bright out. It's going to get really hot. The last week of August.

The train comes and I get on. A guy about thirty-five, wedding ring, tries to get friendly as I go along the aisle, I pretend I'm sitting down, he takes the seat across the aisle and I go on and take a seat at the other end of the coach.

The world moves. Streets that end and old cars parked against a fence and drab houses with peaked roofs with painted shingles in the front in inverted V's above the porches, and mud lanes back of one storey brick warehouses and four tall stacks sliding by above moving roofs and a few trees and the rush of the stones by the rails and roofs of cars and trucks underneath a bridge flicking by as we go by above them, and the end of the freight train starting by the window as we catch up and pass it, blocking everything else and me getting farther away and I feel so used.

I look down the aisle.

There's people standing at the end where the steps go down to the doors and the trains rocks,

I'm always worried it'll tip over,

two stories like this or whatever they call it,

some kind of green double decker,

at the station,

we walk along the sides of long lines of trains and go down greasy stairs and in a wide bright tunnel,

I remember when the trains crashed people waited while the crews brought the passengers out on stretchers,

I wonder what they thought as they waited for their trains and the crews brought out passengers on stretchers with needles and tubes in their arms,

they just waited, that's what gets me, and the people on subway platforms getting pushed,

that girl who died when some crazy guy really sick a mental case shoved her, a total stranger, and the train ran over, sliced her up like a cucumber or something, in chunks, ever since I stand with my back against the wall of the subway and I kind of feel like

that, and I wonder if Stan's at work, still, or are they going off looking at his lot, working out

their plans, they've got the whole day, Melissa is, I was such a fool, I don't

know why, I'm always trying to please, and I really thought

Stan, but you don't know about people, you can never trust,

in the meantime, I've got to think about my job, and exactly what to do today and I'll see when I get there at the Registry with the two floors Toronto and outlying and

figure out, when I get home, if he's

there what I'll say, how I'll act, it hurts more than I thought it would, right now what they're doing I know I didn't think it

would hurt so much

I spend all day talking to his clients, trying to calm them down, they're angry, I'm sure he's losing some, I do what I can. He's losing his grip, they say. I do what I can, so he won't try to blame me, and make sure that I go through his list, so it's done and he'll know I'm still worth it. I'm feeling insecure.

And it takes an hour and a half, getting home, and it's six thirty and there's no-one, he's off with Noreen,

somewhere about the lot, something he wouldn't tell me, I get some dinner, and when it's seven fifteen and he's still not home, and

finally, I call, wondering if her father's there or what, and she answers

"Hi Shelley."

There's silence for a second or so.

"I'm not supposed to talk to you," she says.

I laugh.

"How come, Shelley?" I'm relaxed, more than I thought. I can laugh.

"I don't know," she says.

"Where's your Mom?" She doesn't answer. "With Stan, right."

"Yeah." We don't say anything for a minute. From the way she's been talking, the tone of her voice, I figure she's wondering.

"You know I'm living with him?"

"I know," she says.

"She told you? Your Mom?"

"They said at the Registry." She was at the Registry? "They're all talking about it. Making jokes."

"What jokes?"

"His age. Stuff."

"People can't mind their own business, you know that." She doesn't comment. "Did you mother say what this meeting was all about? This meeting they're supposed to be at?"

"Something about a house or something."

"Yeah, right. You believe that, right?" She doesn't say anything. "You believe that, right?"

"She said," she starts but doesn't finish. I really think the little fool believes that.

"Yeah, well all I know is he got all dressed up this morning, and I haven't seen him all day, I've been downtown all day. And I don't know when he's coming home either." I stop and give her a chance to say something, but she doesn't. "This is crap, you know that, I mean this is crap, I'm gone, I'm out of here." She listens, I've got her attention. "She can have him. You can tell her I said that."

"What?"

"They're fucking," I say, and wham down the phone.

3

We're half an hour late and as soon as we walk in the Registry, I go straight to our desk and unpack the briefcases and get us set up, and Stan's already at Noreen's desk, giving her a big kiss in front of everybody, and I see her for a second, four aisles over, glaring at me like she wants to cut my throat, and then Stan moves closer and blocks the view. After a minute they both get up and walk out, all the way across the front, neither of them looking at me, she's walking on the other side of him he's blocking my view entirely and leaning over listening to her, he looks taller than he is, it's just she's so short, and all the time they're gone, I'm working my ass off, and I've already got three searches done and written up and put away in the file folder, and stacked in the completed pile by the time he comes back and turns down the aisle, coming towards me and she continues to her own aisle, marching like some kind of Nazi stormtrooper or Hell's Angels biker. I smile and really feel warm when he sits down and I whisper, "Hi." My headache's better, more than half gone.

He glares, flicks his eyes down like I'm supposed to be ashamed of something, but I don't react as I'm supposed to, that is lower my eyes and act like his slave, instead I keep staring and I search his eyes when he looks at the ceiling, they're fixed, titanium eyes, all surface, no softness. "What's wrong?" I ask. He doesn't answer, he gives me no reaction at all, and turns away and opens his briefcase, which I've placed at the back of the desk like he wants it, and pulls out a handful of files and won't look at me.

"What's wrong, Stan?"

I want to know, but he doesn't have the decency to say anything. I've still got a headache, but I've been working hard, trying to get his work done, and all he can do is harass me.

And he stays like that, all morning. He refuses to answer, anything he wants he just reaches and takes, when he gets up to copy things, he won't ask if there's anything he can do for me, but when I get up to do my copying, I ask if there's anything he wants, I'm damned if I'm acting like he does, and he hands me his stuff without a word, and when I come back and hand him the copies and he won't say a thing, I say, "You're welcome!"

And the bastard turns away.

For some reason I'm being punished, and at eleven he gets up and snaps shut his briefcase.

"Going to Toronto?" I ask, kind of abruptly because now he is irritating me.

He nods.

"Do you want to know what I did yesterday?" No answer. He loves not answering, he's good at that. "You never asked me last night."

He shakes his head.

"I guess you can figure it out, right? You don't need me right? To tell you what to do, right."

He turns and goes off and I'm left here wondering, is he coming back tonight, do I have a ride home -- what?

And the headache stays with me, coming and going, throbbing so bad that sometimes I have to stop reading and lean my head back and beg it to go away. And Noreen stays, all day, at her regular desk, I can hear her, as if nothing's wrong, as if I didn't exist, and every time I look up, there she is, talking loud and laughing, with everybody that I know, up at the front at the documents counter, getting out some transfers, over at the phones, demanding to know when some client's showing up, chatting it up with everybody, causing me just as much possible trouble as she can.

And the florescent lights, rows of them, glaring, painful like squirming shots of laser beams, blaring like sound turned up as high as it can. If it wouldn't look stupid I'd wear sunglasses. And Noreen, talking, laughing, everywhere I look, all day.

He shows up, just before closing. I've eaten 222s all day, my headache's better. He won't talk.

"What's the weather like?" I ask.

"Hot."

But I won't be put down, so I chatter as if nothing's wrong and follow him to the car, and laugh about something my friend Linda said and tell him all the funny things that happened while he wasn't there and finally, when I put my briefcases in the trunk and he slams the trunk closed and walks off to the driver's side, I just stand there.

"You almost slammed it on my hand!"

He ignores that and unlocks the doors and I can hear the latches snap up and he gets in and slams the driver's side, and I stand there, at the back, right behind the car, daring him to back up and run me over.

I stand there, and he sits there and I won't move, and finally, when he sees I'm not budging, he gets out and stands outside the car facing back at me, with the driver's door open, and says, "Will you get in the damn car."

"Not until you tell me what's wrong."

"Not here."

"What's wrong?"

"I'll tell you at home."

He comes around to the back and stands at the corner of the trunk, and I remain in the middle of the car where he can back up right over me. "Will you get the hell in the car." He says it low, he'd like to

15

shout, but not here, not with everybody looking over at us, waiting for something to happen.

"No."

He goes back and gets in the car and turns on the radio, I know this because the aerial whines and scrolls up and I can hear the music and he tilts the seat back. So I come around and open the door on my side, get in, and slam it.

He tilts the seat up, starts the car, and drives off.

"What did she tell you?" I ask.

He won't answer.

This is getting to me.

"What did that bitch tell you?"

He comes to a halt at the stop sign where the drive to the Registry meets the street and touches the brakes too hard and the car rocks forward.

"That whore is making trouble again. – Isn't she?" Even that won't get an answer.

He starts off too fast and the tires squeal and he swings around the corner too hard and he has to correct or we'll wind up on the curb and we swerve back to the right and brake at the light at Highway Nine.

"You are an ass," I conclude. Still he won't say anything. "She's a liar, Stan. You know that. I just want to find out what lies she's told you now. That's all. That's not asking very much, is it? To want to know what lies she's told about me now." I'm being calm, I'm under control. "Answer me!" I shout that. I'm not as controlled as I thought, I guess.

Nothing.

"Answer me!!!" I scream it this time.

Nothing.

That's all I'll say. My voice is hoarse and he's got to me and I didn't want this to happen. If I lose control, I've lost.

So, what it boils down to, if he doesn't like it, he knows what he can do. I turn the radio up full blast. My headache starts again. I don't care.

Just before we reach the base of the driveway, I push the button to raise the garage door and he goes up the driveway slowly enough so by the time we reach the door it's almost at the top of its winding and he drives straight in. He releases the catch for the trunk and I can hear the lock pop and when I get out and go to the back of the car there's a space between the lock and the edge of the trunk door and I lift it and take out my briefcases, and in the meantime he's brought his own from the back seat and has a cream cardigan draped across his arm, in weather like this, and locks the car doors and pushes the button just inside the garage, and the electric motor lowers the door section by section, I watch them turn over and come down one after the other, jointed together, for some reason it fascinates me, the way it does that and he goes ahead and unlocks the front door and when the motor cuts off and his precious Chrysler is shut away for the night I come in and close the front door, which he's left open for me. It's so hot, I'm sweating, just from that short time outside, and my head feels stuffy and the headache is there, at the back of my head, waiting, low key like a motor idling. He sets the cardigan down on the top of his briefcase, which he's put at the base of the stairs leading to the second floor.

"How come you took your sweater?" I ask. "Wasn't it too hot downtown?"

He goes to the kitchen. He won't even let me make polite conversation.

I put my two briefcases beside his single one, snuggled right up against it, and come to the kitchen.

"Could I have some coffee too?" I ask, because he's only got out one mug.

He takes down another, and puts instant in both.

"I think we've got some muffins, haven't we?" I ask, and open the fridge and take out a package with a hole in the cellophane where I'd pulled out the muffins in the morning and couldn't eat. There's two left in the package. He took all the rest.

"Do you want a muffin?"

"Could we have a talk after supper?" he says and plugs in the kettle.

"Aren't you going to talk until then?" I ask brightly, and my headache lurks, and I take down a couple of plates and put a muffin on each and put them in the microwave and push Sensor Reheat. "Do you want yours buttered?"

"Please."

He stands there looking at the kettle. He doesn't want to fight.

"I guess I'll have to get used to your moods, won't I?" I go on. "You've only said two words all this time. It's not very pleasant. Maybe we should sleep in separate beds tonight. The only thing I don't like about that is, it's dusty upstairs. I'll cough all night. You'll probably hear me up there. Coughing."

He mumbles something in reply, "Umm," or something.

"I guess when we've been living together twenty five years or something I'll get used to your moods. But you'll have to get used to my moods too, won't you?"

I pause.

"Won't you?"

"We'll talk after dinner."

"Yes, your majesty." I could shout but I don't, I've been really controlled and I'm proud of myself.

He turns and looks straight at me, his eyes are moist and sad looking, he really seems sorry for me, there's a lot of caring in his eyes, and that surprises me, I hadn't expected that reaction. "Please," he says, really quietly.

I step up to him and stand on my toes and kiss his cheek, like he's my daddy. "Okay." I smile, but he doesn't, he's still so sad. But there's no hatred or anything in his eyes, no anger, not any more.

I put my arms around him and press my body against him, he really is tall. "How come you were so mad at me?" I can feel his penis activating.

"After supper, please." he says, but he doesn't tell me to go away, it feels too good.

"Mmmmm," I say. He loves that, the little animal hum, the kind of contented cat purr with a suggestion of raunchy.

He takes my shoulders and pushes me partly away and looks down, his eyes are really sad. "We have to have a serious conversation."

"Okay," I answer brightly, with the big smile he really loves, he almost smiles now. "I love talking to you, Stan. You know that." I go to the microwave and get out the muffins and take them to the table and sit down and start eating mine. He comes over and takes his, and I reach over and take his free hand and pull him down in the chair beside me and he can't help smiling. "It's not so serious," I say. "We can work it out."

His smile vanishes. "Let's have supper first."

"I hated it when you wouldn't talk to me." The bitch has got to him. He's clamming up again. But once he's had something to eat, he'll feel better. He's had a long day. He's hungry.

He suggests we have coffee in the den. I carry the cups and the pot on a tray, and he follows with cream and sugar. "Do you want me to put something extra in that?" he asks as I put the tray on a footstool near the sofa chair and he sets down the sugar bowl and the creamer beside the coffee pot.

"Sure," I grin at him. "Why not?"

He goes to the bar and brings back some rye and pours about a jigger in each cup and I pour in the coffee, cream and sugar. He sets the bottle on the tray, I sit back on the sofa and he comes around the coffee table and sets himself down. I hand him his cup. We arrange ourselves at each end of the sofa against the cushions and drink and stare at each other, me trying to figure out what he's going to say to start this, and him deciding how he's going to do it. "This is good," I tell him.

The curtains are open. There's a small tree near the house outside the kitchen window, and a larger tree at the back of his yard that you can see from the den. The windows are full of tree, floor to ceiling. A squirrel is searching around in the grass, lifting his tail in an arch like an eyebrow. It's a little after seven, it's still sunny but the shadows are darker. At this time of day the big tree shades the whole back yard. The grass is thin about ten feet out from the trunk and almost gone at the base.

"I talked to Noreen today," he says.

"Don't you always?"

I smile and sip coffee.

He doesn't smile.

"What did you tell Shelley?" he asks.

"What do you mean?"

"What I said."

"I wasn't talking to Shelley."

I smile.

"I'd like to know what you said to her," he says, as if I hadn't just denied I was talking to her. "I want to hear your side."

"My side of what?"

"What you said to Shelley."

"I told you I wasn't talking to Shelley."

We're talking in a normal tone of voice, we're relaxing after dinner, it's the end of a long day, and we should be happy and satisfied, I've done more for this guy today than three people put together, and that's not counting after work, and besides that, I care for him, I really do, I love him, he has to know that, I've showed that, I don't have to do this, I volunteered, so why is he cross-examining me like I'm a criminal?

"I'd like to hear your side." He sets down his cup.

"Do you want some more?" I reach over and pick up the coffee pot and he holds out his cup. I pour the coffee, then the rye, then the cream, then the sugar.

"Thanks." He puts his cup on the tray.

"You shouldn't drink so fast," I say.

I pick up my cup again. I'm only half finished my first round.

"It's better when you let it trickle down your throat," I tell him. "Right? Isn't that what you said? You can feel it all the way down. It's wonderful." My smile is lazy and warm.

"Did you tell Shelley I was fucking her mother?"

"No."

"That's what she told Noreen."

"She's lying."

"Noreen was upset."

"I don't blame her. That's coarse, to say something like that to a twelve year old girl." He watches me, my eyes, my hands, the way I sip my coffee. I take a drink while I watch him, the lip of the cup comes half way up my eyes and I stare straight at him all the time and the coffee slides warmly down my throat and I swallow and keep my eyes on him all the time. He waits, to see if I'll cough or my hands shake or I look away. I set the cup down on the tray, and lean back and put my left hand along the top of the sofa and lean my head against it and look at him with my head sideways. "I didn't say anything like that."

"You didn't?"

I shake my head, slowly, solemnly.

We sit watching each other in total silence and I move towards him and put my right hand on his knee. "I love you." He makes a half move towards me, but then gets up and walks to the window and looks out at the back yard. He stands with his back towards me. He doesn't believe me.

"I mean that. I love you."

"I told you it was business," he says.

"Are you saying I'm lying?" I could make love to him. I don't feel like it. I still feel fuzzy from the headache, it hasn't gone completely. I feel all hollow inside. I feel betrayed. "You're saying I'm lying." He still doesn't say anything, and that hurts even more. He turns and comes back and sits down and takes another sip of his coffee and then puts the cup back down sharply, as if it's the last he intends to drink.

"I told you it was business." He says it angrily. "I told you everything. I showed you the lot. I told you all my plans. I told you I was meeting another person. I'll show you all the legal papers, dammit, to prove I'm not lying to you. It's just a goddamn business arrangement. That's all. That's all it ever was!"

"Don't swear at me."

"Okay," he says. He calms down. "I'm sorry. I shouldn't get upset, should I?"

"No. It doesn't solve anything."

"I wish you had come with me and seen that house today."

"Do you think I'm lying?" And I'm almost pleading with him. This has all been so quiet. He's got upset just once, just now, but he's calmed down. Basically, it's all been so quiet. That's what makes it so awful. He's calling me a liar, and saying it quietly, not upset, when you say something quietly like that, it's serious, you really mean it. If he cared even a little bit, he wouldn't even think that, much less say it. "You've never called me a liar before," I tell him, sadly, not angry.

"Did I? I didn't mean it if I did."

"You did."

"I'm sorry." He sounds like he really means it now, his voice is gentle, he really cares.

I lean over and touch his arm. He doesn't react.

"What's wrong?" I ask.

"She says she'll pull out."

"So what, Stan? I mean who cares."

Obviously he does. He can sit here and say he cares about me, that he loves me even, but he won't do anything to prove it. Words are cheap.

"I've worked so hard on this," he says.

"You're just upset. She's got you all upset. Who cares?"

"She said you told Shelley ...."

"And?"

"You didn't?"

"Why don't you come right out and say it. Why don't you just come right out and call me a liar. Why don't you! That's what you think. That's what you think. Why don't you just come right out and say it!" I've raised my voice.

"Calm down."

"Don't you tell me to calm down!" I'm screaming at him, suddenly, I can feel my headache getting worse fast, "You're calling me a liar! Right to my face!" the pain is getting awful.

"I never said you were lying to me," he objects, he's defensive.

"You did! You did!"

"I didn't," he hates this, he hates it when I'm really upset with him, he's afraid, afraid I'll leave him.

"Bastard!!!" I get up and knock the tray and the coffee and the creamer and the sugar flying all over his stinking carpet and I don't give a damn and I slam the door of the bathroom and pick up the soap dish and fling it against the mirror and it shatters and collapses smashing against the sink and on the floor, just collapses like ice in the winter raining off trees.

"What are you doing?!" he shouts, he's worried. I lock the door. He bangs on it, "Melissa, what are you doing!" I stare at the shards and spears of glass all over the sink. God it shattered. "Melissa!" he bangs on the door, wham, wham, his bangs are angry, scared. "What are you doing!"

"You'd better clean up," I say. I'm calm again. "It'll stain your carpet." Silence on the other side. "Use cold water. It gets the stain out." I pick up the longest spear of glass and gaze at it. There's a nick on the point, just before the end, just a little bit of a semi circle chipped out, and the spear is curved, glass is crystal, it breaks along the fault lines and curves like this. It was a cheap mirror. That's what's interesting about Stan, he likes really expensive things, but a lot of his stuff is cheap, when you look at it closely.

"Melissa," he says on the other side of the door. He's worried. "Are you all right?" The thing is, he can't see what's going on, that's what makes it worse, he can imagine the worst.

"Go away." I don't raise my voice. I wait. He doesn't say anything.

"Go away."

Silence.

"Are you all right?" he says, quiet, but he's upset, his voice is hoarse. "You're not hurting yourself?"

"Yes." I speak normally.

"Please," he says.

"Go away." I speak normally.

"Please don't hurt yourself. I'll go crazy if you hurt yourself."

There's a long silence. Then he starts hammering on the door.

"If you don't go away," I tell him, keeping my voice normal, "I will." He stops hammering. "I'm not now, but I will. There's a big piece of glass and I will." I talk completely calm.

"Please!! Melissa!" He's practically crawling. He's been treating me like garbage all day, and now, when he thinks I'm really serious, he's crawling.

I don't say anything.

A long silence.

"If I do," he says, "do you promise you won't hurt yourself?"

"Maybe."

"Please."

"Okay." I despise him now. "Only for you, Stan." I know he can hear my contempt, the way I say that.

Silence.

Then I hear him going away.

When I come out, maybe ten minutes later, the stain is all over the carpet and I get some paper towels from the kitchen and clean it up, as best as I can, but I don't get the stain all out, I do the best that I can, and as I'm kneeling down trying to get it out, I can hear him standing behind me, "I'll get that," he says, I don't answer, he comes down, says very gently, "I'll get that honey," I whirl and stand and throw the wad of paper towels in one motion and it whaps on his face and falls off and I shove him out of my way and go to the bedroom and get my stuff and he follows me and says, "Melissa, please, for godsake," and I whirl and slap him hard, "Get out!" I scream, and he starts crying and I slap him hard again, "Get out! Get out!" I'm screaming as hard as I can and he stares at me the tears rolling down his face, "I hate you, I hate you, I hate you!" I'm shrieking, he turns and goes out and he's crying, he won't stop me, I can hear the front door close, he did that, he told me, every time he'd have a fight with his wife he'd leave and walk and walk, for hours, the neighbors knew what was going on, they could see him walking, walking, walking, I drove him from his own house, I did, I'm calm, I'm amazingly calm, and I know that, when I get back to the apartment, I won't be so calm, right now I'm calm, but I won't be so calm then, thank God I've got the lease, you never know, something you think is negative is positive, I was stuck with the lease, thank God, at least I've got somewhere to go.

I'm calm. I've got somewhere to go. I'm calm. Much calmer than I ever thought I'd be. I'll have to take some blankets. I'll get the rest of my stuff later. Right now

I drove him from his own house. I really did.

That makes me kind of smile.

What will he do when he comes back from his big long walk and I'm not here?

Calm. Be calm.

I have to be careful. Marshall still terrifies me. I've got to have something to protect me. I'll be there all alone. I just want something to protect me. Marshall doesn't mean it. He gets crazy sometimes, that's all. I need something to protect me. To make him think, before he does something stupid.

I'm calm. After all that, I'm calm.

I just want to talk to him. I just want to see him. He came before. I know him. He'll come again. All I have to do is call. I don't want to be alone. I hate being alone.

Everything happens for a reason. It does. Even stupid Stan's collection.

Something to protect.

Yeah, this will do it. The blade's dull but the saw edge looks menacing. It's big, it'll scare him off if he tries something. Stan probably won't even notice it's gone.

Dark and cold and right back where I started from, up these stairs, door at the top on the left, key still works dull clunk push open, thank God I kept the lease, must have known this would happen. Cold, God it's cold, dark in here, lights on, what time is it?

Everything's fine, lights on, water runs, stove works, fridge still humming, nothing there.

I'll get a Tim Horton's in the morning. Or something. Get in some groceries. The toilet flushes. Bed still here. Thank god I thought to bring some sheets, almost forgot, blankets, smell musty, keep me warm.

Heat works, thank God the heat works, blowing out. Cold. Middle of the summer and it's cold.

Bet Stan comes tomorrow, picks me up like always, eight o'clock sharp like nothing ever happened. Right back where we started from.

Like always. Never stops. He can't stay away.

Thank god I kept the lease. It may not be much, but it's mine.

Not much here though, bed, dresser, table, lamp. Not like Stan's place. Packed. The place is packed, more than anyone ever needs.

Not like this place.

Nothing here.

Nothing.

God I'm tired. My back hurts. Oh God, I wish that was all. I have to see the doctor. A doctor. Not his.

Two and a half hours. You'd think I'd know better. Not even the cops out. What time is it? Late. Really late. I can't believe those seats are so hard. Cold. No wonder no one uses the bus. Except me.

When you look around, there really isn't much here.

Kitchen. Sink. Toilet. Dresser. Bed.

Come on, answer! You know who this is, Marshall. Come on, come on. I can't believe I'm doing this.

Still ringing, you know who this is, I know you're there.

Not ringing. He's picked it up. Someone with him.
Silence.
Waiting for me to say something.
I can wait.

A voice in the background. Can't make it out.
A woman.
Giggling.
He says something.
She giggles again.
Tells him to stop it, laughs, shrieks a laugh.
He says something, she gasps.

"Hi, Melissa," he's right over top of her, holding the phone while he does it to her, she's kind of hoarse, half strangled. "You like that," he says to her, "you like that," he's talking to me, "don't you," I know that tone of voice, "You're hurting me," she says, "you're hurting me."

Oh God.

I wish I'd hung up sooner. I had to keep listening, driving myself crazy.
Linda.
What a stupid thing to do. Phoning like that.

I can't believe it was Linda. I hope he gives it to her good, good and hard, as hard as he can, I hope she's got something to defend herself with.

I am sick.

Sick sick sick.

How could I be so stupid. How could he be so stupid. Linda. He has no self respect.
So much for Marshall.

So now what? There's nothing here. I hate this place.

Dark. Really dark. What time is it?

I'm getting hysterical. Wipe my eyes. The bastard isn't worth it. Mocking me. The bastard was mocking me. I hate the bastard. I'm crying. He's not worth it. I'm crying.
God I won't get to sleep all night.
What time is it?

4

Breeze. Chilled. Kids outside. Street hockey. Must have left window open. Cold. Why?
What time is it? Morning, some time. Slept in.

Is the lock on? Not sure. Left the lock off, in case Marshall Crazy.

What time is it? Did Stan come? Why didn't he come? Must have. Came. I wasn't out there. Left. Didn't bother to come up, to see if I'm okay. So much for all his caring. Couldn't be bothered, to see if I'm okay.

It's late. Bright. Noon. Close to it. No Sun coming in, must be noon, Sun straight up.
Some kids outside, shouting.
I really should get up and lock the door, close the window.
Don't feel like getting up. Where did I put that knife?

Sun shimmering on the ceiling. Reflecting off something. If he comes, let him. I'm sick. If he comes, I'll let him, do anything he wants. The door's open.

Sick.

Sick.

Sick.

I really am sick, after all he did to me, even to think that.

I think that's what he likes.

I can do it. If that's what he likes.

I'm tired, though, I don't think I slept last night, not once. Must have fallen asleep this morning, just about the time that Stan came, probably. Kids outside, shouting, must be noon, close to it. Hockey in August. Ridiculous

Someone downstairs, opening the door. I guess the door's wide open. Coming up. Heavy steps. Marshall. Couldn't stay away.

Who cares. Whatever happens, happens. Close my eyes and let it happen.

Up the stairs, clunk clunk.

Outside the door.

Waiting.

Opening the door and coming in, crossing the floor, standing right, over top of me. With a knife. Maybe.

Nothing. He's standing there. What's he doing? If you're going to do something Marshall, do it. He clears his throat.

Stan.

"I thought you were asleep." He looks like my father, my god he looks so like my father. "Are you okay?" I can't answer, I'm surprised it's him, I thought it was Marshall. "Melissa?"

Standing there, staring down at me with his dumbass grey eyes, old age puffs, scrappy grey hair. Doesn't look like he's slept much either.

You look like an asshole old man, Stan. Stan the man.

"I was worried about you."

Big deal. He was worried about me. So what.

Neither of us blinks. He stares at me. I stare at him.

"You weren't there when I came home. I didn't know where you were."

"So?"

"I was worried about you."

"So?" I'm hoarse, my throat feels parched, my gut hurts, I can hardly talk, it hurts bad down there, I need a doctor.

"Are you okay?" What does he think, do I look okay, does he think I look okay? He picks something off the floor and spreads it over me, a blanket, like I'm some kind of corpse on the sidewalk. Maybe I don't have anything on. I can't remember. No breeze any more.

"You look cold."

I was I guess.

"Can I get you anything?"

Privacy, Stan. I'd like some privacy.

He sits down on the edge of the bed and puts his hand on my forehead. It's cool. He looks at me like my father. "They're all asking about you."

"Who?"

"All your friends. At work."

"I don't have any friends."

He bends down and kisses my forehead. "More people love you than you can possibly imagine. I love you." I'm crying, goddammit I'm crying, he wipes off my tears with his thumb and kisses me again, on the forehead like a father. "I'll take you to a doctor."

"I'm okay."

"I think I should."

I can't stop crying.

"Have you eaten?" I shake my head and push his hand away and wipe my face with the flat of my hand. "What do you want?" he asks. I push him away, he stands up, stares down, sad like a puppy dog, his eyes have bottom waters, he's about to bawl like a baby. Neither of us says anything.

I can hear the kids outside, shouting. Playing hockey, for godsake, at this time of year.

"Soup."

"You want soup?" he asks.

"Yes! Soup! Asshole! I want fucking soup!"

He knows not to argue, not when I'm like this. So he goes to the kitchen and in the meantime I'm lying here, underneath the blanket, I've got pants on. No top. But pants.

I take them off and throw them on the floor and pull the blanket back over, I want Marshall, oh god I want Marshal more than I've ever wanted Marshall in all my life, goddammit I'm crying again, I wipe my face off, stop it, stop it.

"I'll order pizza," he shouts, "you're probably just hungry." Where's that knife? Where did I put that damn knife? I am not going to a doctor, where the hell is that damn knife?

5

Thank God he's gone. You can't trust anybody. Not even that stupid old man.

Those damn kids. Playing street hockey for godsake. At this time of year.

The whole thing was ridiculous, he wants his clock, I threw him the stinking clock, straight at his stinking head, god he ran.

I don't understand it. He left it lying there, on the bureau in the second bedroom, covered with dust, covered completely with dust, from his wife for godsake.

I thought that was over.

I didn't think he'd miss it.

All I wanted was something I could look at, to remind me, I wanted to remember him, something to remember him, what was wrong with that? Crying again. Stop it. He didn't even have it in his bedroom, it was sitting on the dresser in one of the other bedrooms. He's got a whole house with four bedrooms and a den and a big TV and a bar and a huge glass cabinet with all that war stuff, and a kitchen with everything electric you could ever imagine, and a living room he never uses and all that stuff, I coughed when I went in there and couldn't stand it and it took me half a day just to clean it up, that one room, and I never told him and he never even noticed, he never noticed anything I ever did, I had to have some knives and forks didn't I, I took all my knives and forks over there and they're still there, and I don't even have any plates here, and to say that, to say that....

Everything I've done for him and he says that. So he comes here this morning, all worried, all because I walked out and he'll give me the day off he says and makes me soup and orders in a pizza and sits here and has lunch and I could see him, looking around, at the little clock his precious wife gave him, the wife that walked out, that wife, Stan, remember, that one, and the knives and forks in the kitchen, pretending he was so worried and looking all around, what does she have here he wonders, what's she got, as if he never cared anything about me, ever.

I've got one chair and a desk and a bed and a table and some chairs in the kitchen and nothing to eat, and I have, I don't know what I have, in the bank, not much, and I won't have a salary and I'm not going back there, he can have them, all of them, all his damn knives and forks and plates and clocks and whatever the screw else he wants.

I feel tired. It does hurt. I need to go back to the doctor. Stan will cover it. He said. It hurts. I'll rest here this afternoon, get some rest, maybe it will go away a little, and I'll see the doctor after that. I want some rest now.

It really hurts.

Marshall.

That's what hurts so much. I still care about that rotten freak.

The door's wide open. Anybody can come in here. Stan did. Anybody could.

Where is it? That's one thing he didn't find. Stupid Stan. That's one thing he didn't know I actually had, besides that idiot clock. Under the mattress. I think. It was right there in the cabinet, the one with the glass door, right there in the den, displayed, the first thing you see and it was gone, right in front of his face and he didn't miss it.

Have to make sure I don't cut myself, getting it out, I should get off the bed and fish it out, instead of feeling around like this and lying on top, the handle's down. Here it is. I'm lying on it, hard to get it, yeah.

It is long. Bayonet. Strange sound, really, French or something. Bayonet.

Why would he have a huge long thing like this with a saw blade. So wicked looking? Stan is a strange man.

A big long saw-edged thing, reflecting light, only dull, not shined, strange, holding it up while I lie here, it's odd, peaceful, innocent, god what has it done, so innocent looking.

It's dull though. It hardly cuts at all.

Makes a long red line across my leg, across and up.

Not a deep cut, more like a scratch, like if you're walking through the woods with your shorts and bare legs, just scratches, it doesn't cut very well at all. I should get it sharpened. Won't help much if I need it, dull like this. I should get up and lock the door. Another cut, across the other way. Marshall.

Dark blood. Just veins.

Who used it, I wonder, how many guys did he kill, stabbed them through the guts and pulled their guts out with the sawed edge. Marshall would love this thing, love the way it cuts, the way it runs across my leg and the blood follows, dark blood, vein blood, dark, like a river opening up.

Funny. I don't have any feeling. I can see the point running across my leg and I can see the blood coming and I don't feel a thing, I still hurt down there I have to get the doctor, to do something I don't know why I'm doing this, five cuts now, criss cross across my legs, like plaid.

I thought he cared, he seemed to care, we had wonderful, I really cared, he could come up here right now and yank me open and hurt me, hurt me bad, hurt me bad, hurt me worse than ever, I wouldn't mind, I'd enjoy it, I'd give him the knife, if he wanted he could use it, pull my guts out.

I'm getting hysterical. Wipe my face. I'm getting hysterical. Calm down.

Friends.
Friends.
I don't have any friends.
I can draw this knife across my leg and watch the blood, oozing, following the point in a long red streak and I don't feel a thing, I don't feel a thing about anything except the hurt where it hurts sometimes awful I wish he was here I wish Marshall was here.

6

Suddenly Noreen is just standing there, I must have been asleep.
"Where's Shelley?" she demands.
She's always been a bitch and that's always intimidated me, all the time I've known Noreen, I've got an awful headache and as soon as I jump up everything goes all black and I slump on the edge of the bed and my head drops and I hold it up with my hands and I feel dizzy, "I said, where is Shelley!" she barks, like a dog.
I have no idea what's she's talking about, I feel sick.
"Where is Shelley!" she screams it, the bitch is getting hysterical. Why is she so hysterical? It's weird.
"I don't know."
That doesn't satisfy her. "I said where's Shelley!" she screams, she's totally out of control, and I say, "Oh God Noreen, don't shout, okay, I feel like crap."
"I want to know where Shelley is," she grabs me by the shoulders real hard and I shove her away real hard, and my stomach almost turns inside out.
She's standing back, she knows better. "She said she was coming over here." She's lowered her voice and I stare at her shoes, I'm almost throwing up, this headache is hideous. "I want to know where she is."
"I don't know." Her shoes disappear and I can hear her walking to the kitchen and opening doors in there, "I want to know where my daughter is!" she shouts, as if I've got her idiot daughter hidden in some cupboard in there, all folded up in a box or something. I get up and go out in the hall and watch as she walks to the bathroom and opens the

door and goes inside and comes back out and stands facing me. "Where did she go?"

"Where do you think?" I ask.

I'm feeling better and I'm getting sick of her accusations about her stupid daughter. She walks toward me like she's going to give me a smack. "Don't!" I warn her and she stops.

"I want to know where she went."

"Where do you think she went?" I ask and turn and go back to the bedroom and sit down on the bed again and she follows me and I smile up at her. "Is she gone?" I ask. "I must say I'm not surprised."

"What happened to your legs?" she says.

I shrug.

"Don't you think it would be wise to get something on?" she asks.

"Does it turn you on?"

"I want to know where my daughter is!" She comes at me and I stand up and push her and she staggers back and gains her balance in the doorway and she's all set to charge me only she sees I mean it and she stops.

What's her problem? I don't know why she's here. Why does she think Shelley's here? This is weird.

"Where is she?" she says, real low.

"Gone, I guess. If you say so." She glares at me. "I can't blame her for going, to tell you the truth." We stand facing each other, she is acting really weird. "But I don't know where she's gone."

"I told you to stay away from her."

"You didn't tell me a thing, actually."

"I told you to stay away from her!" Her face is red and I really think she's going to lose it. She's breathing hard. I sit down.

"You shouldn't get all worked up like this," I tell her, really calm, I even smile a little. "It's not good for you. Shelley says you get all worked up and she can't talk to you." She glares at me. What is it, what's her problem? "I won't be able to tell you where she's gone if you keep shouting at me. Will I?" Total silence. "You'll have to ask those kids out there."

Maybe that makes her think and she comes closer and sits down on the chair by the desk. The room is bare except for the desk, the chair, the table in the corner and the bed, there's nothing here, I don't know

34

how I could have stood it. I had it all, all that house, all those things, and he didn't tell me anything and she kept undermining me and now I'm here, if it hadn't been for her I'd still be there. There's nothing on the desk, just the phone, all the stuff in the desk I've moved to his place and it's still there. I just brought enough to wear for a couple of days, and I don't have any food, all the stuff I really cared about is at Stan's house, and I don't have anything, I've always been denied everything, even when I was young, I was treated like shit, I had nothing, not even my own body.

"I'd suggest you put something on," she says.

"I think you like it this way."

A long silence. We stare at each other.

"Where is she?" Noreen asks.

"When did she leave?" I ask. She doesn't answer, just stares at me, trying to figure out what my motives are, what I know and what I don't know. "What makes you think she's here?"

"She's not here, obviously," she's getting more reasonable. "I want to know where she's gone."

"I know she isn't here, Noreen. I can see that. I told you that. I'm just interested in knowing why you think I know where she is. It's weird."

"I'll have to let the police ask that, I guess."

"And what would they ask?"

"Are you going to tell me where she's gone or not? I'm asking one last time." She stands up.

"Why should I tell you, Noreen? You've been nothing but crap, all the time I've known you. You've turned everybody against me, and you've turned Stan against me, you told Stan you didn't want your daughter to have anything to do with me, you couldn't stand it, could you, he liked me and he didn't like you and you couldn't take that, you're too old and wrinkled." She doesn't answer. "You had to turn him against me, didn't you."

She turns and walks to the door I am not finished talking I am not finished talking yet she's walking out the bitch is walking out I grab it as I jump up the kids have started yakking outside again it doesn't sound like they're playing street hockey or anything some boys are shouting at each other and there's the sound of a plastic tricycle rattling along the sidewalk and a girl calling somebody Noreen's almost at the door, I grab her hair and pull her and she stumbles backwards and regains her balance faster than I thought she could and I miss completely with the knife and she hits me in the cheekbone hard and my whole face is filled with pain, it feels like she's broken a bone and somebody screams and she tries to grab my hand but I can't let her grab my hand and the knife hits her arm up near the shoulder and goes in much easier than I'd thought and I yank it out it's harder to yank out than I'd thought and there's more blood than I thought there would be and the expression in her eyes is completely neutral, she looks like she looks at the Registry, when there's a job she has to do and she concentrates on the job she has to do, there isn't anger, she's just concentrating, she's amazingly calm, she watches what I'm doing and I thrust at her again and she blocks it and somebody keeps screaming and I thrust again and the knife goes in again and I can see her worried now there's more blood than she thought and it's gone in below her shoulder, in the upper part of her torso on the right and the next time it's lower yet and it weakens her and when she tries to block me I go underneath instead and it goes in just below her ribs and she falls back she's terrified she didn't think somebody this small could do this I'm stronger than she realized she's older she's not as strong she's always underestimated me she misses again when she tries to block me and it goes in and again and she's sliding down holding her hands up blocking covering her face it goes in in in in in in in somebody's screaming, trying to get away, so the knife won't go in straight, I stop, for some reason I don't want to do this any more she's not fighting any more she curls on her side, moves a little in her blood and curls like a baby in a fetal position, stops moving like I've seen a groundhog clubbed behind the ear, blood comes from her mouth, her nose, and then she's not moving hardly breathing just gulping breath a bit I feel suddenly so weak I black out for a second the pain in my face is terrible she must have broken a bone there and I lean back against the wall and I slide down the wall I'm so weak I almost faint, I'm all wet it must have been me, me screaming, she wasn't shouting or anything her mouth wasn't moving, I'm so weak I have to sit here the pain is terrible, the kids have stopped, it's completely silent.

She didn't have to come here.

If she hadn't come here, this wouldn't have happened.

It was her attitude, her whole attitude.

She should have come later. I would have dealt with it later, I wasn't ready to deal with it now.

Why did she come here? It doesn't make sense.

I'm getting another headache.

I was afraid of Marshall. I brought the knife for Marshall. It wasn't for her it was for Marshall. I didn't hate her that much, I don't hate her that much, this was all an accident.

Kirsten

1

Shelley. She turns the corner and walks towards us, on the other side of the road. Maybe five hundred meters away, so far she's still a line against the lighter trees and the grasses and the sand. She's been walking by the house every day for the last week. It took me almost that long to figure out who she was. I knew there was something familiar, the way she walked. Her right foot swings out and turns in again, just slightly, you can see it when she walks straight towards you head on, once she gets closer. I've never seen anyone else walk like that, she was twelve when I saw her last, at the trial. She comes along this road every day, walks by our place, up to the corner by the old school, and then turns and comes back. She's got a cottage somewhere, renting probably, which is why she showed up a week ago.

She was twelve. Thirty five plus twelve -- forty seven. She's forty seven.

I can't believe it.

I'm fifty four. As old as Stan, the last time I saw him. Dead for ten years. Poor old Stan. He never got anything he ever wanted. I'm not sure he ever knew what he wanted.

A whole lifetime ago. She takes me back a whole lifetime ago. She was still a kid.

I haven't told Page and Erica anything about -- any of that, Noreen or any of that. They're too young, I tell myself, I don't have to tell them that yet. I'm more afraid of those two little girls than anyone else I've ever had anything to do with. They're the only people I've ever been afraid of. Afraid of what they'll think when I tell them about their mother, where I was for twenty five years. Why I was. Afraid they'll hate me, their mother the convict. All that stuff. So small, and they scare the living shit right out of me.

I take their hands. She's still far down there. Erica looks up, I don't usually do this, she picks up on these things.

I knew this would happen one day. The inevitable. Something I'll have to face.

So face it.

"Why are we walking?" asks Erica.

"If we were Indians," I say, "we'd be carrying canoes."

"That's not why we're walking," says Erica, she knows there's something, she watches me, tries to gauge my expression, tries to figure out what's behind it. She's older of course, more mature. Mature at nine years old. Page edges ahead of us, pulls on my hand. I could hold her. She'd suspect. I let her go, she's seven, she's heard this all before.

"We're walking because it's good for us," I say. We're walking because the car broke down.

"Slow down, Page," says Erica. My younger daughter stops dead, and stands so still by the side of the road with her eyes clamped shut you'd think she was paralyzed. We walk by her. She doesn't move because she knows this drives her sister crazy.

"Page!" Erica snaps. Page doesn't move. "We're going to leave you there!"

"Ignore her," I tell Erica. She falls for this every time. We keep walking. "There'd be nothing but woods all around us. Stunted trees, with oozy marsh, and bushes with sharp branches. We wouldn't be able to see anything but the heels of the person right in front of us. And probably some broken branches and tree roots. Which we'd fall over." Erica keeps looking back at Page. "I said ignore her!"

"She's so stupid."

"Don't say that. It's not true. You know that."

"She is."

She can tell, by the tension in my hand, by the way I squeeze her much harder than I need to, that I'm getting irritated. I'm unreasonable when I get irritated. I'm trying to fight this, sometimes I say awful things and regret them afterwards.

She's still a long distance away. Shelley. Down there. There's a few low flat clouds above the lake, over behind the dark green trees down there in front of us, where there used to be islands. Beyond Shelley. The road has been graveled and tarred and compacted into blacktop. There's some patches up ahead where the tar has worn off and the cars have pounded out potholes. Shelley's got blue jeans today, and a white t-shirt with a picture and something written on it. There's no reason for her to be walking along here. There's nothing to see here.

"The sweat would be running down our faces. Stinging our eyes," I tell Erica. "We couldn't wipe our faces. The sweat would be running off our noses right in our eyes, and stinging. Driving us crazy." The canoe trips Jacob used to take us on. I wonder if they remember them. They were really young.

Page runs and catches up with us. "Why?" she asks.

"Why what?" She has short blonde hair and blue eyes that demand answers.

"Why did they do that?" she asks.

"They were women."

"So?" Erica asks.

"Because women do all the work," I say. "You know that."

"Why?" asks Page.

"You are so stupid!" Erica snaps.

"Erica!"

"I am not!" Page objects.

"Stop it! Both of you."

"I want to be a man," Page says.

I stop and glare at her. "Don't you ever say that! Don't you dare!"

I don't think Shelley can hear us yet. I don't think she's close enough yet. What if she says something, with my daughters here, I haven't told them anything yet. I know what Page would say. "Why did she call you Melissa?"

Erica wouldn't ask. She'd notice, but she wouldn't ask.

But Page would not shut up. "Your name's not Melissa. Why did she call you Melissa? You're Kirsten, your name's Kirsten, your name's not Melissa, she doesn't know anything, you're Kirsten!" I can see the way she'd look at me, running ahead a little bit and looking back and up so she could see my face better, and the way her voice would rise, demanding an answer.

I take her hand again, she's my daughter, I want to protect my daughters, I know better, I know they have to learn what the world is like, they have soft, vulnerable hands, my little daughters. "They used to portage, right along here. Hundreds and hundreds of years ago. Across Bark Lake, and along the trail somewhere around here, and then out to the big lake. Sometimes they'd be attacked. They didn't dare make a sound. They had to carry all those things on tiptoes." Marshall with a club.

"Why?" says Page. Erica wants to know too, for once she doesn't mock her sister.

"There were people called Iroquois. Everybody was afraid of them. If they found you, you were dead. They had big clubs. They'd club you to death. They'd wait for you."

"Why?" Erica asks. Now she's interested.

"There's people like that. I've told you that." I hate to scare them like this. Page squeezes my hand tighter. "That was a long time ago," I assure her. A long time ago. She looks around, at the trees on each side of the road, Shelley gets closer. "It's okay now," I say.

"Why did they do that?" Page asks.

"Because they did."

Shelley's getting closer.

I can hear the lake, faintly behind the trees, across the sand and the weeds and the wild rice, a faint washing, a soft undertone, delicate, ancient.

Everything is so unreal. Alien.

Sometimes I have to touch a weed, a tree branch, to make sure it's really there. And run my hand down a branch, a weed, feel it running through my fingers, the coarse weed, the slippery needles, squeezing, feeling the crinkled weed, the soft sensuous needles, in green bunches sliding through my fingers.

And I'll touch my daughters, to make sure they're really here, that I'm not just dreaming them. I never would have thought I'd be here, in a place like this, with two wonderful daughters I have to touch to make sure they're really here, on a beautiful day with the trees all around me, and up ahead there, softening the skyline, the trees of the islands, what used to be the islands. And two daughters, and a car going by on the crossroads, and Shelley getting closer. Jacob, with his custody papers. Trying to take his daughters. From their dangerous mother. Who wasn't dangerous for so many years, until it was convenient. For him. To claim.

Erica stares at me. She's the older one, she understands what I'm going through. Sort of.

I think.

Shelley is stooped, crushed by whatever life has done to her. By everything she thinks life has done to her. Crushed by the way she reacts to it. Everybody loses their mother, eventually.

We approach each other, on opposite sides of the road, and she stares like she's looking straight through me.

"Hello Shelley."

She looks away.

"Hello Shelley," I say, louder.

She doesn't look at me.

She's a wreck.

Her face is lined, she's shriveled. Her blue jeans bulge, she's got hips, her t-shirt has a picture of a woebegone Charlie Brown, faded out, looking lost, out of date and ridiculous. "IT COULD BE WORSE, BUT I DON'T KNOW HOW," says the message.

She's had at least two nervous breakdowns, more probably. I'm sure of it. She doesn't talk, we pass each other on opposite sides of the road. They know there's something, my two little girls clutch my hands tighter. "I don't want you to talk to that woman. Don't look back."

"Yes," says Erica, looking back.

"I said don't look back." She faces ahead. "Did you hear what I said?" I stare down at Page. "Did you hear what I said about that woman. I don't want you to talk to that woman. Ever. … Page?"

"Yes." A small scared voice. I hate doing this.

"I don't want either of you to ever talk to that woman. For any reason. Do you understand that?" I jerk their hands. "Both of you."

"Yes," they say in unison.

"I'm your mother. I'm doing it for your own good." I sound like my mother. I hate it. "Do you hear me?"

"Yes Mom," says Erica. I can hear the resentment. And the guilt. The fear. Just like me. I hate this.

"Make sure you don't."

"Yes."

We walk for a moment without talking.

"Go ahead if you want to," I say, and they release my hands instantly and race towards what used to be the lakeshore road, where it meets the road we're walking on. "Wait for me at the corner," I shout. I so want to protect them. Maybe I'm too protective. I don't want them to do what I did. I want to protect them from their mother.

She didn't say anything. And neither did Page or Erica. "How come you know her name?" The question they never asked. Erica would be more likely to ask it, actually.

That was stupid. I know that's Shelley. There's no doubt in my mind.

Stupid.

If she didn't recognize me before, she'll start asking questions now. How come that woman knew my name, do I know that woman? I don't know any woman named Kirsten.

I shouldn't have said anything.

She's been walking by our place for a week now. There's nothing up this road. The only reason she'd come by here, every day, is to walk by our place. It's deliberate.

I had to confront her. I didn't have a choice. She knows who I am, she knows what she's doing. She deliberately ignored me.

I could have made a mistake. I'll have to face that possibility.

I've changed. It's been thirty five years. And the name wouldn't mean anything. Melissa would have meant something, not Kirsten. And she wouldn't expect me with kids. Neither would I, thirty five years ago.

I could have made a mistake. Like everything else I've ever done.

Erica and Page look back when they reach the corner, and when I don't say anything, they cross the road to the weeds and the wild rice and the grass on the other side and run along the trail through the sand, picking the wildflowers, even though I've told them they mustn't. I don't know how many times I've told them, those flowers are rare. The trouble is, they look so beautiful. So tempting.

Mauve orchids with petals splayed like propellers. Sitting on spindly grass-like stems.

Small purple iris on tough stalks, delicate as glass.

Pale yellow flowers with round petals on tough prickly bushes with tiny lime-green leaves.

And red pitcher plants, holding up cupped leaves to trap ants, to hold them in, to drown them, to digest them.

Stems and petals flexible, thick as leather, tough and ant proof.

Shark flowers.

Page is totally uncontrollable, nothing affects her for longer than five minutes. Light blonde hair. I comb it and five minutes later it's like she's never been combed in all her life. It's light and goes wild like the weeds, like the wildflowers. And yet. Sometimes, when I look at her, at night when I'm combing her hair, I start to choke up, and when she senses, I smile.

Erica is dark and thin and serious. She absorbs what she hears and what she sees and what she tastes and what she smells. I never know what thoughts are brooding behind those large black eyes. I know what it's like, living with a dark, something, that swallows your heart, that suffocates. She's the older one.

Page is young and slightly chubby and doesn't know, doesn't care, what's in there, in her heart.

Erica does.

Already, it swallows her spongy bones, and her blistering skin, and her thin stick body, and her great dark eyes. I try to help. Jacob wouldn't know. Jacob would ruin her. This bitch he's married would destroy her.

I wish I could dress them in something decent. It hurts me, the way their jeans are so faded and patched and out of fashion, the way their t-shirts are all full of holes. I hate it. I get mad when they look at what other kids are wearing and ask me why they can't have that too, and I snap at them, they don't need that, they've got no use for that.

But it makes me mad, that I can't give it to them. That the world treats them like that. And I hate myself, for getting mad at them.

It is not their fault. I don't deserve them. Oh god I don't deserve them.

There was a program on TV, on the outdoor channel, a week or so ago, about the millionaires who came to Muskoka over a hundred years ago and started a settlement that's still there. Huge cottages, one after another, that've been there ever since. They started in tents, and there's still a big cottage with nothing upstairs but a bunkhouse with beds side by side, where these rich guys still come, to fish. But the thing that hurt, the thing that really got me, was the video, the boat ride past cottage after cottage, vast things, with vast boathouses. Boathouses. Their boathouses are bigger than the houses for ninety-nine point nine-nine percent of everybody in Canada. Boathouses! One place had a little railroad that took the steamer trunks up the rocks from the boathouse to the cottage, and a machine that lifted them to a special trunk room in the cottage. The cottage had a trunk room! A room just for trunks. And servants to unpack them, and the locals who looked after their water pumps and their flower beds and their lawns and their boats in the winter, and a huge rock wall all the way around an island, as a work project for the locals, who would otherwise be unemployed. You go along the water, and you look at these huge old cottages with acres of glass and boat docks and flower beds, and people, sitting on their docks with their sunglasses, watching, like they're sitting behind a glass watching a parade, and you can't touch, you have to keep going, you can look but you can't touch. Look what I've got! Look what you haven't got! It hurts. I see my daughters and they have no idea, they're so young, so innocent, they have no idea how much they'll never have. I see them, standing, on the other side of the glass, looking, like they're not even fully human. Some kind of subspecies. Looking, looking at everything they'll never have. It wrenches my gut. These people, they've been rich, these people, for over a hundred years, they're living where their grandmothers and grandfathers lived. Nothing touches them. And they read about people like me. -- I'm paying for that! I can hear them. I'm paying for that! Like they own me. Like they own me. Like they own Erica. Like they own Page. My own daughters. These people. -- Those people. That's what we are. Those people.

The hardest thing. The really hardest thing. -- Those places are just their cottages. Their cottages.

This is wrong. I am supposed to just accept it. This is wrong. I don't care, how long it has been this way, how long the world has worked this way, I don't care, if the world, is supposed to work this way, if the world has always worked this way. A hundred years. A thousand years. Ten thousand years. This is wrong. Do it to me, but not to my daughters.

I still haven't reached the corner. My daughters run along the trail across the sand on the other side of the road, their laughter bright like angels, along the narrow trail that thousands of feet have traveled before them, through sun and wind, out towards the lake, where it's bright and vast like an ocean, where winds come ashore and blow away the dark.

I want. I'm always wanting. I've had thirty five years of wanting.

I want peace. Just leave me alone. I want respect. I want my daughters to have some happiness. To have something to wear that they feel proud of. Some place to stay that makes them feel human. To run through the sunshine, through the clean cold air, through the bright beige sand, through rare orchids, through scraggly, picturesque, dangerous weeds, happy with who they are, happy with where they are.

They stop, they pick them, they run on.

I've had so much trouble, I'm numb. When they come, my troubles, I can deal with my troubles, as they come. Until they do, I don't think about them. And sometimes they stare and walk by.

The hole in Page's heart.

Sometimes I dream about her lying with her chest all opened up, and doctors cutting at her, and I wake up and I'm shaking and I can't stop. If I could only wake up and it wasn't true. She was born with it. It's there. When she's old enough, when her heart has grown, when she's old enough to fix it, they'll open her up like a clam, pry her apart. And fix it, if they can.

And that's one trouble that will not go away.

It's a hot day, Jerry's got his windows down, he drives by and waves, a big smile on his thin face, "Hi Kirsten." He always calls me by my full name. Never Kirsty. I keep threatening to call him Jeremiah. I smile at the back of his car, so he can see me in his rearview mirror smiling at him. When are you coming to fix my car, Jerry? It's been sitting there for two days now. How long do I have to wait? His back wheel drops off the pavement and the sand dust rises in a puff behind him. He waves. When are you coming, Jerry?

This road used to go right along the lakeshore before the lake receded and left nothing but sand. I go across it and enter the path through the sand and the weeds, my daughters are far ahead, they've almost reached the trees now where there used to be the islands, Page ahead, Erica behind. They stop and wait for me. They're brave, but the darkness in among the trees scares them a little I think. I've told them, I don't want you getting too far ahead, they're so far along the path someone could come out and grab them and I wouldn't be able to do anything. They know they're not supposed to get so far ahead like that. So they've stopped.

They're still kids, I have to remember that. They're good for kids. I've taught them well, I think. I hope. It breaks my heart they're so good.

Better than kids whose mothers who are good and respectable and upright and law abiding. Meaning, they haven't been caught yet.

My daughters have each other, which is good, because the other kids won't play with them. They're alone, like I was. Getting punished for what I did. As if I've passed on some kind of disease, some HIV of the heart.

And the watchers are waiting, to take my kids away.

Twenty-five years. And another ten out. Locked up. Still. It teaches things. It teaches silence.

Jacob didn't learn. He wants his daughters back, he leaves them and now he's met someone and wants them back. He gave them up and now he says he can raise them better, he's got money. She can raise them better. That's what he really means.

Forget it.

My daughters come back, bringing me flowers, and hand them to me. "You shouldn't have," I say, and take them, and almost break down. I talk miserable to them, and they give me flowers.

Erica stares, Page wants to get going, but they both know I'm upset, they're sensitive.

I'd hate raising boys. I wouldn't know what to do with them.

"They're beautiful," I say.

"You're not mad?" Page says.

"Not too mad." Kirsten means Christian, in Scandinavian. Melissa means bee. My stupid father's name. I like the one I chose.

There's no one left but me and Shelley. Her father must be eighty by now. Stan is dead. Marshall is dead. My father is dead. My mother was never alive.

Weird. I'm so old I've replaced Stan. And she's replaced Noreen. Yeah. Almost as miraculous as me, having kids at my age. Miraculous, but not impossible. Life is so damn weird.

So, I'll have to deal with her. Sit down beside the path and wait for her to come back, to see where she goes, I doubt if she'll come through the path to the lake, she came around the corner from the lakeshore road, that's probably where she'll go, so I'll see where she's staying. Maybe.

The name wouldn't mean anything to her. She must know. There's a reason why she keeps walking along that road every day. Walking right by our house every day. Looking in.

"How come you're sitting down?" Page asks.

"I'm hot. It tires me out." Actually that's true. All that tension, from twenty five years, and watching, every day, for twenty five years, watching my step, making sure I did the right thing, said the right thing, it affected me, it was bound to. I've got a heart murmur, something with my valves, so I get tired, I have to sit down. The doctor's not sure, was it tension, was it genes, was it pregnancy. Page has got heart trouble too, of course, and she didn't have any of that.

She goes off among the weeds to pick some flowers, and I know it and I watch, I don't want to hassle her, I just want to know she doesn't get, too far away. So I can see where she is.

Erica sits down beside me. She's become a watcher, like me, I have practice, twenty five years, you get good at it. Lying, looking up, a plane grumbling over, high up, silver gleam at the end of a long thin white stream, grumbling way up there, long after the gleam had passed and the cloud stream in the sky had spread out, was dispersing. The horn of a freight train, I remember the freight trains, there's nothing lonelier or more empty sounding than a freight train, freight cars rumbling, off somewhere in the heat haze on a silent hot day. Heat haze that megaphoned the sound. Blank empty sky. They knew not to bother me.

Page brings me another flower.

"You let her get away with too much," Erica says. The wise one, watching her sister run off, to get into more mischief. Thank God at least she's healthy, Erica, the only one among us that's healthy.

Shelley. She's turning left at the corner, walking along the road looking over here, I really don't think she can see me, though she might see Page running around through the grass, though it's tall. Still, if she's looking for something, she'll see, she can hardly miss.

So the thing is, where she turns off, assuming she's staying along here somewhere, she can't be too very far down the road, she's already walked a long distance, just to go by our place, so I'm assuming

Turning up a driveway, I knew it, only about three cottages from the corner, and she's been there a week, so she's seen everything that's gone along the road here and up the road towards our place. Three cottages from the corner. Perfect place.

So I think that's pretty clear. It's deliberate.

She'll be able to see if we come back by the path here, so we'll have to go around another way, once I've made my rounds, why I didn't think. I must be getting tired. Old for sure. Slowed down. Not so angry. I can't afford it. I have to control it.

"We're going," Erica shouts and gets up and follows me and Page comes running and goes by us both. I don't want to hurry, to call attention, we'll be in among the trees in two minutes anyway and if she sees us, well she knew where we were anyway.

It's sad. I liked Shelley, when she was young and I was. When I was someone else.

So now I know where she is. I'll have to deal with it.

2

So now that I know where Shelley is, we can get on with our day, this is wasting our time, it's Monday, Jerry, maybe you didn't hear, I've got work to do, I need my car, I do not want to be walking through the woods like this, I've got better things to do.

How did I get involved with a runt like Jerry? I think of Marshall sometimes, when Jerry's naked. It's embarrassing. Definitely not Marshall.

I can't think of that, I can't torture myself. I can't live in the past.

Sky spaces between the trees, and the sound of the waves, unmistakable now, and my daughters' voices. They'll be throwing stones and watching the splashes. I wish I had their energy.

That's the one thing I'll always remember about camping, coming to the end of a portage and the breeze off the lake, how it hit me, what a relief it was, the worst was the mosquitoes, I sweated and my skin crawled, I'd throw off my pack and run straight in the water.

I shouldn't let my daughters get out of my sight, like this. There's rattlesnakes, I've never seen them, but Dee claims they're here. Deirdre of the sorrows.

My whole life is shouldn'ts.

I shouldn't let my daughters get out of my sight. I shouldn't drag them every place I go. I shouldn't get so tired. You'd think, with all the exercise I get. And I used to do weights, I could kick ass. Not now. Life has kicked my ass.

I shouldn't have to work so hard.

A thousand years. At least that long. It doesn't seem like it, to look at it, but this is really an ancient site. They'd launch their canoes and load in their packs and step in and shove off, all in one motion, and vanish beyond the point, beyond the doorsill of the horizon.

This is irritating. If Jerry had fixed the car, I'd be halfway through the cottage already, getting set to do the next. I'll never get through all my work today, Jerry, you owe me. I just wish

They're sitting on some rocks, waiting for me, talking to each other like they're the most peaceful little girls in all the world. You'd think they'd never had a fight in all their life.

Page jumps up, all set to rush off again. "I have to rest," I tell her. Erica doesn't move. She knows.

So I sit down, and Page comes over and sits on my lap, and Erica does the same, so her sister doesn't get something that she doesn't get.

They're wonderful, my daughters, it's good just to sit here. The waves make foamy white curls along the grey rocks, and the lake is a deep concentrated blue, and the dark green spears of the trees on the point are almost black against the sunshine. Everything is harsh and clear and slightly cold.

I brought you into a rotten world, my daughters. I know teachers who put in for maternity leave and get five years off and then come back and push out the teachers who've replaced them. I couldn't do that, I'm not the right class.

And it's a crazy world too. I know a woman who broke into her lover's house in the middle of the night and shot him dead while he slept, so now he's asleep forever. She told the judge it was all a big mistake, all she wanted was to commit suicide. She didn't explain how come the guy wound up dead. It worked, though, she got off. And went on a lecture tour.

Unlike the rest of us, who spent twenty five years.

What I should have done, I should have shot a man dead and told the court the guy had abused me so much I was completely traumatized and didn't know what I was doing. The gun loaded itself. I think of Marshall. I couldn't do that.

Not me.

I kept my mouth shut.

Don't do that, kids. Talk loud. Find excuses. Lie like hell.

They pick their way along the shore toward a beat-up aluminum boat at a rickety leaning-sideways dock, a few boards resting on posts. An outboard motor leaks rainbows in the water. Page runs tilting along the dock and clambers in and stares over the sharp edge of the boat in the water. I worry about sharp edges, I don't want my daughters to have to deal with sharp edges. And they'll have to.

I sit down on the corner of the dock beside the pathway that leads in to Deirdre's cottage. The boat sloshes. I close my eyes, I get tired too easily now, there's something wrong. I could kill Jerry. I'd be done the whole cottage by now, and instead I haven't even started, and I'm already worn out. Fifty four. I feel like ninety. I never used to get tired like this.

Sunshine and no clouds, not too cold, rocks and trees and a perfect day. Erica searches for rocks with holes in them. I turn and look at Page, to make sure she's all right. She's reaching down and sloshing the water with her fingertips. She could fall in. And drown. I have to close my eyes, look away, forget it, forget all the hazards I want to protect them from, and I can't. I love them so much it hurts.

Where the lake meets the sky it's pale and blank.

"I'm going to the cottage," I announce and stand up and start along the path. Erica follows and Page jumps from the boat and comes after us. She runs by us half way to the cottage, goes up the steps to the porch, opens the door, and dashes inside.

"Find anything interesting?" I ask Erica.

"Some fish."

"How big?"

"Just little."

"Not enough to bother with?"

"No."

Dee finds fish among the rocks, big ones sometimes, and Erica wades out and helps her throw them on the shore. And Page loves to squat down and watch them flopping and gasping, and throw them back, if she's a mind. There's a car in the driveway, a black Chrysler, I've seen it around in the last few weeks, driving here and there. "I want you to play outside today," I tell Erica.

"Page is inside."

"I'm sending her out."

"I don't feel like it."

I stop and face her. "You can play in the tree house."

"I don't feel very well."

"The fresh air will do you good."

"What about her?"

"I'm sending her out, right now. You stay out here."

"Why?"

"Dee has guests."

"So what?"

"Stay here." I go up the steps to the porch, go inside, and cross to the second door between the porch and the living room. Erica follows. I can hear Page, but can't make out what she's saying, a man is talking to her. "You stay here," I tell Erica and head across the living room to the small hallway that leads to the kitchen. Erica is right behind me, but I pretend not to notice.

Dee is sitting at the table looking at a sheet of paper, she seems older than seventy five, wizen and thin, and uncertain. Monica, the loudmouth overweight woman who owns the store at the corners, and a balding man in a dark suit about medium height who looks to me like a lawyer, are sitting in kitchen chairs across from Dee. Page stands beside Dee, staring at the paper on the table. Dee is holding her hand. Erica walks over. "What's that?" she asks Dee.

"I've come to do the cleaning," I announce. Dee nods and doesn't look up.

"What's that?" Erica demands, and Dee hands it to her. An offer to purchase, how many of those have I seen. Poor Old Stan.

"Go outside and play," I tell my daughters.

Dee releases Page's hand and smiles at them both. Erica reads the offer to purchase.

"I'll have to use your cleaning things," I say. "I don't have the car."

Dee nods. I don't exist, as far as Monica and the lawyer are concerned, I'm just the cleaning lady.

I walk to the closet where Dee keeps her broom and mop and pail and dustpan. "I'll start upstairs. Page. Erica. Go outside and play!"

I'm standing by the door, waiting for my daughters and they wait until Dee takes the offer to purchase back and shoos them away and they come over by me and pass through to the living room. I set down the cleaning materials in the hallway and escort my daughters to the porch and down the stairs. "The first three branches, no higher. Watch for poison ivy."

I wait until they've almost reached the tree, and then go inside, shut the door and lock it. As I pick up the broom and dustpan in the hall, the lawyer says, in the kitchen, "Now's your chance."

Dee doesn't respond.

"All your neighbors are selling."

"You're holding it up," Monica tells her.

"I don't know," Deirdre replies. I'm standing so I can see the vultures framed in the kitchen door, Dee is out of sight.

"I don't see what the problem is," says Monica. "Do you, Adam?" He shakes his head. I should go in there and stop this, but it's none of my business. Instead I go upstairs to the two bedrooms she never uses but wants me to clean every week, I'm getting allergies from the dust up here, she tells me, do some sweeping, change the sheets, so that's all I do. I've tried to talk her into some serious spring cleaning, you'll feel better, more healthy, she refuses, she never goes up there she says. I open the windows, dust off the dresser and the chairs with the cloth I've found in her broom closet, and do a quick job on the picture frames, the bed posts, the window sills, around the window frames, the hanging lights and have to stop, this could go on forever, she said she wants a quick job and that's all I'm getting paid for. I'll sweep the floor and the cross ventilation should clear away the dust. Some of it. What's going on downstairs is none of my business. If I had the car I'd have some allergy masks. When I'm old, I'll say all this out loud, and humiliate my daughters. What will they be like?

Once I've finished sweeping the front bedroom, I glance through the window at the white pine my daughters call the tree house. The ends of the lower branches have died and fallen off, but left long stumps that form a ladder that goes half way up the tree. My daughters are not there.

Down by the water, collecting driftwood, which they've set in a little pile beside the dock. Right now they're bending down together peering at something among the rocks. They're all right, they're not in danger. I wonder if they can feel me, staring at them like this. I go back to my sweeping.

As I come back downstairs, Monica says, "You're being very foolish."

"What can I tell you?" Adam the lawyer asks. "What's the problem?"

I walk in the kitchen and head for the closet, they ignore me, I'm invisible.

"You're not as young as you used to be," says Monica. "Suppose you fall and you can't reach the phone? – And nobody knows you're in trouble?"

"What's going on Dee?" I ask and open the closet door. Nobody answers. "Do you have any more dusters?"

"This is a good offer," says Monica. I'm invisible.

"Don't sign anything until your lawyer reads it," I add, close the door and go out and head upstairs to the second bedroom, I don't think they'll think I'm invisible, not now.

"There's nothing wrong with this," Monica says, loud enough for me to hear as I climb the stairs, I've given Dee my best advice, it's up to her.

It bothers me, what they're doing down there, I've seen this so many times before, I can't erase it from my mind as I clean the second bedroom and go to the front and look out the window to make sure my daughters are all right, and finally can't stand it any more and go downstairs again.

"You're the only one holding this up," says Monica.

"Take the cheque and think about it," Adam says. "You can always give it back."

"What do you have to lose?" says Monica.

"I just need you to sign to acknowledge you have the cheque," says Adam as I come in the kitchen.

"What's going on, Dee?" I ask again, go across to the table, glance at the cheque, for twenty thousand dollars and pull it aside and read the offer to purchase. "Don't sign anything or take anything. Show this to your lawyer."

"This is none of your business," Monica snaps.

I put my hand on Dee's shoulder. "Are they pressuring you?"

"No," she says, a little uncertainly.

Adam reaches over, takes the cheque and the offer to purchase, puts them in his briefcase and walks out.

Monica remains at the table. "You've just lost half a million dollars," she tells Deirdre.

"He'll be back," I say and keep my hand on Dee's shoulder, I can feel her bones, she is so thin. "Don't let them pressure you."

"Damn you," Monica says and she stands up and we stare at each other.

"You've been pressuring her," I state. "I'll testify in court."

"Nobody will believe anything you've got to say," Monica declares, and walks out.

I go to the side door and watch as she gets in the Chrysler and when they're safely down the driveway and the rear of the car has vanished around the curve by the trunk of a large white pine tree, I go back to the kitchen. "I've finished upstairs. I won't do the windows today, if that's all right."

"I'm seventy five," says Dee.

I go to her cupboard and open the door to the right of the sink. "I'd like some tea, if that's all right."

"I'd love tea," she says. "I'm a little tired."

I get down the teapot and the tea cozy. The teapot is black with faded flowers, the tea cozy is knitted from orange and black wool and looks exactly like a hat. The holes for the teapot handle and the spout are meant for the old man's ears, says Erica. "I'll call the girls. I think we'll have lunch."

"I have my lunch at twelve," she points out. I get out the box of Tetley Tea from the cupboard below the sink. "Where are they?"

"Down by the lake."

"There's some juice in the refrigerator." She's sitting with her hands clasped. "I don't know if I've done the right thing."

I'm feeling good right now, maybe Dee doesn't appreciate it but I've done what I can, if she doesn't appreciate it too bad, I have to have lunch and then we'll go to the other five places I have to clean by the end of the day, maybe on second thought I can talk Dee into keeping them here, damn you Jerry, I need my car, this is a huge dark living room, she doesn't need a cottage this big, they're not at the tree or along the shore, oh my god what if something's happened, I rush to the door and as soon as I step out I hear their voices and find the place at the side of the cottage where the slats have broken and they've crawled underneath.

"Hi Mom" Page says brightly, they're flat on their backs lying there listening to footsteps above them, smiling at me with their heads turned sideways.

"Get out of there!"

"We're not hurting anything!" Erica objects.

"I said get out of there!"

They crawl towards me and I grab them when they emerge.

"Just look at your clothes! Just look at them!"

I swat the sand off, hard.

"Ow!" Erica says. Page tries to get away.

"Don't you dare go!" She stands while I finish with Erica.

"It's not that dirty," says Erica. Their clothes are shabby, they're the best I can afford, I hate it when they do this, they're always doing this, I was thinking of leaving them here, I can't do that now, it would be so much easier, I could get my work done and Dee would look after them, damn you Jerry damn you.

"Get in to lunch!"

They hustle ahead of me. I feel awful, I do things without thinking, I'm horrible.

Suddenly Page starts running, "You're mean!" like she's reading my thoughts, she runs up the steps and across the porch and through the living room to the kitchen where Dee waits.

Erica stays behind, and we go in together. "I worry about you," I tell her. She doesn't reply, my words sound hollow, she's heard it all before, they both have, she may be more understanding than her sister, my Erica, she's older, but still a child and she's too angry to talk, why is it so hard to be decent to your children, why, why am I such a terrible mother?

"I'm sorry."

I don't know if she's heard me, she walks beside me looking straight ahead, they were not hurting anything, they were just being kids, she walks erect, proud, her brown hair below me, my daughter.

"Tell Page," she says.

3

Steve drove us home. Three waifs, sitting at the side of the road. Too tired to walk any farther. My muscles are sore, tense, especially across the shoulders, I'm too exhausted to think. The girls have gone inside with grit in their eyes and I'm standing here, watching Steve back out the driveway. He's sixty and blocky and quiet and not feeling all that well.

His pickup smokes. It's painted green, but the paint has been dulled and whitened with road salt and acid has eaten holes. The hood is flat, the parking lights are strange slit puffy eyes receding, staring. round owl headlights. They've made him an offer.

I feel sad for Steve. We're a lot alike. He takes care of other people's property. Shoveling snow off roofs in the winter, starting people's pumps in the spring, fixing wiring and siding and shingles in the summer, and now someone is buying off everything. He's sixty and separated and not all that well and he's offered to be the janitor for whatever it is they plan to build here, once all the cottages are down, but they're not interested. The mysterious they. He waves and drives off.

Erica and Page are curled up at either end of the old upholstered swing on the porch. It's almost six. I've dragged them to six different cottages, we were so tired we had to stop half way home and almost fell asleep right there, thank God for Steve, there must have been twenty, thirty cars that drove by and just stared, the people did, smirking. I'll get a blanket from the bed, and cover up my daughters, they can sleep on the porch until I get dinner. It's a little cool out here, a breeze comes through the screens, the porch is open on three sides and we're underneath the pines. In Spring the pollen bothers them. I have to ask Dee if they can sleep at her place if their allergies get too bad, the lake breezes help. I won't be able to do that if she sells.

I'll have to remember to bring water bottles the next time, and I'll have to call Jerry right away, as soon as I go back inside, I'd better latch the screen door, it will not stop anyone for long, I should probably wake them up and bring them inside the house, I hate to, they're so exhausted, they'll be okay out here, I'll be back here in a minute. Do some reading, have a beer, keep an eye on my daughters. I'm probably being paranoid. Better paranoid than sorry. I can read for an hour and start dinner, after, they'll probably go to bed early anyway, though it won't be very early by then. I'll have the evening, what's left of it, to do some work. Earn some money, at something I enjoy doing. Do at least one thing every day that you enjoy. Though I'd rather live on money than cute sayings.

Phone. Maybe that's Jerry. Probably heard what I was thinking.
"Yes."
"Hi Kirsten! It's Bob Nielsen." I don't respond. "Your lawyer," he explains. My whole life has been lawyers, lawyers. "You sound tired."
"I haven't said a thing."
"We've got a date for a hearing. October."
"October!"
"These things take time, Kirsten. You know that. Things are fine."
"Things are not fine, Bob. I want Jacob the hell out of my life."
"And that's what's happening."
"Jacob O'Rourke has not given a shit for ten years and all of a sudden he wants his dear little daughters and who's been looking after them all this time and trying to do the best that I can do and working at two and sometimes three jobs at the same time and wearing myself out all for them and now he wants them."
"Yes."
"This shouldn't be happening."
"He is their father, Kirsten. You know that. The father has certain rights."
"Which he signed away."
"And that's good and that's our second strongest argument. You know that."
"Stop talking down to me."
"And you also know, Kirsten, that our strongest argument is the one you've just been talking about. Okay. The marvelous way you've been raising your daughters for the last nine years, ever since Erica was born. You've said that. I've said that. The judge knows that."
"Good!!!"

"So relax!" He pauses. I am not relaxed. I will not be made relax. I want this goddamn thing over with. "You are being calm and reasonable about it, Kirsten. And fair. Remember that. He is not going to get custody as long as you keep thinking that. As long as you keep doing that."

"Don't tell me things I know a shit of a lot better than you do, Bob."

He doesn't say anything for a while. I hadn't meant to say that, I try to think relaxing thoughts. I tell myself, nothing is ever as bad as I think it is. It is only as bad as I think it is.

"You haven't been like this for quite a while," he says.

"I'm being stalked."

"Oh?"

That is so -- That attitude makes me so -- "Oh?" -- That's all he can say! "Oh?" As if –

Avoid screaming at him. It will do no good screaming at him. He does not necessarily know who Shelley is. He knows I made a terrible mistake, he knows about my background, he's intentionally avoided the details, he's told me that, he's told me it's a long time ago, he wouldn't necessarily know who Shelley is, even though he knows what happened with her mother, it would do no good to go through all that stuff now, it's a long time ago. The very fact that I brought this up, the very fact that I even mentioned being stalked -- I did it, not him, I did it -- this means that in fact I am not as calm as I think I am. Because if I was, I wouldn't have gotten into this. I would have kept my mouth shut. He does not have to know about Shelley. That is all in the past. Long past.

"You know what to do," he says.

"I'll deal with it."

"No, Kirsten. You know what to do. You let the police deal with it. Understand?"

"I'll deal with it, Bob. Trust me."

"Kirsten, you let the police deal with it. The one thing you don't want, are you listening, you know this – Kirsten?" I look through the glass of the inside door, I can see the hook sitting in the eye that's screwed on the porch door, it's locked, I can't see the girls, but I know they're there, the only other way out is through here and I'm standing here. It's hooked from the inside, so no one got in from the outside. They are safe.

"Kirsten?"

"I'm here."

"If you confront this person – I have to assume that's exactly what you're thinking – if you confront this person, do you hear me?"

"Yes."

"If you confront this person, you'll only hurt yourself."

"Why?"

"Think about it. The position your ex is taking – fair or unfair, right or wrong -- the position your ex is taking is that Kirsten O'Rourke is emotionally unstable. That your daughters would be better off living with him, now that he has a stable relationship, and the money to support them." They are safe, the hook is in place, it's locked from the inside. "Kirsten?"

"Yes."

"I want to tell you about a case that came up a few years ago. Okay. You need to hear this. I'm not telling you something you don't know, I'm reminding you, okay."

"Okay."

"You've got a strong case. I'm not saying you haven't. You've been caring for your daughters for nine years, and it's obvious you're doing a wonderful job. It's obvious your daughters love you. It's important to keep it that way. All right. Right?" He pauses. "I want you to listen. Are you listening?"

"Yes."

"There was a court case, about ten years — no, fifteen years ago. Listen. The mother had custody for eleven of the twelve years of the child's life. A boy. Remember this? There was a separation agreement, okay, and the father left the child in the mother's custody. He'd had the kid for one year, and the mother had had the kid for eleven. Remember? And on top of that, the boy wanted to stay with the mother, and he was twelve by this time, old enough to know what he wanted. And the only thing on the other side, on the father's side, was a report from a psychologist that claimed that the boy might benefit from the influence of a male, and on top of that he was gifted, okay, and the father could afford to send him to a much better school. Much better schools. Are you listening? The lower court gave custody to the father, despite what the boy wanted, and despite what the mother had done for eleven years. And the appeals court upheld the decision of the lower court. And on top of that, when the case went against her and the mother applied for joint custody -- she was refused."

"Yes."

"Don't say 'Yes.' Are you listening?" He pauses. Silence gives consent. "There was another case, you probably remember this one too. In this one-- Kirsten? The guy had a housekeeper and more money than the mother had, but that's all he had, and the mother gave the kid really strong emotional support and the court recognized that and admitted as much in its judgment. You remember the hooker in this one? The woman was on social assistance-- okay -- and went from job to job, but she was always there, and she supported the kid too, not in luxury of course, but she gave the kid everything he needed. And the father got custody in that one too. In another case, the guy had a grandmother who said she'd take care of the kid, and in another case, a sister. The deal is, in every one of these cases, the guy had what they call a quotes quotes reconstituted family unit. It could be a housekeeper, it could be a grandmother, a new wife, a live-in, whatever. You see what I'm saying? And then there's the most ridiculous case of all. Maybe you haven't heard this one. The guy wasn't even interested in the kid until they split, and then all of a sudden he's a daddy, and the judge even admitted that. And on top of that, the judge said, the guy's evidence was quote less than reliable unquote, and the woman was a damn good mother, and the reason the judge gave custody to mister daddy and I quote here, I've got it here some -- here we are -- quote if the father does not get custody, he will lose interest unquote. I am serious. That is exactly what the judge said. If he doesn't get custody quote he will lose interest unquote. And mister judge goes on to say that because the mother is such a strong person and that she is so all together and so forth, she can deal with it -- even though she won't have custody, she'll still be a good mother, she'll deal with it. In other words, Kirsten, she got screwed because she was so good. It sounds like something out of the sixteenth century, right."

What can I say?

"I'm not saying that any of this will happen in your case. Every one of these decisions was challenged, people screamed like bloody hell, as you can well imagine. You know that. The thing is, they stood. And you know that too. Remember what your profs told you, Kirsten. In custody, never assume anything."

"Yeah."

"Yeah. You bet. Let the police handle it, Kirsten. You're being stalked, you keep out of it, let the police handle it. You've got better things to do."

"Yeah."

"You'll do that?"

"Yes!!! I'll do that!!!" I didn't mean to shout.

"Relax! Relax!"

"Okay." He's right, I lost control.

"Good girl."

I hate that. I am not a girl.

"I'll let you know as soon as anything happens, Kirsten. Keep cool. Everything is fine. You're doing a good job. You're a perfect mother, you're in control. Prove it. Okay?"

"You still want to meet on Wednesday?" I ask.

"Maybe. I hope."

"I need something more definite than that, Bob."

"I'll call and let you know."

"Thanks for being so definite!" He can be very irritating sometimes.

As soon as he hangs up, I phone Jerry.

He answers.

"Get over here! Tomorrow!"

I slam down the receiver. He knows who it is.

The screen is unhooked. I walk out through the porch and stand on the steps. Over in the sand underneath a tree, out in the late afternoon sun, my two girls are digging. Page is digging, Erica is holding the pail. She's too old for this now, but she's entertaining her sister.

I walk down the steps and cross the driveway and bull through the weeds getting madder as I go, "I told you never to go outside when the door is latched!"

Erica looks up, her big serious eyes filled with guilt.

"Was the door latched or not?"

"Yes."

Page says nothing and keeps digging, looking down at the hole she's making in the sand, stabbing at a minuscule tree root.

"Look at me!"

Page looks up.

"Was the door latched?"

Page nods.

"Who unlocked it?"

Even in my rage, I am glad that neither one blames the other.

"Get inside, both of you!"

They get up and go to the house. I glance toward the road.

Shelley is walking by, looking in. She's heard me shouting at my girls. Of all the people in the world, she was the one person I did not want to hear me being rotten to my two daughters.

When I get back inside and lock the door, I hug them both. "I am so sorry," I tell them.

And still being little girls, they forgive me.

4

It's silent. Except it isn't. Light inside, blackness and walking silence outside, the noise of the trees when the wind moves, the coolness of the breeze, the sofa turned sideways with its back against the side screen, and the swing where my daughters slept this afternoon, my dictionaries and thesaurus and file folders and pencils and laptop.

I should be back inside, at my desk, but the night is cool and I love sitting here listening to the mosquitoes on the other side of the screen with their stingers and I'm in here and they can't get me. Little violins.

A few times I've heard feet going by along the side of the porch. I was tempted to get up to see what kind of an animal it was, but I like the mystery better, mysterious feet padding through the night behind me.

The sofa is musty. On one side of me is a pile of manuscript that I've already edited, turned face down with stickies poking out, notes to the author, I suggest you do this, avoid saying this, does this follow from what you've said two pages before? On the other side is the stuff I have to do yet. A bigger pile. The edited stuff is sloppy, furred with stickies. The unedited stuff has roughly even edges, more or less.

This guy teaches law. Arrogant. Arrogant as hell. He won't let me edit on the laptop, he's got to see everything, and an explanation for everything. Every damn comma.

The bulb in the ceiling is getting dim, giving out. Or maybe my eyes are. Tiny flies beat against it. I don't want to get up and go inside, and reorganize all my stuff in there. I like it out here. The kids are asleep, I'd wake them if I went in. A slat is coming loose in the ceiling. I'll have to get up there, one of these days, and tack it down. Up. Tomorrow. Don't put it off. Do it tomorrow.

And get back to your job.

Fifteen pages.

Light from my bulb paints the lower trunks of the trees. The rest is greyness.

The ceiling in this place is so low it feels like it's moving down. Slowly. We're squatting among the trees waiting for the blow. Me and Erica and Page.

The trees make it musty in here, but they keep it cool. They protect us from the snow in the winter, though branches snap off and crash on the roof. I fix the leaks, but can't afford paint. A one storey shack in the woods, with a screened-in porch and a light bulb at night among the trees.

It's snug, though, I feel protected. Which is strange, given all these other feelings. How can I feel threatened and protected too?

Back to your job.

It's hard to meet my quota some nights. Fifty pages per night.

I've done twenty three, and it's taken me -- an hour and a half. I'll be out here until two a.m., at this rate.

So tomorrow, I've got my Tuesday cleaning, and there's the car, enough to fill the day, especially if it breaks down again.

I should phone Jerry and smooth his feathers. As soon as I get finished, what – the next five. I shouldn't have shouted at him. Made me feel good, though.

A car going by, blinks of light through the trees, like some kind of bigger fireflies.

Took me ten minutes. I've speeded up a little.

Damn.

Just when I think I'm doing fine, some galumphing sentence passes by and all the issues I thought I dealt with fifty, sixty, seventy pages ago. -- I hate this. -- Every time I hit something like this I can't remember how I dealt with it the last time. Or where. And I have to go back hundreds of pages and it takes longer to find what I'm looking for than it does to solve the problem. Once I've found....

Whatever I'm paid, it's not enough. I'll have to tell Tom that. I'm not paid enough, Tom.

Neither am I. He'll answer. That's publishing. I don't believe it. He'll say.

"Jerry?"

"Yeah."

"I wasn't very nice to you."

"Who is this?" I laugh. "Someone phoned and hung up on me."

"I had a bad day."

"That would do it." Yeah Jerry, and you drove by and didn't offer us a ride either.

"Steve got my car going. He said the problem's the alternator. I thought you said you fixed that. The car keeps stalling."

"You told me that already." I didn't and he knows it, he wants me upset and screaming so he doesn't have to come. If you're going to act like that....

"Steve told me I had to get it fixed right away, Jerry. I need your help." There's a bang on the other end of the line. "Jerry?" Swearing, whatever he's dropped. "Aren't you going to help me, Jerry?" More rattling around. "Jerry?"

"You know what to do about it." Distracted.

"You have to come over here. I'm better when I'm not irritated."

"Yeah." In his own good time.

"I need it done tomorrow, Jerry."

"I can see that." He's really trying to irritate me.

"So what time will you be here?"

More noises on his end. "Don't know right now."

"The better job you do...."

"Yeah." He doesn't sound very enthusiastic.

"Jerry, I really need your help. I really appreciate everything you've done for me, okay. And I know how to show it. -- Eight thirty?"

"I'll try."

"It'll be worth it."

Back to the manuscript. Should I make more coffee? I've had too much coffee. Twelve thirty.

Sometimes I can see Noreen, sometimes when I'm just waking up, I can see her face for an instant so vivid, the way she looked.

We were a lot alike. Once she got hold of something, she never let it go, even that last day, when she showed up at that funny little apartment on that rundown street with those kids screaming, I have to stop thinking this, you'd think after all these years.

Shelley showed up. Stan never told me. He said he went downstairs and told her I wasn't there. I had to find that out at the trial. He never told me that.

I am tired.

Get back to the manuscript.

Finishing this is like crawling across broken glass, thirty seven pages what time is it don't look keep working, usually something happens, I make a breakthrough and it goes good after that.

By the time I'm finished I'll be wide awake, editing exhausts me even more than cleaning, I feel hollow, like my bone marrow has been sucked out.

One thirty.

I don't care what Bob says, what does he know, he's a lawyer, if she pushes it too far I'll confront her, maybe, knowing what I'm capable of, she'll back off.

She should know what I'm capable of.

5

I was up by six. Jerry knocked on the door at seven thirty. I was shocked. "Yeah," he said, "I'm more surprised than you are." He's got the hood up, and his toolbox sitting on a tarp underneath the tree by the driveway where I'm sitting, handing him tools as he asks for them. I've got his wrenches laid out on the grass, biggest to smallest.

There isn't a cloud anywhere. It's getting hot.

"Number five wrench," he says and throws a screwdriver on the ground and holds up his hand like a surgeon with his head inside the engine. I put the wrench in his hand and pick up the screwdriver and drop it in the bottom of the toolbox. He's not organized.

Jerry is emaciated. He's abused his body but he knows cars. He's never achieved much because he drinks and does drugs and rots his brain, and he's been caught doing a few stupid things. And he's on parole. He's a friendly guy, though, pretty harmless, given my background, I don't have much to fear from Jerry, I figure he's got more to fear from me. If I didn't think of Marshall. Everything Jerry isn't.

Page walks up, I didn't hear her coming. "I thought you were out back," I say. "Where's Erica?"

"Hurry up! We need the car!" she tells Jerry.

"Shit!" he says.

"Don't talk like that," she says.

"Where's your sister?" I ask. I wet my finger and rub a smudge of dirt from her forehead.

"When's he going to finish?" she demands. I look towards the house and see Erica coming from the living room and going across the porch to the screen door.

"Fuck!" says Jerry. The screen door claps and Page goes off up the driveway towards the road. She and Erica have had a fight.

"Don't go too far," I call after her. Erica comes up beside me.

"Hi Rick," Jerry says, standing and bending backwards to flex his muscles.

She sighs, "Will you tell him I'm not Rick."

"That's what I've heard," he says.

She stares at the top of the trees on the other side of the driveway, she will not communicate with Jerry when he's talking stupid.

"Not too far," I say loudly to Page.

"I'm only going to the road," she objects.

"You can play back here." I won't raise my voice higher than necessary.

"I'll just be at the road."

Jerry pushes the hood down until it's almost latched, "I'll need to get some parts."

"Page, come back here," I shout.

"I'll get her," says Erica. She passes Jerry, who is coming back towards me.

"Hi Rick," he says, and she tosses hair from her eyes and will not speak. He smiles. "I need to get some parts," he tells me.

"How much?" I lean so I can see around him to see what is happening with my daughters. "Page!" She stops and turns back. Erica tries to take her hand but Page won't let her.

"Twenty five, thirty dollars," says Jerry. "I'll see if I can save you some money." Erica follows Page. "Maybe less," he throws down the wrench he's been using, I give him a cloth to wipe his hands and put the wrench in its proper place in line. "How are you today?" he says to Page when she gets back.

"When are you going to get it fixed?" she demands. He smiles and wipes his hands, his truck is parked on the other side of the driveway, if Shelley comes along she'll be able to see his license, not that she needs it, all she has to do is describe the truck and anyone can tell her where he lives, she's been going around causing trouble, I know that for certain, I don't need evidence.

He sits down beside me, continuing to wipe his hands. "Melissa."

"When are you going to get it fixed?" Page demands.

He smiles. "Going somewhere?"

"I'd kind of like to know myself," I tell him.

He looks at Erica, who has returned. "Isn't your majesty going to say anything?" She shakes her head. "I'll call you Rick."

"You're impossible!" She heads for the house.

"Get me a beer while you're there," he shouts.

"When?" Page demands, standing in front of him so he can't ignore her. "When are you going to fix it?"

"Today. Maybe."

"That is not satisfactory," she says and goes after her sister. Jerry roars but I don't laugh, it's not funny.

"So what about it?" Jerry asks, once they're out of hearing.

"What about what?"

"I wouldn't know," he says, stretches out beside the driveway full length, puts his hands behind his head and stares at the tree branches above us.

"Is that all you're going to do? Lie there?"

"Were you called Melissa?"

"Who told you that?"

"Was it?"

"No."

He pulls the peak of his cap over his eyes. "When do you need it?"

"Today. Now."

"What time is it?"

"Eight thirty."

"Canadian Tire doesn't open until nine."

"You'll just make it."

"I need some money."

"Bastard."

I get up and go inside and go through the living room where the girls are watching TV. "Where did I leave my purse?" I ask Erica.

"He's a jerk, Mom," she says. "Why do you have anything to do with him?"

"Do you know where my purse is?"

"Bedroom."

She's right, underneath the mattress, I probably would have found it in a few minutes anyway, I often leave it there, just so it isn't sitting out. I've got sixty five dollars. I never have enough for anything, I am so tired of never having money for anything, even when Jacob was here and we had a lot more money in the house, there was never enough. There is no way I'm giving anything to Jerry, we'll all go to Canadian Tire and I'll pay the bill myself.

The phone rings.

"I've been trying to get you all morning. You won't answer."

"Hi Dee!"

"You have been refusing to answer your telephone all morning."

"How long have you been phoning?" I keep it light, just like I do with my kids when they act silly.

"I've been phoning all morning. Ever since I got up." She's raspy and miserable.

"I've been up since six, Dee. This is the first time the phone has rung, as far as I know. Did you leave a message?"

"I've left you ten messages. You haven't phoned once." She never leaves messages, she hears my tape and thinks I'm right beside the phone refusing to talk to her.

"Was there something you wanted to tell me?"

"My living room is a mess. You didn't clean a thing when you were over here yesterday. I paid you more than I owed you and you didn't clean anything. This place is covered in dust."

"You told me you didn't want me to clean the living room, Dee. We talked about it for an hour. Don't you remember? You said I worked too hard."

"You think you can cheat me any time you want. You think you can take advantage of an old woman."

"I did what you told me to do, don't you remember?" I'm bass, soft and low.

"I don't remember any such thing!" She's treble, loud and harsh.

"I asked you if you wanted another cup of tea. You'd just been talking to some people who wanted to buy your cottage. You were quite upset and you wanted to talk to me about it, you weren't sure what you wanted to do."

"I don't remember that!"

"You were talking about some driftwood that Erica and Page had brought inside for you, you were telling me what wonderful little girls they were, and how much you enjoyed talking to them."

"Well yes, I did say that. I remember saying that."

"You were telling me you just wanted to talk. You told me to forget about cleaning the living room. I had already done the upstairs. You told me I could do the downstairs the next time."

"Did I say that?"

"Yes."

"I forget sometimes, you know."

"I understand. Do you want me to go over and clean the living room?"

"I'd like that."

"I can't do it today, Dee. I've got a lot of places I have to go to today and my car is broken down. I won't be able to go there today."

"Won't Erica and Page be coming over?"

"They can't. They'd like to."

"What day is it?"

"Tuesday."

"Really."

"Yes."

"I am such a silly old woman. I'm surprised you put up with me."

"We enjoy going over there. We just can't today."

"I get lonely sometimes, you know."

"I have an important meeting tomorrow. I'll drop by the day after. I promise. Put it on your calendar."

She fusses around and I wait until she gets down the calendar and brings it to the phone and laboriously writes in that we will be over there the day after tomorrow. I tell her I have to hang up now, I have some things I need to get done, that I'll have to get them done now if I'm going to get over there the day after tomorrow. I stress that, the day after tomorrow. She apologizes for taking my time like this.

"Just do one thing for me."

"What's that?" she asks.

"Don't sign anything until I see it. Will you do that? If someone comes over there and wants you to sign something, don't. Not until I see it."

"I wouldn't do a silly thing like that. Why would I do a silly thing like that?"

I make sure all the windows out back are secure and check that the back door is locked and go to the living room and stand in front of the TV. "We have to go into town with Jerry."

"Oh," Page objects.

Erica is too disgusted to say anything.

"I want to stay here," Page says in the whiney voice she knows irritates me.

"We're going into town with Jerry."

"I don't see why," Erica says.

"To make sure he spends my money on car parts." They stare at me like I'm one of their TV programs. "Let's go."

"Oh," objects Page once again, and gets up. Erica remains cross legged on the floor, staring at me defiantly. I turn off the TV and make sure the windows in the living room are locked, and wait at the front door for my older daughter, who gets up and goes by me and out through the porch to her sister, standing outside. I lock the door behind her and my daughters go straight to Jerry, who is lying under the tree dozing from whatever he ingested last night. They stand looking down at him like two cops who have come to arrest a suspect on a drug charge. He senses their disapproval and stirs.

"Let's go," says Page.

He looks at her from underneath the peak of his cap and grins, and then at me when I come up beside my daughters.

"We're going with you," I announce.

"Don't trust me?"

"No," Erica says.

"I was just getting relaxed here," he says, sitting up and grinning at me with his arms resting loosely on his knees. He looks at Page. "Your mother's been working me too hard."

"We have things we have to do today, Jerry!" I snap at him.

"So give me the money and I'll pick the stuff up," he says, squinting up at me. "I can't fix the car if I don't have the parts."

"Let's go."

"We haven't got all day," Erica adds.

He looks at us, one by one, standing here in a line staring at him. He laughs.

"You can be very irritating," says Page.

He reaches out his hand like a football player who's been decked, like he expects me to pull him upright, I know what he's thinking, as soon as I take his hand he'll pull hard and I'll fall on top of him, and it'll be all a big joke, the whole world's a big joke, as far as this asshole's concerned. None of us moves. He gets up by himself.

"I don't know if I can work with people who don't trust me with their money," he complains, and we follow him to the truck. "I've got some things I have to get," he adds.

"After you're done," I say.

"See what I mean," he says to Page. "She works me too hard."

The parts cost thirty three dollars, and he stops at the LCBO and buys some rye and vodka, and a couple of cases of Molson at the Beer Store. "Would I have been paying for that?" I ask when he puts the cases underneath a tarp in the back.

"Your mother's a very suspicious person," he says to Erica. He has been getting more and more irritated by my daughters, how Page jumps around and gets in the way of his driving, and how Erica half sits and glares out the window. "What is it," he asks, "you can't talk any more?" He resents her silence, and of course she knows it, I love the way she's getting to him.

The truck rattles and squeaks and clunks and the muffler is going and I ask myself, how can he fix my car if he can't do a job on his own, I curse this stupid backwater and the time I've wasted on a car I should have gotten rid of five years ago, if I could afford it. I have never had a new car, ever. I'm always putting up with someone else's second hand problems.

None of us talks on the way back, and Jerry has the car fixed and running half an hour after we return, and when I hear the motor revving, I go out as he's closing the hood. "She's fine now," he says. The girls are inside watching TV, it's eleven thirty, I can get lunch and have them ready and we'll be off for my Tuesday cleaning, a little late but still okay, I can get through it all before supper. He follows me inside and we go by the living room where the girls are sitting cross-legged watching cartoons, Erica pretending boredom. "Go outside," he says to them.

They don't move, I close the bedroom door behind us.

"Shouldn't they go outside?" he asks, taking his shirt off.

"Why?" I start undressing.

"The TV," he says, taking his pants off.

"What about the TV?" My skin is coarse, I have to get serious about my diet.

"I can't do anything with that..." the TV roars, he opens the door and screams at them. I close the door, get dressed, push him out down the hall he hops and gets his pants on hopping across the porch and down the steps I throw his shirt after him. The TV volume is turned down behind me.

"See if I fix your fucking car again," he says, loudly.

"Don't you ever talk like that in front of my daughters," I am barely in control, my voice is soft but I feel like

"You're too fucking old anyway," he says and pulls his shirt on, "I don't know what the fuck I was thinking." He goes to his truck, starts it and backs out the drive, staring at me until he gets near the road and is forced to look behind him so he doesn't sideswipe a passing car or run down a pedestrian and I'm thinking, where is Shelley when I need her? But she's not there to flatten and he turns on the road, brakes, and spins away like a teenager. He really is childish. I have to smile, he'll be seeing his parole officer tomorrow, he'll be subdued the next time I see him.

"Don't let the flies in," Erica shouts. I smile and shut the door. She meets me in the hall. "I'm hungry." They calm me down, my wonderful daughters, just when I'm thinking how hideous the world is, they restore my faith and make me smile. Jerry is such an ass.

6

Kids should not grow up too soon, life is hard enough without rushing it. And they hate being dragged from cottage to cottage like they're prisoners, because their mother cannot afford a babysitter and they're too old for babysitting anyway, Page says.

I can see her in my rearview, asleep in the back seat among the brooms and the mops and the dustpans, she's leaning on a green plastic garbage bag of dust rags, I don't want to stop and wake her up, and I don't want her to fall over and choke on the plastic bag. The car lurches back and forth on this hideous road as I dodge the potholes. Erica is sulking. I made them help me today, even though she hated it, the dust bothers her allergies she said. The sad thing is, it probably does. I hate this life, I hate what I have to make them do. What's saddest of all is, she's offered to help me, and I've turned her down, and now that she has to, I really understand, I'd be the same. That really hurts, I can't do what I want to do, I want them to be kids, I want them to play, I want them to not grow up too soon. Round and round.

"I don't always ask you to help me," I tell her. She's tired, sitting beside me, but she's grown up, she isn't going to fall asleep in the back like her sister, she's too old for that. "I wish I didn't have to."

"That's okay." She'd resent it if I didn't include her, she's pouting out of principle. I had to use them, I'd never have gotten done, Jerry held us up.

"Could you make sure Page is okay?" She turns and glances back and looks ahead again almost instantly. "Is she okay?"

"Yeah."

"Could you look more carefully?" She sits rigid in her seatbelt. "As a favor to me." She unlatches the belt, turns, kneels on her seat and pulls the garbage bag on the floor. Page sort of slides down until she's resting sideways in the space her sister has created. Erica eases her feet up underneath her so that Page sleeps in a fetal position with her head on the cushion of the seat. "Thanks."

"You're welcome." She turns back and buckles her belt.

"I don't think we'll have to do this again."

"That's okay."

"I'll work out something with Dee." I should be able to talk to my oldest daughter. I can't. "We'll have to work out some kind of arrangement. A contract." I'm too protective, even before Shelley showed up. Long before Shelley showed up. I'm probably using Shelley as a handy excuse to continue doing what I've always done. I don't want them to grow up. It's perfect the way it is.

There's a cop car in our driveway, underneath the big Norway Pine where Jerry sleeps when he's supposed to be working on the car. I can already see it from this distance, so everyone else must see it too, it's the main road into town, everybody drives by here. They used to harass me when we first moved in, but nobody has bothered us for years. So probably people won't think anything about it. I don't like cops in my driveway. There's nobody in the car. He's either out around back, or inside the house snooping around. I know I locked it.

When I pull off the driveway the bumping wakes Page and she sits up. "We'll wait here," I tell Erica.

"I'm thirsty," says Page.

"I think there's some water still in the cooler," I tell her. "If you didn't drink it all." She leans over to the floor behind Erica's seat, where I set the cooler.

There's no movement in the house.

"Can you get the top off?" I ask Page, for she's still bending down behind Erica's seat.

"It's difficult."

Erica turns and looks. "It's coming," says Page. I am not getting out and going inside the house. Whatever confrontation is going to take place is going to take place right out here, where we can be seen by everybody. He'll have to come to us. "Got it," says Page.

"Is there enough for all of us?"

"Two."

"Give one to your sister. We'll share."

"How come?" Erica objects and takes the plastic bottle of water her sister hands up to her.

"I'll take a swallow of hers and a swallow of yours."

"Oh," Erica says, opens the bottle, and hands it to me. I take a swallow and hand it back. "I don't really want it," she says.

"I've had enough," I say.

A young cop emerges from the path to the left of the house and heads toward our car. I've never seen him around before. From behind my seat Page's water bottle appears in my grubby daughter's hand. I look down at it, she raises it to my lips, tilts it, I take a swig, and she pulls the bottle back. "Thanks."

"You're welcome," says Page. I wipe some surplus water off my lips.

"I wonder what he wants," Erica says. She's screwed the top on her bottle and is gripping it more nervously than she's letting on. "Probably some damn speeding ticket."

"I don't speed."

I roll down the driver side window and the cop bends over.

"Mrs. O'Rourke?" He has a broad, eastern European kind of face, the open, slightly naive expression of a cop just starting. "I was just passing by ma'am, and thought I saw something out back. I was checking it out. -- Hi." He smiles at Page, who's leaning over the back seat grinning up at him.

"Did you find anything?"

"Could I talk with you alone, ma'am?"

"What about?" Erica demands.

He smiles at her and glances at Page. "I'd prefer if we talk alone."

I get out and walk to the back end of the car where we can be seen from the road.

"I understand you do a lot of cleaning in the area," he's watching my body language, interpreting the tone of my voice, watching the way my eyes move. "I was wondering if you'd seen anything, we've had a lot of breakins."

"No." He takes a notebook from his shirt pocket and jots down something, presumably what I've just told him. "No one I work for."

"I'm afraid that's not true, ma'am."

"No one has said anything to me." He listens for any hesitation, any inflection, any change in tone, but I've been answering questions long before he was born. So old. God I'm so old.

"They asked us not to say."

"That's odd," I reply.

"Perhaps they're feeling a little insecure."

"I suppose." He watches me. I smile. He checks his notebook.

"Do you know a Mr. Gerald," he looks at his writing more closely, "Soroka?"

"He was over here this morning, fixing my car. Maybe you saw him when you drove by."

"Did he say where he was last night?"

"He doesn't tell us much."

"Nothing about last night?" I shake my head, and he notes that. "You've been here at least ten years?"

"About," I admit.

"And before that?"

"I'm sure your records show." My calm surprises him, I think. "Is there a problem?"

"Just getting acquainted," he says, puts away his notebook and starts buttoning his shirt pocket. "I'm assuming your children know." It's none of his business how I raise my children. "I really wouldn't know what to say, ma'am, if I were you. I'm sure it's a problem." And if he thinks I'll react to that, he's a fool. He turns to go.

"I didn't get your name."

He turns back. "Constable Norman Maclean."

I ask him to spell it and he rips off a sheet of paper, hands me a pencil to write it down, then goes to his cruiser, gets in, and backs out the driveway. It's the constant surveillance that wears me down, though I don't always admit it, it's so much a part of my life I hardly notice it any more. Worse than that, it's a part of my daughters' lives too, which I really hate.

"There's been a break in," I explain as we go towards the house.

"Did he think we did it?" Erica asks, I'll have to tell them, I really will, she assumes there's something to be suspicious about. Page lets go of my hand, runs up the stairs, flings open the screen door and waits at the inside door. When I unlock it, she scampers to the living room, turns on the TV, and squats before it.

"It's your turn to help with dinner," I tell her as I pass through to the kitchen. Erica joins her and they have an argument, but in a minute Page comes out and I give her a hug. She helps set the table, get out the potatoes, dump the frozen corn in a pan, fill up the kettle and plug it in, and search the fridge for dessert, even though she knows there won't be any. We'll get groceries tomorrow, on the way back from town and my meeting with Bob Nielson about my damn divorce.

7

We sit surrounded by trees, playing cards, Twenty-one, Ninety-nine, I teach them some euchre, and I can see Page getting tired, her eyelids sandy, she fights to keep them open, they've both decided I've had a hard day and they want to stay up and entertain me, but they can't, Erica is almost as sleepy and finally I put both of them in bed. I won't get my quota done tonight, but maybe I can do twenty pages, ideally twenty five, I can make up the rest tomorrow, and do tomorrow's quota too. I trust. So the end result will be the same.

But I don't feel like doing it, my whole body objects, I'm tired, my brain isn't working, how much should anybody be expected to do?

Turn on desk light, get out the manuscript, arrange it on each side of me, find a lively tape not something soothing that puts me to sleep, that's not what I need right now, shove it in, clip it on, put the earphone in my right ear, turn it on. Strauss. Loud.

It's a quarter to ten. I can get at least an hour in.

A call. Knocking at the front door, on the other side of Strauss. At this time of night?

This is not the time of night I want to answer the front door.

I assume they see the lights in the front room, knock again more loudly.

I go to the living room and turn out the lights.

That doesn't stop them. Knock again. And again.

Monica. "Hello! Anybody home? Kirsten?"

Somebody is with her, I can hear her assuring them that it's all right, Kirsten never goes to sleep until at least eleven thirty, the lights are usually on here until twelve or sometimes later. How she knows that I wouldn't know, unless she keeps an eye on this place every night.

Knocks again. "Hellooo!!" she warbles.

Okay, out through the hall, and talk to her through the screen, which I keep hooked.

"The kids are asleep."

"We won't take a minute," she promises. "I'd like you to meet someone."

I should have turned on the outside light, the person with her is standing three or four paces from the foot of the steps and I can't tell who it is.

"Just a minute," I say, and go back to the front door and lock my daughters inside the house and unlatch the screen door to the porch. "We can talk out here," I half whisper. "My daughters are asleep."

"I know this is a terrible time of night," says Monica coming in talking loudly all the way, "Leslie tells me she has to get back for some kind of meeting tomorrow morning, she won't tell me what it is though. We were going by on our way to the airport, Leslie has her own private airplane can you imagine that. I saw the light and suggested we should see if we could find you in, this is Leslie Wyzeman."

Leslie doesn't let on she already knows me. She's the same woman Stan invested with thirty five years ago. Seventy years old. Leslie Wyzeman is seventy years old. Trim and tall and rich, and a wrinkled old woman who doesn't think she's old. If she could only see herself. But she's rich and doesn't have to.

"We'd like to make a proposal," says Monica, sitting down on the porch swing that my daughters slept on yesterday afternoon. It squeals and rocks. "I feel like I'm sitting in a row boat!" I don't think she should call attention to her weight like that. "I'm totally exhausted, I've had the pleasure of escorting Leslie around our little town all day. I really think the experience has made me a little disoriented. It's not often you get to meet a legend."

Leslie sits in a wicker armchair, sets her handbag on her lap and her legs together comfortably, she still has nice legs, for a woman her age. I don't want to think what I must look like, these blue jeans let my stomach out and emphasize my fat legs and my hips, my skin has gotten rough, my hair is stringy, even when I've got a perm, which is rare, and then a day later it's as unmanageable and coarse and thin as ever, I'm going bald. I've ruined it with dye. You can see the grey.

"I can't take too long," says Leslie, sizing me up, asking herself probably how it's possible I've got daughters and a settled life and people who accept me when I was never accepted anywhere.

"We wanted to talk about your property," says Monica, I have the sense that she's just about worn Leslie out with her loud voice and her big phoney grin.

"I wasn't thinking of selling," I tell them.

"Maybe I can offer you something that would make it worthwhile," Leslie says.

"She can do that," says Monica.

"I don't think so."

Leslie opens her handbag, which is long and flat with a long gold clasp along the upper edge and takes out an offer to purchase and hands it to me.

I honestly don't see why they need this property, we're back along the road that leads away from the lake and there's nothing here but bush, anything it might be useful for can surely be realized on the vacant land on either side of us. All the building will be going on near the lake, from what I understand. That's why people come here, for the lake. I glance at the offer and reach it back to her.

"It's no use to me," Leslie says. "Throw it away, if that's what you want."

I continue holding it out.

"That is a very good offer," Monica butts in.

"How would you know?" I keep staring at Leslie.

"At least look at it before it walks out the door forever!" Monica snaps.

"I don't think it will help anybody to get into an argument about this," Leslie says and stands up. "I've made my offer. Throw it out if that's what you feel like doing. It really doesn't matter to me." She goes to the door and looks at Monica. "I really have to get going."

"I don't believe you're being so rude about this," Monica says and has a brief struggle with the unstable swing, "This is a really good offer," she gets up, "far more than your dumpy place is worth."

I smile. "It's late and I'm tired and my daughters are asleep."

"I would have thought you'd want to think of them and what's good for them," she sounds like she wants to arm wrestle me about it. "All the things you could do for them."

"It is very selfish of me, I'm sure."

"I'll be waiting in the car," Leslie tells Monica, and leaves.

"Do you have any idea who you've just said no to?" Fat Monica glares like she's ready to punch me. I shrug, she goes grumpily down the steps, I switch off the porch light, hook the door shut and go inside the house. The only thing that might be done back here would be a golf course, but the drainage problems would be massive, the offer doesn't make sense. I put it on the bureau beside my computer.

Ten twenty.

Obviously there's no point doing anything tonight, I'll pull down my e-mail and send the publisher a progress report and get a fresh start tomorrow night.

So why the sudden interest in Kirsten?

Yahoo.

Type in my name.

Search.

Twenty sites.

Not that it necessarily means anything, Melissa is a common name. I'm surprised there isn't more. They'll match both names first, first name and last name. Then last names. Then the first name. Something like that. So there might not even be any site that recognizes both names. And even if it is on here somewhere, my name will be one of hundreds of thousands listed for who knows what reason.

A new site.

"The Murderers Among Us."

Five pages of listings, with names, aliases, when convicted, when released, where they're living now.

My name.

Noreen's.

The date. When it happened. Where.

Kirsten is wrong, spelled wrong, both names spelled wrong, not even close. A completely different province.

Almost like a warning -- we'll fill in the correct stuff if you don't do – do what?

We'll get back to you, the implication seems to be.

Who are these people?

"The Family Vigilantes. We fight for the right to make our homes safe for our children."

Fort Worth, Texas.

An e-mail address, of course. "Send us the information we need to know. Where are these people? Who are your neighbors? How can we tell them? How can we protect your children? The American Family Strikes Back!"

And a quote from the Bible. Make sure you always have a quote from the Bible.

"What hast thou done? The voice of thy brother's blood crieth unto me from the ground. Genesis 4:10."

See, God says it's okay, so it must be okay. Thy brother's blood crieth. Strike back! Vengeance!

This is on the Internet. It goes all over the world. Everywhere. My name goes everywhere.

I've got a Bible here somewhere. On the third set of bookshelves, back behind the first line of books, back here somewhere. Black cover, with gold letters. A small thing. King James Version. Where? I know it's somewhere on this shelf. I'll have to take the books out, so I can see what's back there. I know it's here, the shelves are the right height, it's a small, small black -- got it!

Black cover, red edges, $1.10 at the E P Book Shop, wherever that was. The Bible. Authorized Version. Authorized by who?

So what does it actually say here. -- Genesis. -- Chapter Four. -- Verse 10.

"And the Lord said unto Cain, 'The voice of thy brother's blood crieth unto me from the ground. ... And now art thou cursed from the earth.... A fugitive and a vagabond shalt thou be in the earth.' "

And what did Cain say to that? – "Now what? I won't be safe anywhere."

The Lord needed reality checks.

And so the Lord said to Cain -- what?

"Whoever slayeth Cain, vengeance shall be taken on him sevenfold."

Okay. The Lord did not -- *did not* -- give anyone a license for vengeance. Anyone who takes vengeance shall answer to the Lord -- it says so right here. "Vengeance shall be taken on him sevenfold."

I really wish these people who quote the Bible so glibly would actually read it.

Now what?

This is a direct threat to my family. And there is nothing I can do about it. Even if, by some miracle, I shut down this website, whoever set it up will relocate. Anywhere. Whatever I do, I will have to do, nobody will help me.

I put it there five years ago, up above the kitchen in the hanging ceiling, wrapped in plastic so it wouldn't get rusted. I think the ammunition is there too.

Think about this, Kirsten.

What's the up side?

What's the down side?

You're taking a risk. You're not supposed to have a gun.

I'd better get it down.

8

Bob Nielsen has an office above a craft store on the main street, there's a small reception room but his secretary left early and there's no one to watch Erica and Page. I don't want them to hear any of this, so I close the door behind me as I go into Bob's office. He hands me a fax as I sit down. "This just came in."

I fold it in half.

"You don't want to look at it?"

I shake my head.

"Believe me, you want to." He's put on at least twenty pounds in the last year. I tell him he should diet, it's not easy, finding a good lawyer.

"You haven't heard anything from Jacob?"

He shakes his head, he's told me this already. "What's the problem, Kirsten?"

Is there any point? What can he do?

"Kirsten?"

"My name's on a website."

He tilts his head and waits for me to explain, he knows me well enough not to make some stupid joke. It's not worth bothering about, whatever has to be done I'll have to do myself. But I can't stop myself, apparently.

"I want to know what I can do to get it off."

"Where from?" he asks.

"Texas."

He spreads his hands, what can he do about it, speech is free, right.

"This is serious, Bob, it affects my daughters." He stares at me. "I've got a life here. I will not be driven out. I've got a right to be here." He nods. "You're my lawyer, dammit."

He tilts back in his chair. "From Texas."

"Texas."

"Right."

"Don't be irritating Bob. What do I do?"

"Ignore it."

"Don't be ridiculous!" He can see I'm on the verge of throwing a fit, this has really got to me, I thought I had more self control.

He picks up a pen and opens a note pad. "What's it say?"

"How can I make someone take my name off a website? That's pretty straightforward, isn't it. Isn't it!"

He sets the pen down. "What does it say?"

"Bob!"

"I need details."

He waits for my reply, and I wait until I calm down. It was stupid to raise this at all, he can't do anything, what's the point. When I still don't say anything he cocks his head.

"It's a website from Texas." He waits for me to continue. "It mentions my name, Bob, and the names of a lot of other people. It invites people to log on and give them all sorts of information, where I live, what I'm doing, how long I've been there, do people know who I am, what can they do about me. That's exactly what it says, Bob. What can they do about me."

He picks up his phone. "Give me a minute, okay." He punches in some numbers. I relax, as much as I can, while he stares at the ceiling and waits for someone to answer. I unfold the fax he's given me.

An offer to purchase. She's found out who my lawyer is. Godammit, everybody knows my business, they know things about me I don't know.

Across the bottom she's written in big blocks letters, "Immediate Possession!" That's Leslie.

"Norm, Bob Nielsen here," he says. "I wonder if I can put off our appointment for an hour." He looks at his watch. "Can we do it at three, do you think?" He listens for a moment, and I examine his law library, which is stored on four shelves to his right against the wall, law reports, Ontario Real Estate Law, The Rules of Evidence, Torts, The Ontario Family Law Reform Act. "I can appreciate that," he says, "the point is I've got an emergency here and I need a bit of time to deal with it. What am I asking for, an hour? Can you give me that?" I put the Offer to Purchase on Bob's desk and go to the door to check up on my daughters.

They're sitting on the hardback waiting chairs and Erica is holding a National Geographic, reading to her sister. Page is looking politely at the pages her sister is holding open, but clearly she's bored. "I'll be right out," I promise them. "Fifteen minutes." When I close the door, Bob has finished his call.

"Kids okay?" he asks.

"Yes. Thanks." I sit down again.

"Don't forget your paper," he tells me, glancing at the Offer.

I give him my poor little me voice. "Thanks for taking the time for me, Bob." I feel like a little girl asking for help from her daddy, which is ridiculous, since Bob is ten years younger than I am.

"The Family Vigilantes," he reads from the notepad he's placed in front of him.

"They're from Fort Worth, Texas."

There's a monitor on his desk. He turns it toward him, and starts downloading the website. "When did you find out about all this?" he asks.

"Last night, about eleven."

"You've never seen it before?" I shake my head. "So you don't know how long it's been up?"

"No."

"And why do you think it's a threat to your family?"

"That's obvious, Bob," I'm more rational now, my voice is softer, quieter, he can tell I'm not going to freak out. "I won't be safe anywhere. Anywhere there's an Internet."

"Which is pretty sweeping."

"Pretty." He looks at the monitor again and taps the fingers of his right hand on the base of the keyboard. "Slow this morning."

"This afternoon."

He grins. "Yeah, it is."

"I wish I hadn't done what I did, Bob. It happened thirty five years ago. I wish it hadn't happened, but it did. I can't bring it back now. I haven't done anything since." He stares at the monitor, ignoring my little speech. "For the sake of my kids...." He nods, watches the monitor, types "Family Vigilantes" into the box of the search engine, speaking each letter as he does, and clicks his mouse.

"Pretty soon now," he promises. Behind him is a magnificent view of the bay, achingly blue with vivid white traces of cloud suspended above it. Three or four sailboats are scattered across the water, the bay is a horseshoe with hazy headlands of grey escarpment at each end, the open lake beyond is smooth at the horizon.

"I tried to think of everything we could do about it," I say, "but I couldn't decide on anything. I thought maybe we could flood the site with a million hits and close them down. But I didn't see what good that would do, they'd only be up again in a day or two. I thought we could seek an injunction, but it's Fort Worth Texas, all they'd have to do is set up a new site in Saudi Arabia or somewhere like that. I thought maybe the government.... There might be something the Attorney General or the Minister of Justice could do. But then I decided I wouldn't hold my breath about that either. The thought was ridiculous. I know better."

"Here we are," he says, and watches the site unscroll down his monitor.

"I didn't sleep all last night."

"You look pretty awful," he confirms. "No offense."

"Thanks."

He reads: " 'Send us any information we need to know about these people. Where are they? What should we do about them? The American Family Fights Back.' " He taps the desk beside his keyboard. "Right."

"So what can I do, Bob?"

"You've got the Bible against you," he says, still reading. He can't resist being flippant.

"I'll never be punished enough, will I?" He turns and stares at me. "No matter what I do, I'll never be punished enough, even if I was Mother Teresa. Or Elvis. Or John Lennon. I took twenty five years, Bob, I did everything I was supposed to do, it's on record, Bob, anybody can find it, all they have to do is look it up, I served my parole, nine years, it's been thirty five years, and there's always somebody out there who thinks I wasn't punished enough, and thinks they have the right to decide how I should be punished and how much, what I did was wrong, I admit that Bob, I shouldn't have done it, I've paid what I was supposed to pay and it'll never be enough, no matter what I do, I'll never satisfy them, never, never, not even if they execute me, not even if they execute me, they'll want my head on a pike on the CN Tower and even that won't be enough."

He stares.

"It's the Bible, Bob. Nobody believes in God and they still use the Bible. Hell, they don't even read it, Bob, they don't even know what it says."

"Thou shalt not kill," he orates, his eyes don't flicker.

"Vengeance is mine. That means vengeance is his, Bob. He decides, the big maleman in the sky. He. Nobody else decides, He decides. He decides, only nobody believes in God, and nobody's satisfied, the law is all wrong, no matter what it does, it's all wrong, and whatever I do, nobody's satisfied. It's my kids they're attacking now, Bob, my kids. My kids can't have a life, because of what I did."

He doesn't answer.

"It's wrong. I don't care what they do to me. It's wrong."

He looks down at the offer, which is still sitting on my side of the desk.

"Why should my kids suffer for it?" I demand.

He doesn't answer, he waits for me to calm down, I shouldn't let this happen, it doesn't help to go crazy like this, I can feel the tension all along my shoulders, down my spine, every muscle in my body is clamped up tight, I'm breathing hard, I feel like I'm choking.

I think calming thoughts. I gulp air, I calm down.

"I agree," he says finally, very softly.

I wait, until I'm calmer. "So what do I do?" I ask finally. It's almost a plea.

He reads the entire site, which has finished downloading. There's a bloody knife on each side of the logo, which reads, "The Murderers Among Us," and beside the knives, which are pointing towards them, are tiny groups of mothers and fathers shielding their children with their bodies. The child on the right is about six, a girl, with blonde hair. She looks like Page. "Pretty powerful stuff," he says. "Crude, but effective."

In fact it isn't, not with all the other things on the Internet, things much more awful than this is, from a graphic point of view. "What can I do, Bob? If it was just me, I'd just leave. I'd disappear."

"You had some pretty good ideas," he says, turning the monitor away so it faces the window and doesn't distract us. "I like the idea of overloading the site. It's worked before."

"For a while." He nods. "So?"

"Much as I hate to admit it, the government may be your best bet." He makes some notes on the pad in front of him. "Whatever we do takes time, that's the problem."

"It could be over by then," I point out. He nods solemnly. "So what's the point?"

"Giving up is not an option," he replies. Nice, but not very helpful.

"What is?"

"I have to think about it." He looks at the monitor again. "I'll print out the site and make some inquiries and do some research. We'll work out a strategy. Okay?"

"There's not a damn thing we can do about it, is there?"

"Don't give up, Kirsten. It's too important."

And that's all he can do. Mouth bromides. I stand up. "There's nothing from Jacob?"

"Not a whisper."

"Do you really think he could win?"

"You have to be smart, Kirsten. You can't let anything bother you. Not this, not anything. He's got himself a smart Toronto lawyer."

"Bob, this is so wrong! I've been raising my children for six years, ever since he left. We've got a written agreement, Page doesn't even know what he looks like, and Erica hasn't seen him for three years. The last time she saw him she said she hated him, to his face. She hates her own father, Bob."

He stares up at me. I know this look. I'm getting hysterical. "You have to make it clear that you have not encouraged her to think that," he says. "Understand? You have to make it clear to everyone, to the judge, to everyone, that you are not doing anything to alienate your daughter's affections. Which means, Kirsten, that you have to encourage her to think differently about her father."

"In other words I have to tell her that she is not allowed to have any feelings of her own. I know what that's like, Bob. It doesn't work that way."

"Be that as it may," he says, so calmly it's irritating, "you have to encourage her to think more positively about her father."

"The bitch is eighteen. She's a child."

"Good. Perfect. We'll use it. His wife is eighteen, she is not mature enough to take care of your daughters."

"So why would he even have a chance?"

"Keep thinking that."

"I don't trust the law. Not for five seconds."

He grins. "We try to please."

"You know that irritates me."

"Fire with fire." He's still grinning.

"There's one more thing." Gradually the grin fades. "A cop showed up at my place yesterday. He was out back when I drove in, he claimed he was checking to see if we'd been broken into." I wait to see if Bob is taking me seriously. "I think you'll want to make a note of this."

"You're probably right," he says, but doesn't.

"He asked me about some breakins, and he made a remark about where I'd come from before I lived here."

"So there's a pattern here," he admits, and makes a note.

"He asked me if my kids knew about my background, which obviously is none of his business. And then he added something about, he didn't know what he'd say to them, if he were me." Bob makes another note. "Constable Norman Maclean," I add, which he writes down, and looks up at me, almost smiles, but decides against it. I turn to go.

"Don't forget your paper," he says.

I go up to his desk, pick up the offer, and walk out of his office. He'll flip through some law books, tell me he can't find anything about the Internet, the government won't do anything, and an injunction won't work. He can't do a thing. I'm on my own. That's what he'll tell me. I know that's what he'll tell me.

"I said I wouldn't be long," I say to the girls as brightly as I can. Page is sitting in the rotating chair behind the secretary's desk, swiveling back and forth, and Erica is slouched almost flat in a hard backed waiting chair. I tell her to sit up and put the offer to purchase in her backpack. I'm tired, I've got a headache.

When I zip up the pack, she stands and goes to the door and waits for me. Page keeps swiveling.

"Are you coming?" I ask. Page jumps down and runs around the desk and out the door past Erica and scampers down the stairs. "Be careful, you'll fall," I shout just as I hear her stumble and yelp, and I rush out. She's caught hold of the banister railing and is hanging there. I clatter down as she straightens up, grab her other hand, and shake it hard. "You'll stay in the damn car!"

Erica walks by us both and holds the door open at the bottom of the stairs. I walk out gripping Page's hand and take Erica's as soon as we're on the street. "I don't want either of you to cause me any more trouble!" I command as we go along the sidewalk. "Do you hear me!" People stare and pass by and I feel like turning and yelling out exactly what I think of them all.

"We hear you," Erica says, wearily.

I'm too hard on her. I'm too hard on both of them, Jacob always told me that, he was always full of big advice. That's all he had to offer me, advice. The whole damn world is full of damn advice. I forgot the Tylenol.

"Not talking, eh."

"Hi Jerry," says Page.

He's standing in the middle of the sidewalk grinning down at her. "I thought you guys were gonna walk right by me." People go around us on both sides.

"You think you don't deserve it?" I ask.

"Why?" He gives me a big smartass grin.

"Guess!" says Erica.

"I met a friend of yours," he tells me, but I don't answer and he shrugs and walks away.

"He's a jerk," says Erica, looking back as he heads down the street.

"He'll get what's coming to him," I assure her.

"Why are you so mean to us?" Page asks.

"You said you wanted to buy something for yourself?" I ask Erica.

"Maybe you could use some Tylenol," she suggests.

The thing is, can I trust him to do my car?

"We could get some," Page chips in.

It's not worth going back for. Still, I hate letting that smarmy little jerk get away with something.

"Mom!" says Erica.

She's right, I have to pull myself together. "We can do your shopping first, if you like," my voice is softer, I hope, if I lose my daughters I've lost the only friends I've got in the world.

"We need groceries," she reminds me.

There's a Shoppers Drug Mart at the end of the street, we can stop and get the Tylenol there, and then they can do their shopping. That should take an hour and a half, they deserve it, and then we can drive to the supermarket and get our groceries and after that go to the picnic tables along the shoreline right behind the parking lot and eat our supper from the good things in our grocery bags. I can buy them some treats while I'm in the drug store, some chocolate bars and M and M's, they can tell me what they want, we'll work it out together.

"Can we eat at Wendys?" Page asks. How does she do that, how does she know what I'm thinking?

"Wouldn't you like to have a picnic?"

"No." The tone of her voice makes it clear that there is no doubt in her mind at all, a picnic would be a huge damn bore.

"You can feed the seagulls."

"I want to go to Wendys."

"We can't afford Wendys," Erica tells her.

"Oh!" Page says. Her life is one big disappointment.

The headache is almost gone. They like the sunglasses I bought for them, Page looks cool and aristocratic, like a movie star, especially the way her straw hat covers her forehead and shades her face. She reminds me of lady so and so in her English garden, taking tea on a sunny afternoon. Erica seems more high strung, and more modern and with it, she's taller of course, like a healthy young college girl off to play beach volleyball. Her sunglasses are thin and oval, Page's are big and round. Page has accepted the picnic, and Erica is trying what she can do to entertain her sister, they have small colored stones lined up on the far side of the table, and sand falls from some as the sun dries them out. Page has put her shoes back on, at my insistence, you have to wear shoes for supper, I told her. Erica kept hers on and directed her stone-collecting sister from the shore. I told them, stones look better in the water than they do when you take them out and let them dry, they can be quite disappointing, they don't have the bright colors any more. They look like jewels in the water, says Erica. Page gave me three of the best ones, and I've placed them beside my plate. We're all sitting on the same side of the table, so we can face the water and watch the sailboats. Small things, graceful scraps of paper on the water.

Across the bay from us and stretching out to our right, is the long line of the escarpment, and back behind us, partially hidden by the supermarket and the other buildings, warehouses and so forth, is the opposite line of cliffs. The escarpment forms a U, and the town is in the trough of the U, though the cliffs become low hills as they curve around the base of the horseshoe at the end of the bay. The ancient portage started somewhere here and went up through the hills to a small stream and across the height of land to a river and then through the lakes near our place and along a trail by our house somewhere, and out to the inland sea. According to Jacob. He loved that expression, the inland sea, it made it seem so much more important. It really is an inland sea, he said.

"Your father and I went along that shoreline over there," I tell them, "as far as that headland," pointing to it. "It was a lot rougher than I thought."

"What was he like?" Erica asks.

"Don't you remember?"

She shakes her head.

"I do," says Page. "I know exactly."

"You weren't even born yet," Erica says.

"Actually she was," I correct her.

"Told you," Page says.

"Okay, what was he like?" Erica demands.

"Nice," says Page.

"You don't know what the hell you're talking about."

"Erica!"

"She doesn't," Erica insists.

I tear up a slice of bread. "We haven't fed the seagulls yet."

I throw a couple of pieces of bread on the sand in front of our table, and immediately every seagull within sight rises and heads straight for our table and they hover, six feet above us like sixty shrieking white helicopters. The sound of their wings are like whirling blades, an undulating thwish thwish, right above our dinner laid out below them. Page shouts and waves her arms, but they won't go away, like they're nailed to the sky directly above us.

"Good shot, Mom," says Erica.

9

It gets so dark here. No street lights, no house nearby, no Moon, the trees around the driveway shut off whatever faint light there is. They were polite, they said they enjoyed the movie. I would have been better to go to Wendys, I would have spent less.

Page is sleeping in the back seat. Erica tried to stay awake to keep me company, but she's leaning against the door and hasn't talked for the last half hour. The headlights on the front of the house make a stage setting, with the porch in the center, a tree trunk and a few branches sticking out on one side, and scrub bush on the other. There's a birch tree to the rear of the house, and its trunk is faintly illuminated like a spirit of the dark woods. The car hasn't been acting right, it hesitates on the corners and doesn't have much pep.

When the motor is turned off, Erica stirs.

"We're home," I announce. She mumbles and doesn't move. I turn and reach into the back seat and shake Page by the arm.

"We're home. We have to go in."

She reaches across her breast and places her hand on mine and holds it there, and keeps sleeping.

God I love them.

"We're home," I say more loudly, and shake Page again. "We have to go in now." Neither moves. "Page. Erica."

Erica sits up. "What time is it?"

I turn around and turn off the headlights. "Nine thirty. It's dark."

She opens the door and sleepwalks to the porch. I pull up the latch on the back door of the car, get out, open it, look around to make sure all the others are locked, and shake Page. She stirs, I reach in and lift her, lock the door, carry her to the porch and set her down there.

"You're heavy," I tell her. "You're growing up." She stumbles up the steps and I hold the door open for her and then go across the porch to the main door where Erica is waiting, drunken with sleep. I unlock the door and as they go in, I look back at the car to make sure I remembered to turn off the lights.

I have.

By the time I'm in and locked up, they've already gone to their bedroom. I find them sprawled in their clothes on their pallets on opposite sides of the room. I strip them down to their panties, tuck them in, stand at the door just to look at them lying there, and then close the door softly.

It's so silent in the house I'm afraid they'll hear me, and I move softly to the back door, check it and all the windows for signs of a break in, find none, get myself some orange juice, and check the messages.

One new message:

"I never know how to do this." Dee's voice. "Am I doing this right? I want to speak to Kirsten. Are you there Kirsten? I was thinking, when you come over here to finish up your cleaning tomorrow, see, I remembered, you didn't think I'd remember, did you. Maybe we could all go out. I was thinking we could all go out in my boat, to one of the islands or something like that. I know the girls would like that. They're always down at the dock. We could take a picnic and motor out to an island and eat our lunch and maybe dinner out there. Is that a good idea?" A long silence. "I don't know if you heard this or not.... Kirsten?" Another pause. "I guess I won't get an answer. Maybe I'm not entitled to one. The way I've been acting." Another pause. She hangs up.

Poor old Dee. I sit down at the kitchen table and drink my juice.

I forgot the groceries, they're still in the car. It's almost ten. Maybe I should leave them there, I could bring them in tomorrow.

The stars are ten million spots from the other side of the universe. So far away. I feel so alone. The girls are the only thing worth living for. Despite the seagulls, I did enjoy the picnic. I'll need to take two trips to get all this in. Up on the porch and inside the screen door. I hate mosquitoes. And back outside. It's so damn dark. We're so far back from the road, in among the trees. If someone wanted to do something, they wouldn't have a problem. I'm imagining things. The trees create shadows, and the shadows look like anything, bears, people, someone waiting. And me, getting stuff from the trunk, illuminated by the trunk light. The sound of the trunk slamming.

I'll have to get another lock. There's a deadbolt at the back, and one on the inside front door. But the porch door has a hook and nothing else. Someone could break in and be waiting on the porch when we open up the door in the morning.

We're completely isolated here. The house is so far back from the road you don't even know it's there, in among the trees, not one house close by.

Metal and chemicals, and it can kill someone. The last time I fired it was five years ago. I'll have to get some practice. Out in the woods somewhere. I'd feel awful, if someone showed up and I hadn't even tried the damn thing. It feels good. Smooth and deadly. Little pieces of metal.

This was Jacob's idea. Everything we've got is Jacob's idea. And then he leaves.

Ten thirty. I haven't done any work. If I don't do something, I'll get really hopelessly behind. I'm already behind. I'm too tired to edit. I have to. Have to.

We fight for the right to make our homes safe for our children. Their children, not mine.

10

I'm sitting in the car trying to start it, getting more and more frustrated, the motor whirs and stops. Page comes down the porch steps and walks along the path that's been worn in the grass and then along the gravel toward her mother, who is cursing at this damn car. My daughter is wearing an old flower print dress that comes down to her ankles and her movie star sunglasses and a straw hat that shades her face and makes her look mysterious. When she came out for breakfast she had dark rings under her eyes, and I asked if she'd slept all right and she said yes, but that obviously isn't true. She should get her sleep, she's only six. I don't understand what would keep her awake. She's not grown up yet.

I try once more, the motor whirs and dies, and I yank the key from the ignition and roll down the window. "We're going to have to walk."

"Damn Jerry," she says.

"Page!"

"He thinks he's so smart."

"You'd better get your jeans on."

She turns and goes back toward the house.

It's another nice day, a little hotter than yesterday. It's boiling in the city, the radio says, they'll be roasting on the Gardiner. I love to listen to the road reports, to hear what I'm missing, I remember where the 401 dipped down to the Don Valley and the heat waves shimmered like the road was cooking bacon. There's a cool wind at the tops of the trees, the sky is blue porcelain.

There's so much that's nice about this place. It's got good memories, the girls, the first three years with Jacob, the trips we used to take, learning to handle a canoe, portaging, sleeping out at night a million miles from anywhere, the stars like a window on the infinite, finding petroglyphs along the shoreline, wondering how long ago it was they'd been painted, who those people were that did it. Lying in the house at night with Jacob beside me, wondering about the portage that went by here somewhere, almost hearing them going by in the dark, three hundred years ago, really at peace with myself, for the first time.

I lock the car and go back to the house. The morning sun lights the porch and glows along the roof and heats the house like glass. A Blue Jay lands on the Norway Pine and squalls, harsh and raucous, again and again, it's a beautiful looking bird, light grey belly, a mantle of blue along its back with white and black striped highlights, a crest that peaks behind its head, black alert eyes, a sharp efficient ebony beak. A cute crow. We'd never know that, if it learned to keep its mouth shut.

"Jerry. This is Kirsten." God, I almost said Melissa. "The car isn't working." He's smiling, I know Jerry. It's hard to keep my voice down. "Maybe you could come over and get it going." I hang up.

I can't scream at him, that wouldn't work. It's almost nine. He should be up by now anyway.

I wait a couple of minutes, dial again, and the phone rings. When the message comes on, I hang up, wait a couple of minutes, and call again. It rings, the message comes on, I hang up, call a fourth time, hang up. If he wasn't up before, he will be up now.

Erica is in the living room hitching up her backpack. I help her adjust the straps. "Is Page outside?" She nods. "She told you the car isn't working?"

"I heard you."

"Didn't you think I was nice to Jerry?" She huffs. "I'm sorry we have to walk. Did you put in your swim suit?" She nods. "Page's too?"

"It's all taken care of Mom," she snaps.

"If we had any money I wouldn't bother with the bastard."

"I'm going to make a million dollars. I can't stand this."

"I'm sure you will," I give her a kiss. "Think about the boat ride, okay. You're a wonderful help."

"We have to stick together, right." She really tries to be positive.

"Absolutely."

I watch my serious daughter walking straight for the door and across the porch and down the stairs. Page is sitting under the Norway Pine, waiting, and as soon as I've double checked the windows and the doors and locked up everything securely, I come down the steps and march by them like the leader of a Girl Guide troop. "We're off!" Page clambers up as I pass and I assume Erica is behind her and I walk to the end of the driveway briskly, setting a good example, but stop and look back to make sure they're following, I can only go so far before I start to worry. By the time they're grown, I'll be a physical and emotional wreck.

"Just think about the Indians," I say when they catch up, and I lead them down the road towards the lake, "they used to travel hundreds of miles without a rest," I slow a bit so they can catch up, "with big heavy packs and birchbark canoes on their backs, and their kids, at night, through the woods, with the Iroquois all around them, just think what they felt like. Just think. At your age you'd have a big pack, twenty-thirty pounds of stuff and a baby to look after, probably."

"We do," says Erica underneath her straw hat with her blue backpack sticking out back, "I do."

"It's not so bad is it?" I wait until she comes up beside me and pat her shoulder and Page comes over on the other side and takes my free hand.

"Can I carry something," Page offers.

"Forget it," says Erica.

"It's sunny and we're going for a boat ride," I look down at Page, and then at Erica again, two straw hats walking along the shoulder of the road with their mother between them. "We'll have a picnic on the island. The Indians never had it so good."

"I'll be dead before we get there," Erica says.

Tires crackle on the gravel of the shoulder of the road, right behind us. I take Page's hand and grab Erica by the backpack and pull them off the shoulder to the ditch. And turn and see Constable Maclean in his cruiser, with a female officer beside him. He pulls forward and the woman rolls down her window and says "We need to talk." She's thin, blonde, twenty three or twenty four, and her tone of voice and the way she looks at me makes it obvious she has all the answers, and an attitude. "It'll just take a minute," she adds, though she knows and I know that isn't true, it'll take the rest of my life, is what it will take. The best way to handle this is to not say anything. Let them explain themselves.

Maclean leans forward. "We need to talk to you privately."

The woman glances down at the kids. "We can make you," she says. "That's why I'm here."

"I'll look after Page," Erica tells me.

The ditch beside the road is shallow with grass and some tall blue cornflowers, and on the far side is a low sand bank and the woods beyond that. "Sit over there," I tell Erica, and watch as she leads Page through the grass and they sit down on the bank.

"They'll be fine," says the woman.

I turn toward them. "What is it?"

"Could you get in the car."

"No."

She steps out and opens the back door. "In."

"You're going to do this right in front of my daughters?"

"In."

I don't move. "This is harassment. You have no reason to do this." Her eyes are stone. "I'll lay a complaint."

"That's up to you."

I look back at my daughters. Page is digging in the sand, concentrating on the hole she's making. Erica has taken her backpack off and is trying to find something. "It's okay," I tell them, and get in. The woman slams the door behind me.

"Damn you to hell," I say to Maclean, and can see through the windshield, on the shoulder on the other side of the road, Shelley, walking toward us, though she's just turned the corner at the crossroads. My daughters are to my right, across the ditch on this side of the road, but the cruiser has no door handles on the inside and there's a heavy metal screen between me and the cops. There's a metal bar just below the screen where people are handcuffed, and the metal interior of this space feels and smells like a cell. Someone was sick in here last night.

Nobody talks and Shelley walks slowly toward us and then stops and stares at the cop car. She's still far down the road.

"Why am I here?" I ask.

"We want to ask a few questions," says the woman. "We're hoping you'll cooperate."

"You couldn't have dropped by my house. You had to stop me in the middle of the road and lock me in your cruiser."

"Ma'am?" says Maclean.

"I think you heard me."

"We were wondering if you knew anything about a break in at a house down the road," she says.

"What is your name?"

"Answer the question."

"I've asked you for your name. Are you refusing to tell me."

"Johnson."

"First name."

"Louise," she snaps. "Do you know anything about this break in?"

"No."

"You drive by there every day," she says.

"I was in town yesterday. Yesterday afternoon."

"Can anyone verify this?"

"Why is that necessary?"

"It isn't ma'am," says Maclean. "We were just wondering if you might be able to."

"I was at my lawyer's. You'll be hearing from him."

"That's up to you, ma'am," Johnson says. "Where were you yesterday morning?"

"I was working. Why are you asking me?"

"Just asking, ma'am," says Maclean. He's watching me in his rearview, and his partner is looking around, gauging my reactions.

"The morning?" she says.

"At a client's."

"Who?"

"That's all I'm saying without my lawyer. Unless you have a reason to ask me any further questions, I want out of this car right now. I have work, I'll be late. And I've got children to look after."

"We would appreciate it if you could tell us a little more," says Maclean.

"Is there any reason why you won't cooperate?" Johnson asks. I'm no longer on parole, they can't make me answer or charge me with obstruction, not without my lawyer.

"Where was this break in?" I ask.

"Just up the road," she says.

"I can't tell you anything if I don't know exactly where it was, can I."

"The house at the corner," he says. The place where Shelley is staying.

"I didn't see anything."

"Did you go by there yesterday morning?" Johnson asks.

"I will not answer any more questions without a lawyer present."

"Why would that be necessary?" he asks. I don't answer.

"You were on parole for nine years," she says.

"And?"

"Nine years?"

"I haven't been on parole for over a year. I served my time."

"Second degree homicide," the woman says.

"You've got it all on record," I point out. "Do you have any reason for asking me all these questions?"

"It was a pretty horrible murder," she says.

I don't comment.

"Some people say you got off easy."

"Who might those be?"

"Me, for one. I've seen the pictures."

"I've paid for it. I don't owe anybody anything."

Constable Louise Johnson turns fully, lays her arms on the back of the seat, and fixes me. "My father was shot dead. He showed up at the wrong place at the wrong time." There is no response to that, no matter how I react, it will be wrong. "He was a cop. I was fifteen." Neither of us looks away. "He had a huge funeral. Cops came from all over North America. And you know what happened to his murderer? He got manslaughter. Five years. He's walking the streets right now. Between you and me, just between you and me, there isn't a day goes by I don't curse the courts and the judges and the whole fucking legal system for doing that, for making a mockery of everything my father did. The only people who have any rights any more are people like you. If it was up to me and every other cop in North America, you'd be dead. But that's only my opinion. I'm just a cop."

I don't want to give this bitch the satisfaction of beating me, but there's something wrong, I have to look away. Page is walking toward the woods and Erica is saying something, I can't tell what, but she's looking at the cruiser and sitting down and Page isn't stopping, I can imagine from the angry set of Erica's shoulders what it is she's shouting at her sister now, but it isn't working.

"My youngest daughter is in trouble," I say and look back at the bitch who's kept staring at me. Maclean looks out the window. Erica is up and following her sister, she's grabbed her hand and trying to pull her back but Page is pulling away and falls down, her legs working, trying to escape, she's stronger than she looks. Erica is shouting at her.

I try to open the door, but there's no handle. I pound at the window. The girls look up and I gesture at them to go back where they're supposed to be and sit down. Erica lets go of Page, who stands up and hollers something I can't hear. Maclean watches her, but the bitch hasn't moved and keeps staring at me. I don't have to look, I know what she's doing.

"I want out of here," I demand. Johnson doesn't move a muscle. "I'll hold you both responsible if anything happens to them."

"They're fine," she says, her voice even and unconcerned.

"How do you know," I demand. "You haven't looked."

"I've seen the pictures."

"I want out of here now!"

"I don't know what makes you think you have the right to have kids," she says.

Maclean pushes a release and the door pops open, I get out, walk across the ditch, take my daughters by the hand and pull them back towards the cruiser just as Constable Johnson slams the back door shut and gets back inside, my sense is she's disgusted with Maclean. "Why don't you arrest us all?" I demand.

The bitch watches me as they drive off and I'm left here on the edge of the road holding my daughters' hands.

"She wouldn't come back," says Erica.

"I was bored," says Page.

"Let's go to Dee's," I tell them. My lungs feel constricted, I'm having trouble breathing, I inhale three or four big gulps of air, I tell myself, relax, relax, my head feels numb. Erica's backpack is sitting on the bank and I lead them back there. As she puts it on, I brush off Page's jeans and take a comb from Erica's backpack and while I comb Page's hair, my youngest daughter runs her hand through mine, staring at me very seriously, neither of us smiles or says anything. When I'm done, I do Erica's. She complains when the comb gets caught and I pull out some tangles, I apologize, and when we're all straightened up, we come through the ditch and start off toward the corner again. Shelley is almost opposite us now and as we pass she says, "Hello Melissa."

I stop.

For about fifteen seconds I am overwhelmed by the urge to run across the road and grab her by the throat and shove her down and hold her with one hand while I beat around blindly with the other until I can find a rock big enough to smash her skull in, I can feel the heft of the rock and the way my arm muscles knot as I bring it down as hard as I can and the sound of her skull bones munching and the burst of her blood all around the rock as I smash it down down down again again again.

"Are you okay, Mom?" says Erica.

"I'm fine," I say and start off again.

11

When we reach the crossroads, I stop Erica and get my change purse from her backpack and take out all my coins and put them in my pocket, and put the purse back in her pack.

Steve drives by and doesn't wave. "What's his problem?" Erica asks.

"I wouldn't know," I say.

"I'm tired," says Page.

"We'll rest at the store," I tell her. "I have to make a phone call."

There's a bench in front of the big plate glass window, facing the sand flats with a glimpse of the lake beyond the trees, and Erica and Page sit while I pull the door of the phone booth shut, spread my coins out on the ledge beneath the phone and pause for a moment, to rehearse what I have to say. I'm sure he won't be in, or if he is, he'll have the answering machine on. This phone booth is so old it'll go straight to a telephone museum, when they finally haul it away. The lower panes of glass are missing, the folding door squeals, there's sand jamming up the guide track and the door won't shut completely unless I ram it. What if I can't get it open again? It would be just my luck, to be trapped here in this half glassed cage.

The answering machine.

"Bob, Kirsten. Ten minutes ago I was stopped on the road by Constable Maclean, and his partner, Louise Johnson. They made me get in the cruiser in front of my daughters and I finally had to demand to be let out so I could look after them. All this was done on a public road with people driving by wondering what the hell I was doing in a police cruiser. Johnson did most of the talking. There's been a break in, she said, and they wanted to know if I had any information. They locked me in their cruiser, Bob, and she told me that she, and every cop in North America, wants me dead. She didn't think I had any right to have kids. According to her, I have too many rights. That's what I can remember right now. As soon as Johnson started going on about my kids, Maclean let me out, he knew she'd gone too far. I'm laying a charge of harassment against them both, Bob, and I want you to handle it. I'll talk to you later."

For half a minute I'm convinced I really will be trapped in this jerkass telephone booth and then the door pulls open just enough so I can get out and I sit down by my daughters, we don't talk, they know I'm upset, and then I stand up and we go on. I agree with Erica. I don't know why Steve didn't offer to drive us, he could see we were walking, he knows what the situation is.

I'm usually so worried about damaging my tires or ripping off a muffler I don't notice the details along this drive, the little areas of swamp and the curved white trunks of the birch trees back in off the road and the bright yellow of the sunlight they let in and the butterflies that come tumbling by and the trees like a tunnel ahead and how hilly the road is, how hard it is to walk up and down through here, and the great round rock mantle underneath covered with moss and grass thatch. It's rocks through here and rotted leaves and tree branches and thin soil and marshy where the water collects and can't get away. Before the lake and the sand silted up the flats back behind us, and turned the water to swampy sand, and the sand to dry land, this used to be an island, a little world by itself. And then the sand filled in and connected it to the rest.

Page has run ahead but we're so close to Dee's cottage now I don't worry, we'll be there in a minute.

Erica has stayed with me. She doesn't have any friends her own age. I was like that too, so it's probably hereditary. It isn't very healthy though. Her only friend is her sister. I've given her that at least.

Come September, she'll be going to Grade Five. The school bus takes them every morning and lets them off at the end of the driveway about five thirty when it's already dark, so they're gone all day and I have no idea what they do or who they talk to, they never bring their friends home or tell me what's gone on at school. At least Erica doesn't.

Page makes friends, at least she says she does, but Erica never talks about the kids on the bus, or the friends she makes at school, assuming she does make friends at school. I've never asked and she doesn't offer.

I'm afraid to ask her.

"How's your headache?" she says.

"Better," I assure her. "I hardly notice."

"Those bastards didn't help." I can't object to her choice of words, it's a scientific description. "They didn't have to stop us like that."

"No."

"I wonder who talked crap about us this time."

"Don't say that."

"People talk crap about us," she says.

"Who?"

"People."

"Who?"

"Assholes."

"What do they say?" We're looking down to make sure we don't stumble on the roots that have grown across Dee's driveway at this point. My daughter is stooped like the weight of the world is pushing on her shoulders. "Erica?"

"Nothing."

"It can't be nothing if you won't tell me." That was too harsh. I'm concerned for my daughter, I don't want to sound like I'm cross examining her.

"It's not important."

Do they talk about me? What do they say? I don't ask her, the last thing she needs is a paranoid mother.

"Stupid shit," she adds.

"It doesn't matter what anybody says," I don't believe it even as I say it, it does matter, it matters a lot, to her, and that really tears at my heart

"They're liars."

"Is it me?" I can't stop myself, my mouth is independent of my brain. "Erica?"

"They're assholes."

A chipmunk is sitting on top of a broken branch that's fallen by the side of the driveway up ahead of us, the trees are tall, evergreens, the driveway twists and winds among the tree trunks. The chipmunk stands on its hind legs as we get closer, and then drops and runs, stops, runs along the branch, flicking its tail above its striped back.

"I guess you don't want to say."

It drops to the ground and scampers off.

I have to tell her what I've done. I didn't want to tell her when she's only nine. She's too young for that burden. But I have to tell her.

"I love you more than anything else in the world. I would never do anything to hurt you, even if it was the last thing I had to do in my life." That has nothing to do with anything, she doesn't respond, she knows I love her, the information is boring. "I did some things a long time ago. Long before you were born. A long long time ago."

"Were you in jail?" she asks.

"A long time ago."

Page is sitting on the steps by Dee's side door, as soon as she sees us she jumps up and yanks the door open and runs inside and I can hear her merry high pitched voice shouting "Hi Dee," and Dee crying back, "Page, how wonderful to see you, where's your mother, where's Erica?" and Erica doesn't ask me the next logical question, "Why were you in jail, Mom?" we're too close, thank God, I don't have to answer that now, we're too close, Dee will see us any second, I'll answer that later, before she asks, I know she'll ask me, she won't let it drop, I'll answer her, somehow, I don't know how.

They'll blame themselves. How do I make them understand that, that they shouldn't blame themselves, kids blame themselves, some jerk makes a comment, kids take it personal. They mustn't. They have to understand that. Whatever your mother did, you don't take crap for it. It wasn't you, it was nothing you did.

Page is stuffing a butter tart in her mouth and all around it and kneeling on a chair looking at a map spread out on the kitchen table and Dee says, "Don't get crumbs on it, dear," and Page says brightly, "I won't," and does. Dee smiles.

"Do you want a butter tart?" Dee asks Erica when we come in and Erica nods and slides her backpack on the floor and takes the tart and pulls a chair up beside her sister and looks at the map. I pick up Erica's backpack and Dee puts her arms around me and hugs me and I lean against her, I can't reciprocate while I'm holding the backpack. "You look tired," says Dee.

I nod and sit in a chair opposite my daughters.

I'm relaxed. That surprises me. We're all relaxed. It's almost like home. Dee goes behind my daughters and leans forward, pointing at a spot on the big sheet, which is a photocopy of a rough map of this whole area with roads and forest areas and islands drawn in. Someone has penciled in amateurish diagrams of buildings and miniature cars and boats in the water. "That's where we're going today," Dee says.

"What's that?" I ask. I am tired, like she says, I've still got a headache, which isn't as bad but I'll need to lie down for a while. I've got two more cottages to do after Dee's, but I don't need to do them until some time late this afternoon, when we get back. She has a Delft porcelain clock on the wall beside her broom closet, it says ten forty five. I've got the living room to do, that's all.

Dee switches the sheet around so I can look at it more closely and Page turns her head sideways so she can read it upside down. "This is what they plan to do here," says Dee. "That friend of yours left it, she said it's the only copy she's got, we have to take care of it. She has something to do with all of this, I'm not sure what exactly. That's my cottage there, what they plan to do with it. Some kind of conference center, she says, you can see what she's written there."

"You've sold?" I ask.

"It's just a sketch. They'll make it better."

"But have you sold?"

"I'm thinking about it seriously."

The map shows everything, a complete plan of Leslie's development scheme, with hotels and marinas and a kind of Disneyland entertainment complex. There's a dotted line that parallels the road that leads in, and a penciled notation, "Ancient Portage Trail." Who knows that? It's pure speculation. I've walked all through there, I know that whole area. It's swamp.

But what stands out, what screams at me, is another notation, "Native Meditation Center," exactly where our house is, in the same handwriting as the commentary for Dee's place.

"Your friend wrote that," Dee says, she can see what I'm looking at, it's so obvious, we both know where my house is.

"I really don't know her," I say. Page is standing up with her feet on the chair and her hands on each side of the map, making an arch of her body like a picture I've seen of the Egyptian goddess of the heavens, with her body curved above the earth and spotted with stars. I turn the map around and she sits down, rests her chin on her hands and stares at it some more. Erica eats her butter tart and watches me.

"Have you heard of Glenerin?" I ask Dee.

"What is that?" she asks.

"It's a slum, Dee. The same woman who wants to do all these things," I gesture at the map, "did the same thing in Glenerin thirty years ago. She bought the houses and drove out all the people who used to live there and then sold it to a third rate real estate company that went bankrupt. The stores are boarded up and the hotels are brothels. She's not my friend."

"Don't you think the girls should go outside and play?" she asks, but neither Erica nor Page move.

"Do you want this cottage all boarded up?" I ask.

"Or used for something awful?" says Erica.

Dee looks at me in horror.

"What?" Page asks.

"Why don't you go outside with your sister," Dee suggests.

"I'm tired," Page says, and besides, the conversation in here is much more interesting.

"I have to finish the living room," I say and get up. "She's not my friend."

"What?" Page asks Erica, but her sister doesn't say and Dee asks if they want another butter tart and looks angrily at me as I go out to finish the cleaning she was so furious about the day before yesterday.

"She said she was your friend."

Oily exhaust boils up from the back of the motor and drifts above the surface of the lake behind us, and sometimes when the wind shifts, chokes us. We're heading along a channel between the mainland and a smaller island, through a corridor of wild rice and small fish swimming among silt covered rocks. Erica is up front staring at the water that glitters by, watching for rocks high enough to scrape our bottom and ding the prop.

The wild rice bends away as we pass by and I can see the V of our wake rippling through the green stalks like wind passing across a wheat field. Erica holds up her hand, and Dee slows down. Page presses against her sister's leg, drags her hand in the water, grabs at a floating weed, pulls it up and drops it in the bottom of the boat. And leans over and drags her hand again. I'm sitting in the middle seat facing forward and

Dee is at the back with her hand on the throttle, steering and slowing as Erica directs. A small lily pad with a long trail of root swirls by, stirred by the wake and Page's hand. Three or four fish dart off the way we've come. Dee cuts the motor once again.

My daughter's hats are straw disks. They've got on their bathing suits and I've insisted they stuff their blue jeans and tops in the shopping bag that Dee provided. Erica's backpack is beside Dee's white and maroon plastic cooler, where we've packed our pop and sandwiches and the cookies. Page grabs at a lily that floats by. I tap her and shake my head, she looks back at me and nods, grabs at another long floating weed and dumps it in the boat. It's a long green vegetable snake with Elizabethan collars. Baby snails like brown transparent gravel are stuck underneath the collars. We're moving very slowly now, the oily exhaust goes straight up.

"It's a wonderful day," says Dee.

I nod. Page has spread her small arms on the gunwale and gazes at the water. Erica watches the channel like a deckhand on a lakeboat. She raises her arm again and Dee cuts back the throttle once more. We're crawling.

"It would be a shame to change all this," I say.

"Your friend thought it was all right."

"She is not my friend."

A dragonfly whirs across our bow, lands on the gunwale beside me, moves its biplane wings up and down, remains still for a moment, and then whirls off. Page stands up and comes back to the middle seat. I move over and she sits beside me.

"Find anything interesting?" I ask. She shakes her head. "I don't think you've been here before." She shakes her head. "There must be something interesting." She grins and closes her eyes and shakes her head. "Are you cold?" She shakes her head, her eyes are still closed. "You don't feel a chill?" She grins, keeps her eyes closed and shakes her head. It's become a game.

"Is it getting deeper?" Dee asks Erica.

Erica nods.

Ahead of us the weeds and the wild rice taper off and the channel opens out into a broad stretch of water. The end of the small island is off to our left. Dee speeds up.

"You can stop watching," she shouts and my older daughter turns around and sits huddles into the cavern of the V at the bow. Dee opens the throttle another half notch and speed bends the brim of Page's hat upwards. She turns it back down and holds it there with her hand. As we emerge from the end of the island, the wind off the lake catches us and I move Page to my other side where she's protected.

"Do you need a sweater?" I shout to Erica.

"No thank you," she shouts back.

Page says something which I can't hear and I lean towards her. "You never swim," she shouts. I shake my head.

Dee leans toward me, "See all these islands," pointing around us and up ahead at a channel beyond which we can see three separate islands. "They own them all. It's already too late."

"They say," I reply.

"Your friend...."

"She is not my friend."

"She said she knew you," she shouts. I nod. "When she was twelve." Shelley! I thought she was talking about Leslie! "She said she knew you."

"She wants you to sell," I shout back, we are going pretty fast now. "She'll say anything."

"What?" Dee shouts.

"They'll destroy everything. All of this."

"I don't care."

"I don't believe that," I shout.

Dee cuts the speed. "Do you think it matters. Even if I did?"

"It would destroy all of this! All of this!" I point at the islands and the wild rice on both sides of us and the wind-blown trees on the mainland. "You know that."

"I'll lose a lot of money. That's what I know."

"They're pressuring you, Dee. Don't give in. It's worth it."

"You have no right to say anything to me, not after what you did." She opens the throttle, the outboards roars and we rush across the water. Her eyes are watering, it's probably just the cold air, she wouldn't be out here alone with us if she was afraid for her safety. Either she didn't believe what Shelley told her, or she knows me better than that. I can talk her around. I've always been able to talk her around. She loves my daughters, she doesn't want to be cut off from Erica and Page, I'm sure of that, and I'm sure she can't believe I'm as bad as she's been told, not when my daughters are as wonderful as they are. I'll let it die down. She never sticks to anything, she's a foolish old woman. She's already cutting back on the speed, Page is grinning and Erica is turned around leaning toward the wind and the water is rougher, there's a roll on the lake and it's coming through the gap between the islands and the boat is beginning to buck and hurl back spray.

"Speed up!" Page shouts at her. "Go faster!"

Dee shakes her head and slows down and looks at me with a deep, disillusioned sadness. Whatever else she's feeling, she's feeling sorry for me. I can use that. No matter what she thinks I've done, I can talk her around. And I need to find out how much Shelley has told her. I've dealt with everything else, I've dealt with things I can't believe I've dealt with, I can deal with this too.

12

Four thirty. I'll get dinner early, the girls can help me clean up and we'll all get to bed early. There's one message.

"Kirsten, Bob. It's one thirty right now. I'll be in my office until three. If you get back after that, call me at seven tomorrow morning. We have to talk."

So that's taken care of.

No message from Jerry, which doesn't surprise me, and no answer when I call, except for his recorded voice, requesting that I leave a message. Okay Jerry, I'll leave a message.

"You know who this is. You didn't fix the car, it still doesn't work. I need it tomorrow, Jerry. Call me."

Erica is standing just inside the front door when I hang up. "I thought you said you were playing outside."

"Who said it was us?" She never smiles. Is that my fault? Have I given her nothing to smile about?

"Us?"

"Who told the cops we broke in?" I can see the driveway, framed in the screen door behind her, but no sign of her younger sister.

"Where's Page?"

"Who said we broke in?"

"That woman I told you about."

"What's she got against us?"

"I don't know." I'm gutless, it's not the right time, I have to deal with Jerry first and get Bob to lay a charge and clean up around here and start dinner and I'm tired, I'm not ready to do this right now, I've had enough emergencies for one day. I'll tell her tomorrow.

She turns and goes out.

I like making dinner. It allows my brain to turn off. And I get something good at the end of it. It's a challenge, to take what we've got, and make something good. Out of it.

Spinach.

Three hundred and fifty thousand.

Lettuce.

Three hundred and fifty thousand. I can see the money in every pot and pan. I could do so much with three hundred and fifty thousand. It's summer, they could start a new school in the fall. It's a perfect time. Immediate possession. God it's tempting.

Chicken, with mushroom soup.

Where would I go? I've got a life here. It'd be the same anywhere else. If I don't fight it now, I'll have to fight it somewhere else. Might as well be here.

Three hundred and fifty thousand.

Dinner's ready but I don't want to call them, they look so peaceful, underneath the tree, playing. I love the way those branches reach out like great green umbrellas, upturned palms, almost touching the ground on the far side, shading my daughters on this side.

It's their quiet time. My quiet time too. Just watching.

They look so small, really. Erica. The one in charge. Page. Who's allowed to be a child yet. Hard to know which is better off.

I love this place and they're trying to push us out.

Don't get mad, get even. Old T shirt slogan. Push back. Push back.

Three hundred and fifty thousand.

Like Dee says, can I afford to turn it down?

Would they like it? Whatever I do, I have to tell my daughters....

What I have to tell them.

Tomorrow.

Erica, the serious one, the one who has to solve the problems. So focused, digging in the sand, thinking things out, really pissed at that woman who's been telling all those lies, making trouble. Erica will be in charge some day, somewhere important, giving orders, taking crap from no one. Doing what I could have done.

"Come in for supper," I call.

"It's early," Page objects.

"So we'll get it over with," I point out.

They get up.

"Don't forget your things." They pick up the sand pails and the shovels and their sun hats and come in.

It's five thirty. Monica is knocking and there are three people that I can see standing behind her and a couple more walking up the driveway toward the house.

"Hello!" Monica shouts cheerily, "Anybody home? Kirsten, are you there?" Framed in the hall standing at the door, leaning and peering in.

Page jumps up and is already running down the hall, I don't want to shout at her and embarrass my daughter in front of other people, but I wish she'd stayed where she was. Now I have to go and find out what this woman wants that is so important that it interrupts our dinner.

Monica is standing on the top step smiling at Page and asking if she can unhook the screen door, darling, she'd like to talk to her mommy, the woman turns my stomach. "Hello Monica," I put my hands on Page's shoulders and make no effort to unlock the door.

"We were wondering if you could give us a few minutes of your time," Monica says, smiling big and broad and insincere. Another car has just pulled in the driveway, and there's already seven people standing behind Monica. Steve and Monica's son and his husband and four other people I don't recognize. I can see Jerry's pickup on the shoulder across the road and himself getting out and slamming the door and watching for the traffic before he crosses to join the rest.

"We're sort of a delegation," Monica says.

"Oh?" I keep my hands on Page's shoulders, standing on the inside of the screen door, blocking their passage.

"Can we come in?" Monica asks. There are five more people coming up the driveway, including Shelley.

"We can't come in?" she says.

"My house is a wreck."

"You should see my place." She smiles and they collect in a semi-circle behind her.

"What did you want to talk about?" I make no effort to be friendly with any of them, they look as dour as a posse, although Jerry is coming up the rear grinning at me.

"We won't be half an hour," she promises.

"I still don't understand."

"Can we come in?" she insists.

I know a lot of these people, there is no reason why I shouldn't let them in, I've tried to be a good neighbor and I've helped them when I can, I work for some of them, they all know me, they all know I'm dependable, I've been here longer than most of them in fact. "I've been cleaning everybody else's place," I apologize, just to remind them, and unhook the door. As they go by I stand aside with my hands still on Page's shoulders, and hold her closer as Shelley passes, who looks ahead as if neither of us existed. I can feel Page's diaphragm moving, she's all set to blurt out something, but I give her a little shake and she keeps quiet.

And then I hear Erica, as everyone finds a seat in the living room or moves up against a wall to keep as far away as possible from what is going to get said here. My older daughter is glaring at Shelley. "What have you got against us?"

Shelley doesn't answer, as if my older daughter didn't exist either.

"I asked you a question," Erica raps out.

"We haven't got anything against you, honey," Monica says, pats her cheek and sits down. I shake my head at Erica, she mouths at me and gestures in outrage, but says no more. I glance at Steve, who is back against the wall, and he looks away. Nobody will look at me except

Monica. Jerry has stayed outside on the porch and I'm standing with my youngest daughter just inside the main door, which I've left open. Erica comes over and stands beside us.

"Why don't you take your little sister outside for a little while," Monica says to her, "we have something we'd like to discuss with your mother," and Erica of course doesn't move. "I think that would be a good idea," Monica insists. Erica looks up at me, I nod, and she takes Page outside.

"We think you should leave," says Monica. Brutal, blunt, uncompromising. Nobody will look at me except Monica with her real estate eyes, and Shelley, who has won and wants me to know she has won. "You have a good offer, much more than this grubby place is worth," Monica goes on and I'm thinking, how does she know I have a good offer, "you'll be able to buy a good place somewhere else. But it has to be somewhere else. No one feels comfortable with you around here. Not any more."

"You'll have to live with it," I tell her. "I'm not moving."

Immediately Steve and four other people walk towards the door, none of them will look at me, and when I say hello to Steve and call him by name, he makes a sort of mumbling in his throat and goes by. The screen slams behind them.

"Isn't anybody going to talk to me?" I ask. The rest of them stir and look down, the only people who meet my eyes are Monica, her son, and Shelley. "Is there anything else you want to say?"

"We're prepared to help you move," Monica says. "It's the least we can do, I think. For the sake of your daughters."

"Have I ever done anything to any of you?" I demand.

"That's not the point," says Monica.

"What is?"

Nobody answers.

"Get out of my house," I say, and they all do that except Monica, who remains exactly where she's sitting and stares at me while everybody crosses our sight lines and crosses the porch and down the steps and the screen bangs after the last one leaves. "I meant you too," I say. She's an immovable object, a boulder with a voice.

"Nobody knew what you had done," she says. "I know I didn't." She waits for me to comment. "We were asked to come here by everyone else in the community," she goes on, "in case you think we're the only ones who think this way. Most of them couldn't bring themselves to come in here, knowing what you did, they were frightened, quite honestly. We knew you'd been in trouble, and most of us were prepared to ignore it, it happened so long ago. And even when we found out, and this is what really astonishes me, I have to tell you, most of us were prepared to ignore it, I wasn't, but most of us were. But not when we saw the photographs. A picture is worth a thousand words."

"I will only ask you one more time."

"Take the money," she says. "It's really the smartest thing you could do. You can build your life somewhere else."

"Nobody is driving us out."

"It can be quiet," she says and stands up, "or it can be very public, whatever you want. I wouldn't want to put your daughters through it, if I were you." She moves to the door and I am tempted to stop her, but I know there are at least ten people out there waiting to see what will happen and anything she can use she'll use, she'll lie about it, whatever is convenient, and I'm not going to give her an excuse to say I threatened her. So I step aside.

About five people are standing just beyond the steps and move off when they see her coming out, and Steve has been talking to the girls and leaves when I appear at the door. They all get in their cars, back out and drive off, except Jerry, who's standing across the road leaning against the fender of his pickup looking in here and when the last car drives off, he stands for a minute or so longer, straightens up very leisurely, throws his cigarette on the road, opens the door of his truck, and climbs in, slams the door, grins at me, starts his truck, waves at me, and drives off.

Erica and Page come up the steps, staring at me as they do. Page looks away and goes by me and Erica stops. What the hell is going on, her eyes demand. "Did you bring all your things in?" I ask.

"We didn't take anything out."

"That's good."

"Don't you trust us?" she says.

"Of course I trust you. Why would you say that?"

"Because you don't trust us!" Her logic is inevitable, it comes right back to the place I don't want to deal with right now. "Why were all those people here?"

"Someone has offered to buy us out. They'll pay us three hundred and fifty thousand dollars to buy this place."

"Who?" Erica demands. Page has come back and is standing, sober faced, just inside the main door while Erica and I confront each other on the porch. "I'm tired of not being told things," says Erica. "I'm not a goddamn child."

"Erica!"

"I'm not!"

Page, the talkative one, is not saying a thing. I put my hand on Erica's shoulder and she pulls away, I'd do the same myself, so I sit on the sofa swing, she sits on the sofa chair against the side wall of the porch and Page comes and sits on the swing beside me, pushing up against me. I put my arm around her. "So?" Erica demands. I cannot put her off like I can put off her sister. She is beyond mothering.

I look down at Page, and over at Erica. "A woman is buying up all the land around here and putting in some kind of hotel slash entertainment complex."

"We saw the map."

I ignore Erica's tone. "Her name is Leslie Wyseman. She has millions of dollars and she can do whatever she wants, and what she wants is to buy our lot and tear down this house and put in some kind of, I don't know what, a meditation center, something, whatever that is."

"I saw that," Erica says

"You didn't say anything."

"I saw it."

"She wants us out. We're not getting out."

"Why?" says Page.

"We're low class," Erica says.

"Don't even think that!" I bark.

"I don't. She wanted to know." I love this feisty little woman.

"Why don't they want us," Page asks, looking up, hurt and mystified.

"I told you!" Erica says.

"There are some people," I tell Page, and look over at Erica, and back at Page, "there are some people who think that nobody else is as good as they are. That's their problem. We know better. Maybe we don't have the money they do, that doesn't mean anything, they just got lucky. We're as good as anybody, and better than most."

"They can buy us," Erica says, this cynical streak gets worse the older she gets, maybe I've taught her that, I probably have, she's too young to have life so sour so soon.

"They can buy us if we sell out," I tell her. "Only if we sell out," I say to them both, gently, "only if we think we are less than we really are. But we're not, are we. We're as good as anyone."

"You said that already," Erica sneers.

"And I'll say it as long as I have to. I'll say it until both of you believe it, I'll say it until you both think it automatically, without even really thinking about it. Okay."

"Okay," says Page the peacemaker, who doesn't understand any of this. Her sister is older, things are not so simple any more.

"Let's finish our dinner." I get up.

"How come Jerry didn't come in?" Page asks as we go along the hall toward the kitchen.

"He's a goddamn coward," says Erica.

"Erica!"

We still haven't finished our cold interrupted meal when I hear someone in the driveway, go to the door once more, and see Jerry leaning in the open hood of our car. I walk down the steps and stand behind him.

"I forgot to fix this," he says to the engine, as if it was all a big joke. "Nothing but a few loose bolts. The guy who installed this didn't do a very good job." He works for about five minutes, stands up, slams the hood, and turns around and grins at me as I stand here with my arms crossed, tense with rage. "I'll give it a try," he says, not quite so smartass now, gets behind the steering wheel and turns it over. The engine roars, calms down, runs smoothly, and he switches it off. "Everything is working perfect!" he says, gets out, and hands me a newly cut key. "I forgot to give it back."

"You said my car wasn't good enough to steal."

He smirks. "It isn't."

"Bastard."

"I came to make sure you'd be okay. I swear."

"Who?"

"That woman. Shelley. You knew that."

"Get out of here."

"I didn't have anything to do with it. It was that woman, Shelley." I'm getting dangerous and he knows that, he gets in his truck, backs out the driveway, looking behind to make sure he doesn't run off the track. Just before he drives off, he glances at me again. The smartass grin has gone.

I have to talk to Bob tomorrow morning. I'm always one step behind, by the time I get to talk to him about one thing, there's something new.

They've got up a petition, you can be sure of that, Monica made sure of that. God knows what deal she's worked out with Leslie.

My daughters are standing in the porch as I walk up the stairs and they turn and head back to the table, they know not to cross me, they know my moods. I'd be the same, if I were Monica, I can imagine how her business will take off if something like this really gets going, there'll be tens of thousands of people, swarming in here, murderers not wanted, bad for the image.

My daughters are eating and don't look up and I sit and say nothing, I've lost my appetite. Tonight will be a bad night. Another bad night. By three o'clock in the morning I'll be ready to kill someone, anyone, my eyes will be blood. I know what I'm like. It's a process, it's a cycle. By tomorrow I'll be clearer, more rational. Still enraged, but more rational.

In the meantime, the girls and I will have to keep out of each others' way. They know me by now, they know how to handle me. They'll get up from dinner and go to the TV and I'll go to my computer but I don't think I'll work, I'm not clear enough, my head is stuffed I feel weird, the light in this room, blares at me, they'll probably be nurses, or some sort of caregivers, they've had lots of practice.

13

Pine branches waving on the blinds, shadows sharp and perfect, perfect summer day, blue uncluttered sky. I fell asleep. I stay awake all night and the light starts up and I fall asleep. It's eight fifteen.

I feel dizzy. The start of another crappy day. Hot. It'll be real hot.

I have to phone Bob. He'll think I'm crazy. Maybe I am.

Thirty five years ago. Your mother lost control. She did things she would never do again. Things she regrets.

I have to tell them.

Later.

He'll be in by now. Get it over with.

"They don't want it on the CBC News," Bob says. "That you can count on."

I've thought of that, Bob. I can hear him rapping on the keyboard, thinking with his fingers.

"It's discrimination. There's no doubt about that. They're not allowed to do that. For any reason."

"She said they would."

"How many people?"

"Fifteen. About. I didn't do a count."

"She said this in front of everybody?"

"Yes."

"Probably overstepped her instructions. Assuming she had instructions." He's tapping on his keyboard. "There's one thing you can do for me."

"What."

"Don't say a thing. Nothing. Not to anybody."

"Yeah."

"I know you, Kirsten. Don't say a thing, not to anybody."

"I hear you."

"We'll send a letter, okay. They're not allowed to do this."

Except Shelley.

"Dee? Hello."

"Yes," she says, she's not in a good mood, I can hear the resentment on the phone.

"I hate to ask you this. It'll only be an hour. Are you there?"

"Yes."

"I'd like to take the girls over there, for an hour okay. I have something I have to take care of. Could I do that? I'd really appreciate it."

"I have to do some shopping." She can be very abrupt.

"It'll only be an hour. Maybe you could take them with you."

"I won't be able to do that." She does not want to be bothered with them.

"Just an hour. Surely you can spare an hour. They love to be with you, Dee, you're another mother to them. It's such a short time."

"I have to do my shopping!" She makes no effort to disguise her anger.

"They'd love to go." She doesn't know how to say no to me, she never has. "It'd only be an hour. Just an hour."

"I have so much I have to do," she's changed her tone already, she's making excuses. "I only have today."

"It'll be all over before you know it."

"I have so much to do."

"They'd love it. They really would."

"Oh all right."

"We'll be right there," and I hang up before she's had a chance to change her mind.

And now I'll have to get the kids up, get them dressed and fed and off to Deirdre's. We can do it in three quarters of an hour, she'll wait, she could never say no.

"Why do we have to go to Dee's again," Erica asks as soon as I wake her up.

"Yeah," Page agrees from somewhere in her blankets.

"You're getting up now," I tell them both, I'm sounding angrier than I intended to, I don't have time for their objections, "I said get up now." Page moans. "Now!" I didn't want to shout at her. "Please. For me." They don't move. "It's after eight."

"Let's go," Erica says wearily, dragging herself up and going over to Page's bed and yanking the covers off. "Another day at boot camp."

She gets a clean pair of blue jeans and panties from her dresser and a T shirt with little holes in the collar and I want to tell her, don't wear that one, get a good one, but I've given enough orders for now and she takes a pair of blue jeans and panties from Page's drawer and another T shirt and puts them on her sister's bed.

"Aren't you going to wear socks?" I ask her.

She shakes her head.

"You should wear socks."

She shakes her head. Page is getting up and I go to the kitchen and make toast and pour them orange juice and get out the cereal bowls.

"What cereal do you want?" I shout.

"Trix," says Page.

"Erica?"

"No thanks."

You should have cereal, Erica, you need a good breakfast, breakfast is the most important meal of the day. But I don't say it, she's had enough hassle, life is tough at boot camp. I smile when I think of that. She gets more like her mother every day.

God I hope not.

Eight forty five. The blinds bang on the windowsill. I didn't close the window last night. I switch open the venetians, the sun paints a slatted parallelogram on the kitchen linoleum. It's damp, I'll have to air this place out, the wood is rotting behind these walls, it would be a good thing if this place was torn down, I can feel the floor sagging underneath me as I walk across the kitchen. I'm tired of this place, of these people, of everything here, and I love it, this is where my daughters are, this is where I rebuilt my life. Erica comes out and sits at the kitchen table and drinks her juice and takes a piece of toast. "Eggs?" I ask her.

"No thanks."

"You should eat some breakfast."

"I don't feel like it."

"I worry about you. You don't get enough to eat."

"Mom!"

"Page," I shout.

"Coming," she says.

"Yeah sure," comments Erica.

I'll carry the gun in a handbag. Too obvious in my jeans.

"See that cottage right there," says Erica. I've stopped at the crossroads, waiting for a car to come through, an irritating driver, going slow, as if people don't have places they have to get to. There's a truck coming the other way, if he doesn't get by soon I'll have to wait for the damn truck too.

"Where?' says Page.

"Right there. You can see it through the trees. It's white."

"Oh yeah."

"That's where that bitch lives."

"What's her problem?" Page asks.

"She's a bitch."

How does she know where Shelley's staying?

"How do you know?" Page asks, she's read my mind, my younger daughter is growing up.

"Remember that day we were walking to Dee's," says Erica, "when we stopped on the path and you were running around irritating Mom?"

"I wasn't," Page objects.

"I saw where she went. She went in right there. Right there where that black car is."

You never know what your daughters are seeing.

"Why doesn't she like us?" Page asks.

"Ask Mom." Page doesn't.

Finally the truck is by and I turn right on the lakeshore road. "You are not to have anything to do with that woman. Do you hear me?" I say. "Erica. Page."

"Yes," says Erica.

"You are not to go anywhere near that cottage, you are not to have anything to do with her, if she talks to you, if she tries to say anything to you, you are to ignore her. You are to keep right on walking. You are not to have anything to do with her. That's an order. Do you hear."

"Yes," says Erica.

"Page."

"Yes," Page says, in a smaller voice than her sister's.

"I want you to promise me. Both of you. I want you to promise you are to have nothing to do with that woman. You are not to go anywhere near her. That's an order. Do you hear?" They say nothing. "I want you to promise.... Erica." No answer. "Promise."

"Yes," Erica says.

"Page."

"Yes."

"I don't want you to just say that. A promise is a promise. When you make a promise, you do not break your promise. Do you hear me?" No answer. "Do you hear me? I know what you're like, I know what you're thinking, I want an answer. Do you hear me?"

"We hear you," says Erica.

"Be as mad as you like. I want you to do as I say."

"We hear you!" Erica says, loudly, she's angry, she's made her promise, she's tired of being treated like a child, she is not a child any longer, she can make her own decisions, she knows what she's doing.

"Okay," I say, "I'll back off. I'm only saying this because I love you. I don't want you to get hurt, either of you."

"Why does she hate us so much?" Page asks me.

"She's a bitch," says Erica, "I told you that, there's some people who just like to cause trouble, that's life, you'll have to learn that. You can't let them get to you. You have to take a stand."

It's ten to ten, Shelley usually takes her walk down by our place at ten thirty, I'll just catch her in, she'll be up but not yet ready to go. I'll say what I have to say, it won't take long, I'll be back at Dee's well before eleven and Dee can do her damn shopping. I turn into Dee's driveway. "Did you bring some peanuts for the chipmunks?" I ask Page.

"Yes," says Erica.

"I can answer for myself," says Page. "I don't need you telling me what to say."

"Did you remember?" Erica demands.

"Yes."

"Then how come I had to put them in?"

"Please don't fight," I say. "Be nice."

"Tell her," says Page.

"Both of you."

"Yeah," Erica says triumphantly. Sunlight wavers on the windshield, the branches of the Norway pine at the side of Dee's cottage are moving slightly, I can see whitecaps on the lake.

"Make sure you wear your sweaters," I say as they clamber out, and I back up and turn around without bothering to say hello to Dee, I can talk to her afterwards, the sooner I get this done, the sooner I get back.

There's nothing in the driveway now, the Chrysler is gone, Adam's Chrysler I think as I turn off the engine, the house is white, like Erica says, back from the road behind a screen of cedars that filter out the sand dust and shake it off again when a car brushes by, they've grown half across the driveway, if the cottage wasn't white, you'd never know it was in here, tear down the trees, it's nothing, a four room one storey fisherman's house, a gable like a nun's cowl, white clapboard across the front, a single window on each side of the front door, small porch, sitting up on cedar posts with a painted screen of cedar slats in diamond shapes, no basement, at least one hundred years old, more, probably, the road was a lakeshore then and the sand beyond was water, Dee's property and every other clump of trees out there were islands, they could watch the sunsets from the front windows here, the sun descending behind the islands, water trees rocks sand, a godawful empty land, no one asked questions, everyone had something to bury. My handbag is a soft black leather purse with a thin strap, but it's so small I can carry it in my hand. She lets me in as soon as I knock and we don't say anything and I turn left off the center hall to the room that used to be the parlor where no one went except when guests came, the walls on every side are stuck up with photographs, photographs all over the place, there must be fifty photographs, of Noreen's body, from every possible angle, the blood around it like a Chinese background screen, like a halo on Buddha, the thumb almost cut off, the slashes in the neck, the clothes black where the blood flowed out, the legs and arms petrified at crazy planes and angles, naked on a dolly with the stab wounds circled and numbered, thirty six numbers, the body washed and white, the blood down the stairs where it flowed in the hall beyond the door where she fell, a curve and splash of blood along the wall where it streamed off the blade as it lifted, her feet and the blood how it flowed away from her body, footprints on the floor where my shoes were, every possible angle and direction of sight, numbered and tagged at the bottom right hand corner in white ink markings, thirty five years like it had happened ten seconds ago, the horror I never stop, that lives, the horror that Shelley, displays, like a tourist attraction, the smell the taste the sound the sight, I have no feeling, I can't, I fight to stay standing, I want something to support myself, I fight to stay erect, I feel sick, I feel everything everyone feels who sees this, I know how they feel, why they react like they do and I know what she's doing, I am frozen forever at this second, my life has never stepped beyond this second, nothing that has happened to either one of us beyond this second has actually happened, everything after, was just breathing.

14

She steps forward, into the room. To her right is a picture of Noreen, black and white, taken straight down with her legs at weird angles like she's flying, galloping through the air spewing clouds of blood. A full color picture to the right of me, bright red arterial blood, taken probably a half an hour after it happened. It was incredible, how fast the cops got there. "How could you have done this?" she says. She comes a step closer. I'm in the middle of the room, the photographs around me, in front of me like a panorama, a backdrop, in my peripheral vision to right and left. "I want to know," she says, the pictures behind her. "I trusted you. I wanted to stay with you. That's how much I trusted you. I trusted you more than I trusted my own mother. I thought you understood." There's nothing in her hands. I'm gripping my handbag. I can feel the shape of the gun, underneath the kleenex and the letters and the wallet I've got jammed in there. I concentrate, to see what's really here, the mantra I've rehearsed for twenty five years, so long it's automatic, stay calm, think clearly, see what's there. "Why did you do it?" she says. "How could you do it?" she asks.

"I don't know."

"I want an explanation."

"There isn't any." I insert my fingers in the handbag, I touch the metal with my fingertips. "I killed her. I don't know why. It was wrong."

"You butchered her."

"Would you believe anything I said?"

"No."

She advances another step.

"I don't know why I did it." I think calm. I keep my voice firm and calm. I don't let it waver. The touch of the metal calms me, I have control, if I allow myself to think that I have control, I give myself permission to have control. "What I did was wrong. Your mother hadn't done anything. I took my punishment. I'm over fifty years old. I've got nothing. I've been punished."

"I don't have a mother. You killed her. You murdered her."

"My mother sold me."

"You didn't have a mother. So you killed mine. Is that what you're saying? Is that why you did it?" She's close to hysteria.

"There is no reason." I'm proud of myself. I am in perfect control.

There's five feet between me and her, she's standing between me and the doorway, it's the only way out, but I'm not worried, she isn't carrying anything, I can see both her hands.

"That isn't good enough." She sounds strangely parental. I can understand exactly how odd that is.

"So what do you want, Shelley?"

"I want you to pay for what you've done."

"I have."

"She's dead. You're alive." Vengeful. Whining.

"Do you want me dead?"

"Yes." Decisive.

"Here I am."

She's spent thirty five years feeling sorry for herself, I stare at her straight, she looks away, her face is baggy, her shoulders slouch, her whole body is flab, she's rehearsed this for thirty five years and she can't bring it off. She's weak. She's abused herself. She's thrown away everything she ever had, I can tell by the way she's standing there, she's had kids, she's had a husband, a home, a life, she's thrown it all away, she looks twenty years older than she is, she looks ten years older than I am, her face is wasted. She's come from a psychiatric ward.

"You gave your mother nothing but shit," I say. She doesn't reply. She's a weakling, she talks, that's all she does, she talks. "You keep telling yourself, if I hadn't been so awful, this would never have happened. Isn't that right? Isn't that what you've said?"

"No way." I can see the rage, the denial in her eyes, that's a sure sign she knows I'm right.

"You torture yourself." She doesn't deny it. "You sit in this room, surrounded by all these pictures, and you torture yourself. It's the only way you can think of, to make up for it, for the way you acted, the way you treated your mother. The way you betrayed her. You torture yourself. You've spent your whole life making up for it, destroying everything you've ever got, you want me to make up for it, you want me to pay for it. I've paid for it. I will not solve your problems. That's up to you. That's your job."

"You murdered her."

"I paid for it."

"I'm the one who's paid for it." Whining. Rationalizing.

"You've made sure of that. Haven't you." The window in this room has been nailed shut, I don't think there's a window open anywhere. We're both sweating, I can feel the sweat running slowly down the ridge of my back, beading down, my spine is a drainpipe, my face is slick, the sweat is stinging my eyes. "No matter what you did to me, Shelley, it wouldn't make any difference. You'd still torture yourself. You'd still be a victim. You don't have to do anything, Shelley. You can sit here and whine, surrounded by all these pictures."

"My life has been awful." She doesn't know what awful is.

"Stop causing me trouble."

"She's dead. You're alive."

"It's been thirty five years. Get a life."

"I hate you!" she screams. "I hate you! I hate you! I hate you!" Tantrum.

She is a weakling. She is not a threat.

"I've gone through things you can't possibly begin to imagine," I say, low, calm, controlled. "I've paid for it. I've got a right to a life. Stop causing me trouble."

"Why don't you just kill me," her voice loses all vitality, dull, dead. "I wish you'd just kill me."

"Don't be an asshole."

"I've got lots of knives. You can take your choice." Helpful.

I step forward, and she steps back. "I have to get going now," I say calmly. "I've made my point. I want you to stop causing me trouble. You've caused me enough trouble."

"Are you warning me?" She steps back another pace.

I stay where I am. "I want you to stop causing me trouble." She wants me to threaten her, she wants me to say something so she'll be able to call the cops, to arrest me for making threats.

"Why don't you just kill me," almost begging.

I touch the gun. There in case I need it.

"Just kill me!" she shouts, daring me.

If I didn't have Page and Erica, things would be different, a lot different, I wouldn't have to do this, I wouldn't have to care about any of this.

"You don't scare me," she says.

She was only three years older than Erica when it happened. I've never thought of that before.

"I have to get going now," I say, in a calm ordinary voice, like a guest who has to leave reluctantly, almost apologetically.

She moves back so she's entirely in the door frame, blocking my exit.

"I can wait," I say.

The room has no chairs, no tables, nothing to sit on. I could lean against a wall.

"My father is dead," she tells me, like we're having an ordinary conversation.

The pictures have a strange effect, as if nothing has happened since that time thirty five years ago. I'd get used to them, if I looked at them long enough. You can get used to anything. Study them. Cope with all the details. You can get used to anything. I've learned that. I've faced what I've done. She hasn't. She's spent all her life denying. She hasn't had the strength I have. I can outlast her.

"He died of colon cancer," she says. "I watched him. I watched him become a skeleton."

It's been a terrible shock, Noreen, splattered on the walls, I'm getting used to it, I've seen them all before, they tried this, the intimidation.

She could lock the door. The window isn't boarded. She wasn't thinking either. She wanted lots of light in here, you need lots of natural light in an art gallery, so people can see them all. If she'd boarded it up, I'd be in trouble, I'd be trapped in here.

"I don't have anybody," she says.

"I'm sorry to hear that. It must be terrible."

"Just kill me."

"No."

She steps into the hall, away from the door.

I walk to it carefully, she's standing aside in the hall towards the back of the house, she's sweating, she's looks white and sick, she can hardly stand up, I go carefully out, watching her, my hand on the bag, I can feel the shape of the gun inside, I go down the hall sideways with my back to the wall, feeling ridiculous, watching her.

"Keep away from my kids." We're both feeling sick. She couldn't take it, she's backed off.

"I don't have anything," she says. She starts following me.

"Keep away from my kids. You know what I can do. Stay away from my kids."

"You could kill me." She's crazy.

I stop.

She does.

She knows what I'll do it if she goes near my kids, if she harms them in any way, I'm out and in my car and starting the motor and backing out, watching her every second as she stands at the door, I ease the car forward when I get to the road, I don't want to spin the tires and give her the impression I'm running away, but I'm glad I am out of there and I feel ashamed, I have never run from anyone ever and who is she, nobody, I'm running from a nobody.

I'll take the money.

It's not worth it. I'm so exhausted I'm sick. It's not worth it. I'm shaking.

15

The cops will be showing up, I'll give them an hour, maximum. She knows where Dee lives, they might come there, or back to our place.

The first thing I have to do is get rid of the gun, I'm not supposed to have a weapon, I'll get rid of it at Dee's. And work out my defense. She shook me up more than I thought, I've made at least one mistake, you know what I can do, that was stupid, damn, damn.

Figure it out. Be calm, and figure it out.

First. I didn't threaten anybody. The only witness to what I said was Shelley. She could have taped it, so I'll deal with that in a moment. Follow through this line of thinking first.

Assume there's no witnesses. Whatever she says, and it will be real good, you can bet on that -- she's biased. I killed her mother, so she won't have anything good to say about me, right, and that makes her testimony tainted.

So it's me on one side, and her on the other. The presumption will be, I've been jailed for murder, so I'm likely to make threats. But the victim was her mother, so she's not reliable either, not without corroboration. And there's no weapon. That I'll make sure of. And I didn't touch her.

The road into Deirdre's.

So.

Assume it's taped.

What did I say? "You know what I can do." I was talking about my kids, I was telling her to stay away from my two kids.

Stop in the woods, well before the cottage, off the road where I won't be seen if they come down here looking for me. No point making it easy.

Think.

She's been hanging around our house, walking up and down the road in front of our house, over several days, to the point where I had to tell my lawyer about it. Showing up at Dee's, causing trouble with my friends, showing up at the big meeting where fifteen people tried to push me out, without justification, and she's been spreading stories all over, making trouble, my daughters are nervous, they're worried, they've been asking me, who is that woman.

Conclusion: I'm a mother, and I was protecting my children from someone who might be a threat. My words were not chosen wisely, true, but I was protecting my children. I had a reason.

So. I admit what I said, before she plays the tape. Assuming she has one.

What else did I say?

Nothing. I was calm. I accepted responsibility. I said I'd been punished. She said she wanted me dead.

Yeah! Right!

She said she wanted me dead. I told her, here I am.

Right! I didn't threaten her. She threatened me!

Okay.

Perfect.

Okay.

So if she's got a tape, her threat will be on it too, unless she cuts it, in which case, the whole thing is tainted. Make notes, date them, and put down the time, you can never find a paper when you need it.

Pen. Pencil. Dammit, I know I had a pencil in the glove compartment, somewhere, one of the kids.

The paper too.

Damn. I'll write it down as soon as I get to Dee's. A red squirrel, right above me, they've got roads up there, the pines trees their super highways. People say they lock their teeth, if they bite. Crazy, to be scared of a dumb little thing like that. Quite beautiful, in its own way. Blue sky, up through the branches, a Blue Jay.

Get on with it, been sitting here long enough.

This weather has been perfect. Hot at day, cool at night, they're boiling in the city, I can hear them, every morning on the radio, complaining about the heat, the traffic, the accidents, the holdups, reports from cottage country, come on up, the water's fine, the nights are wonderful, stars and moon, and breezes off the lake.

Like right now. Sit here a moment, with the window down, beside her cottage, with the lake right ahead, and the breeze.

Okay. First things first.

Maybe she saw the car and assumes I'm looking for the kids, so she won't be concerned that I didn't come in right away. They're down by the lake, on the dock, with a net it looks like, trying to catch little fish, I assume. That's what I thought, they were digging right under the tree, no one around, Dee somewhere or other. The kids are out of sight, they can't see me here, they're down by the dock.

A hole. She's been digging a deep hole, which she's given up, Page, always digging sand holes, wrap it in kleenex, place it in, cover it up, no one will look here, put some toys on top, a shovel, plastic animal, dig another hole, she'll assume that's the one she's been working on, maybe, can't be too sure about Page, unpredictable. The gun in the sand pit. Probably screw up the mechanism, all that sand, despite my wrapping. Ironic. Took the gun to protect me, bury the gun, to protect me.

Back to the front porch and look down towards the dock and wave hello to the kids. Erica gets up at once and starts for the house, she can't wait to get here, but I have to go in and say hello to Dee, to let her know I'm here, and borrow some paper and a pen and make my notes right away. Hang around, collect the kids, act cool, and have some tea if she offers it. Wipe the sand off my jeans, leave my handbag in the car, "Hi Dee! Are you there?" crossing the living room, my God they're here already, just pulling in behind my car, blocking my exit, "Dee?" as if nothing's wrong.

"In the kitchen," she says, resentfully, I've been holding up her day, and I just get in when they rap on the side door and while she answers I set my handbag on the kitchen table and write down my notes, quick, on a blank recipe card she's left there and stuff it in the handbag as she says, "Hello officer," and I go to the phone and dial Bob's number. I'm still listening to his message when they walk in and Johnson the bitch cop signals, hang that phone up, but I shield the cutoff button with my body when she tries to reach across me and end the conversation. "This is Kirsten," I say, loud enough so everyone can hear me, "The police have just come in. Call the detachment and find out what's going on. I want to talk to you. This is Kirsten, the police have taken me somewhere, call the detachment," because the message was still running when I started talking so I have to make sure he's heard me and I repeat myself, "Call the detachment, this is Kirsten."

I place the phone on the hook and turn around.

"I hope you don't mind," I tell Dee, "I borrowed one of your blank recipe cards."

"These officers would like to talk to you," she says.

"Where are the kids?" I ask her, ignoring them, and then I see Erica standing in the door behind her.

"What are you bothering us for?" she demands.

"We want you to come with us," Johnson the bitch cop tells me as if my daughter did not exist.

"We just want to talk to your mother for a while," Maclean says to Erica.

"We haven't done anything," she says, raising her voice.

"It's all right," I tell her calmly, going over to my daughter and bending down and putting my arms around her. "I'll be back in a little while. I'll straighten it out, okay."

She shrugs me away and stares at the cops. "It's that bitch. I know it's that bitch," she says.

"It's all right," I reassure her. "I'll be back in half an hour." I look up at Maclean, who has come around behind my daughter, so that Johnson is on one side and he is on the other.

"Maybe not," he says.

"It's that bitch," Erica says. "That woman." I'm sure Johnson the bitch cop thinks my daughter is talking about her.

I look around at Dee. "Can you look after them a bit longer? I hate to ask you."

"I have shopping."

"We can leave them with someone else," says Johnson the bitch cop.

"Please," I ask Dee.

She agrees.

"Look after Page," I tell Erica, "I want you to make sure your sister is all right, you are not to let her out of your sight," my older daughter's hysterical, I want her to have something to occupy her thoughts so she doesn't do something stupid. "Maybe you can go shopping with Dee."

I stand up and walk out to the cruiser and they follow and Johnson the bitch cop slams the door so I don't hear what Erica says but I can see her rage as she stands beside Dee and Page watches from the corner of the cottage as the cruiser backs, turns, and drives off. I've parked our car so Dee can get out, if she really wants to shop. Driving makes her nervous, and anyone in the car makes her nervous, and I doubt if she will, the way she drives makes me nervous too, the cottage and my daughters disappear in the trees and the cruiser thumps over tree roots and emerges on the sand flats and turns at the lakeshore road and drives by the store so everyone can see me in the back, being driven off for questioning. "My lawyer knows you have me," I say, and think about my handbag sitting on Dee's kitchen table, they were probably distracted by our little domestic drama and didn't think to pick it up, I'm sure Shelley told them about it.

We turn and drive on the road towards town and right by my house. "Where are we going?" I ask. There's witnesses they've got me, and witnesses that will say I left voluntarily, and witnesses that heard me calling my lawyer.

"Coming in," says Johnson on their radio.

"What questions?" I say to Maclean.

"Did I tell you what I've been reading lately," Johnson says to him, ignoring me. We drive by the old brick schoolhouse and Bark Lake to our left. "A thing about hanging. Sort of interesting, in a gruesome kind of way."

"Yeah," he says, concentrating on his driving.

"Why are you taking me?" I demand.

"Interesting stuff," she goes on. "Did you know, for example, that the last hangman in Canada was a lightweight boxing champion in the British army, that is before he came here and took up the job?"

"No."

"Yeah. I remember my Dad talking about him. He was a big square man you didn't mess with. Traveled all over Canada. Doing his job." The bigger lake on our right.

"I want to know where you're taking me."

"The last woman he hung had her head torn off. Blood all over the place. A real mess. Accidents will happen." We pass the quarry. "He used to use a small string to tie the rope in a little loop, right beside the client's left shoulder. Just before he dropped the trap, he'd take off the string so the client would fall straight down, and the rope would break the neck. He'd set the noose beside the left ear and stretch the rope ahead of time, so it wouldn't snap back. That's why you always see those scenes in the movies with the trap door coming open and a bag of cement or something heavy attached to the rope falling through. He'd leave it hanging there overnight, to stretch the rope. It was a real science. He kept notes. And mathematical tables, I'm not kidding you. So he could figure out how much rope to allow for, see, given the height of his client. And her weight. He always called them clients. Men or women, they were always clients. Personally, I hope they've still got them, his notes I mean, in some government vault somewhere." No one talks for a long time, until we reach the highway and turn left to the detachment, which is off the road just above the long hill out of town. "Probably not," she says. "Have to invent the wheel all over again."

"I'll make a statement," I say. That should get their attention. "I want my lawyer there."

"Ask the victims," she tells Maclean, "how merciful it was for them, you know what I mean? Or painless. The more pain the better, as far as I'm concerned. Rip off their heads. The more blood the better, right Melissa. Isn't that right? I guess you know about that, right."

She turns and faces me. "You talk about closure. There is only one way I will ever get closure. Watching the prick who killed my father get hanged. Twisting and gurgling, I would love to hear that." Her eyes have started filling up and she turns and looks ahead. "Rip their heads off, that's what I say."

16

We are almost back home, the bridge is up ahead, Bob is driving fast, abusing his car because he can't abuse me. "I told you not to talk to anyone," he says. "Isn't that what I said. I said don't talk to anyone, don't say anything to anyone. What do you do? You go straight to her cottage. I knew you'd do that, I knew you'd do that." I can't argue. It must be at least six thirty. I haven't had a damn thing to eat. The shadows are getting longer, the sun looks darker, the birds are flocking.

"Thanks for coming," I say. He won't look at me. "I appreciate it."

"I don't know why you bothered," he says.

"Didn't I do good?"

"You haven't heard a word I said."

"Back there. Didn't I do good back there."

"Six hours too late."

"Do you still have that offer to purchase?"

"Yeah."

There's three canoes on the lake coming toward the bridge as we whip across it, I look back at them, remembering Jacob and the first three years we were here, when everything was perfect and I was building a new life and everything was bright and new. I'm looking around at everything we pass, memorizing it. I hate to drag Page and Erica away from here, it's the only place they've ever known, the only home they've ever known, but I'm tired, I have a right to some peace. Maybe they'll leave me alone.

"So you think you'll take the offer?" he says.

"Assuming it's still good."

"You know where you'll go?"

"Any suggestions?"

"I'm sorry."

"About what?"

"All this. All this crap. You've tried. Nobody can say you didn't try."

"What do you think?"

"The cops?" There's a small house trailer up ahead behind a red pickup, he slows down across the next bridge beside the swamp and the flat open water of Bark Lake to our left. "Routine. I think the point you made about the threat. I think it worked. For godsakes stay away from her."

"Right."

"You were smart to cooperate."

"Thanks."

"At least you did something right." That's all he'll give me. He swings around the trailer and hurtles past it and the car coming in the other direction slows and honks and we get back in our lane and the pickup behind horns us, and Bob lifts his right hand off the steering wheel and erects his middle finger and the driver behind horns him several more times.

Usually I'd be amused at this macho childishness, but right now I'm numb, like I was from the second Noreen stopped moving and all through the trial, until they finally made up their petrified minds what they'd do with me and how long, and not even then, not until the walls locked behind me and that's when I woke up, I had to, to survive, for twenty five years, which I can't believe even yet and it's brought it all back. All back.

That's behind me. That's behind me. I move on, that's always how I've worked.

Only, they won't let me.

"Don't let it get to you," he says. "Think of all the things you've got. Your girls, for example. Nobody can take them away, ever, they've got you locked inside their hearts forever."

"I didn't think you were such a sentimentalist," I say. He slows down and signals for the turn to our driveway. "My car's at a friend of mine's down the road, if you wouldn't mind dropping me off there," I say. "Turn right at the corner."

"No problem." He switches the signal off and speeds up.

"You'll handle my closing?"

"You leave, he'll get custody."

Not if Jacob can't find me, I think, and say out loud, "You'll handle my closing?"

He nods.

The crossroads are as empty as ever. I try to imagine what this will look like, when Leslie starts building, ripping this all up. "Turn right."

He does.

"There's a road that goes off to your left about two minutes down the road, there's a mailbox at the corner."

"Deirdre's," he says.

"Everyone knows Dee."

"How are the kids?"

"Pretty well, considering. All this disruption has got them stirred up, as you can imagine. I'm happy school's out, for more than one reason. That's why we'll have to get moving on that offer right away."

"You heard what I said?" I don't answer. "Right here?"

"Left here." Dee's mailbox is in the shape of a black and white cow, I don't know the breed, Jersey maybe, I can't be sure. I know wild animals a lot better than I know cows. Bob hits the pot holes exactly right as we go up Dee's drive, so we get the maximum bump and bang. "Pull into the grass a bit," I suggest.

"Easy for you to say."

"It won't scratch your car. It's grass."

"Easy for you to say." We hit the next hole square on.

"It's your muffler," I say as we thump down and up.

"I'm thinking about moving myself," he says. "Toronto, maybe."

"I thought you hated the big city."

"I do."

"Somewhere in Northern Ontario, maybe," I think out loud. "The girls will like it."

"I haven't heard a word you've said."

"They'll have to."

"What's Erica, nine?" he asks. "You'll only need ten years, max. And then you can go wherever you want."

"When I'm sixty four."

"Life goes on."

"Easy for you to say."

"I suppose." He smiles.

"The way you're driving." I can see the edge of the cottage through the trees, and Dee's car parked right behind mine. She'll have to move it, my car is sitting with the front bumper against a tree, a stupid thing to do, I wasn't thinking.

"You'll be fine from here?" he says, and turns into the place by the side of the driveway where she usually parks.

"Yeah."

"I'll get you closer," he offers, and backs out into the driveway again and swings around until his rear bumper kisses Dee's rear bumper. "Service with a smile," he says, and I lean over and kiss him. He puts his arms around me and gives me a strong squeeze. "That's better," he says,

I smile as I get out, he's never been so caring before and I feel so much better about everything and everybody, not everyone's a jerk, it's just that there are so few that aren't jerks and it's always hard to tell which is which, at least for me, I always assume the worst.

I've already closed the door when he leans over, raps on the window, and rolls it down. "I'm looking into that thing about the website."

"Thanks, Bob."

"Nothing yet. Just thought I'd let you know I haven't forgotten you."

He rolls the window back up and I stand and watch as he drives off, until his trunk vanishes among the trees and the light flashes off the back window, the sun is low in the sky now and finding a hole through all the branches and illuminating for an instant the automobile glass of one of the most decent guys I've ever known, who is off to Toronto, but I don't hold that against him either.

I don't feel like getting my children and going home and making dinner. Maybe Deirdre has fed them already. She might have. I never know about Dee. The way she's got her car parked right behind mine, tight up against the bumper, she doesn't want me to leave before she's given me a piece of her mind, where was I, it's been all day.

I don't feel like going into that right now, I'm grateful she was there for me, even though I know she didn't want to. I'd rather just get the girls and go home.

I hate to admit defeat. I've never admitted defeat. I'm worn down. I didn't think anybody could wear me down. If it wasn't for the girls. They're my treasures, they're a stone around my neck. A millstone. I never knew what a millstone was until Jacob showed me, outside an old mill one time, set up like a monument, a big circle with ridges cut in, and a hole in the middle. A huge damn big pendant. Around your neck.

Nobody's around. I can't hear the girls. Maybe they're inside. They must have heard us driving up. You'd think Dee would be anxious to get rid of them.

"Hi Dee."
Kitchen empty.

"Dee!" Not a sound. I'd be able to hear something. "Page. Erica." Empty living room. One big room, fireplace, couches all over, driftwood, windows all around, some of them cracked. Pretty clean though. I keep it pretty clean for her. Never been able to get up at the rafters. Spider webs up there. God knows what else. "Erica. Page. Hello! Anybody there?" Empty porch. Rattan furniture. Windows all around. The dock is deserted. The last time I saw them was down there, except when the cops took me off. The first time they've seen me taken away by the cops. Must have been a shock.

Quiet here by the dock. No one all along the shore in either direction. The boat is tied up, hasn't moved since she brought us back from the picnic. They've left their nets down here. Funny. I'm always mad when I have to pick up after them. Feels like they're around somewhere though, having to collect the stuff they've left around. "Hello." Ridiculous. Nobody could hear me out here. This is an empty land. Rocks, rocks, more rocks. Trees, water, useless. Just as empty as it was when the natives were here. Portaging through. Even they didn't stop.

There's no point searching around. Maybe they're all off on some excursion, searching the woods for morels and puffballs. Flowers. Look but don't pick.

Might as well go back to the cottage and wait for them. They'll be back pretty soon. The car is here. So they didn't go off somewhere.

God this land is empty. Beautiful, but empty.

Someone on the porch. Dee, standing in the doorway, like fate, waiting for me to come back, so she can tell me what she thinks. Must have been upstairs sleeping.

"Where are the girls?" I ask, as soon as I get close enough so she can hear me, before she has a chance to say anything.

"You've been gone all day."

"I couldn't help it Dee, it wasn't my idea."

"You told me it would only be an hour. You've been gone all day."

"Where are the girls."

"I told you I had things I had to do. You didn't give a damn."

"The girls?"

"I had a thousand things I had to do, I was counting on it, I had it all planned out, every moment, I didn't have a minute I had to spare. All day."

"I asked a question."

"I don't want you to come here any more. I don't want to ever see you ever again."

"I'll take the girls and leave. Where are they?"

"I will not have the police coming to my house. That has never happened to me, not once, ever, in all the time I've been alive."

"You're getting hysterical."

"I am not getting hysterical. How dare you say I'm getting hysterical. I am not getting hysterical. You woke me up from a sound sleep. I haven't had a sleep all day."

"I'm sorry for your trouble, Dee. It was not my idea."

"I can't take this. I'm too old to take this."

"Where are the girls?"

"I do not want you ever to come here again. Ever. As long as I live."

"I'll take the girls and leave."

"How dare you bring the police here."

I'm standing on the path two paces or so from the foot of the steps, and she's standing above me in the doorway letting in the bugs and the mosquitoes, and driving me away.

Who gives a shit.

"Could you tell the girls we're going home now. Are they having dinner?"

"I don't know where they are." She says.

I wasn't expecting this.

"What do you mean?"

"I do not know where they are. That's clear enough, isn't it? You have the rudest daughters I have ever had anything to do with, I have never heard anyone use the language your daughters use. Ever. I told her I was going shopping and she said the rudest things I have ever heard anyone ever say to me, in all the time I've been alive. She refused. She flatly refused. She wouldn't let her sister come either. I told her, get in the car, I ordered her, get in the car and she stood right there, right where you're standing now, using the foulest language I have ever heard anyone say in all my life. Right where you're standing now. The one who taught her to say all those terrible things."

"Where are they, Dee?"

"She called me a bitch and she used another word too I will not repeat, ever. No one has ever called me that, ever."

"Where are they?"

"I do not know." Why? Why doesn't she know? "She said she would not leave her sister. They refused to come, both of them."

"You left them alone?"

"When I came back they weren't here. I haven't seen them for the past two hours."

"Move your car! Move your car!"

"I will not!"

I am not going to argue with her, every second I argue with her is wasted, I'll spend fifteen minutes arguing, by the time she gets her keys and moves her car and I can get my car out of here, she's a stupid stubborn bitch, I start running, back to the dock and along the shore, the quickest way, I stumble on the rocks, fall, get up, hurt, keep running, ignore it, trying to calculate how fast I'm running, how many minutes I'm taking, already down the shore, trying to think how I'll recognize the path we took the day we walked here, where it comes out and leads back to the road by the crossroads, hoping I'm wrong, trying to think everything I can to pray, hope, desire, will, that I'm wrong.

I told her not to go anywhere near Shelley. I told them.

I shouldn't have said anything. I shouldn't have said anything. It only put the idea

I'm wrong. I know I'm wrong. They wouldn't do anything, she wouldn't do anything, I told her to stay with her sister, I told her not to leave her sister, she didn't leave her sister, both of them, I'm being ridiculous, I'm thinking the worst thing, nothing like

Still can't see the house, back in behind the trees, only when you get, I'm breathing, hard, pain in my side from running so, doesn't matter, car honking and someone shouting, across the road, up the driveway, the house white with the inverted V above the door, door wrenches open, somebody shouts, turn left,

In the center of the room, both of them, she had to have her sister with her when she confronted this woman, she had orders, to not let her sister, out of her sight, both of them in the center of the room with some photos ripped from the walls, lying on top of them Shelley, Shelley, has arranged their bodies, sprawled like her mother was sprawled, like they're galloping through the air, no blood, cold, bruises on their backs where she knelt on them, to hold them down, the hair at the back of their skull slightly flattened where her hands held their faces against a pillow or a cushion, mouths open where they tried to gulp in the absent air where they died trying to gulp in the absent air, my daughters, abrasions on their wrists and legs where she tied them so they wouldn't give her trouble, and a page ripped from a school sized notebook, ragged edge where it was torn off from the wire binder, and the note in Shelley's handwriting, which I recognize from the map she wrote on,

"I don't know why I did this," the note says. "Now you know how it feels."

Journal

Sunday, August 1

6:25 a.m. I can't think about it. It's too new, it's too massive. I want to write stories, novels, wild and improbable fantasies. Every time I try, I wind up writing about myself. What could be more wild and improbable? What life could be more crazy? Squatting by the side of the road, looking at a stone. Thinking. Thinking of my daughters. Dead ten years, ten years ago. Ten years this month. I have to stop thinking. Thinking drives me crazy. It does no good. It won't bring them back.

This funny little stone. So light I can hardly feel it. Place it on paper, draw an outline around it, look at it, while cars go by and people stare and say to each other, there she goes again, crazy Melissa, someone should lock her up. Squatting there writing in that book of hers. What's she writing? We should have got rid of her ten years ago, when all that stuff happened to her daughters and we had to bury them and pretend we were sorry.

They tried. It didn't work. I will not go away. I will squat here as long as I damn well feel like it and write whatever I damn well feel like, and nobody's stopping me.

I saw this little stone because it didn't fit. It was sitting on the side of the road with all the sharp edged gravel, and the stones flung up as the cars go by, and this one out-of-place, rounded, bland little thing. It's a rough oval, not any definite shape, a sort of shoulder at the top as I look at it here resting on the page where I'm writing, a sort of shoulder at its top left hand side and then it sweeps to the right almost straight, then curves down and around on the right hand side in an almost perfect little semi circle and then back towards the left side again, underneath almost straight again, but not parallel with the run at the top just slightly angling down, and now it makes a curve going up, stops curving almost straight vertical on the left side now just slanting away a bit, and curving again to the right and this time the curve is double, a curve, a straight, another curve, and finally back to the top left shoulder where it starts, water slapping the side of my face a derisive shout a red beat-up car racing by really close, a teenage kid leaning out shouting back giving me two fingers, I hope he leans too far and falls out and cracks his skull the little jerk. A half-full plastic water bottle lying in the grass. The scum threw water at me.

I can't let it bother me. He's young, the little jerk. I've seen him around, I think. I can imagine what Page and Erica would say. Ignore him, Mom. They'd be older than him by now, all sophisticated and grown up, advising their mother, he's a jerky little asshole Mom, ignore him. We'll take care of him, the next time we see him. They would too, they'd humiliate him, they'd slice him to bits.

Another jerk just like him, driving. Chunky kid, judging from his head. Not like that skinny little jerk, leaning out the window. One of Jerry's bastards, probably. And his daddy, locked up again.

Ignore them.

It's dry, this little stone. More colorful than it seemed at first, when I first saw it lying there. There's a charcoal black area partially dividing the right hand section of the side facing me from the left hand section, then spilling away charcoal black indefinitely over here and shooting out a sort of burst of darkness over there and surrounding this and mingling in with it, is a mixture of iron and quartz that produces a pinkish tinge on the right and at the top, and random speckles of white quartz scattered throughout. There are a couple of little, tiny circles incised into the surface of this flat side facing me.

The whole stone, the entire tiny thing, is no more than an inch wide and three quarters of an inch high. It had to have been carried here by someone or something or maybe the truck when it delivered loads of stone for the base of this road, picked up at random, it doesn't fit, it shouldn't be here and that's why I noticed it, and for reasons that I don't understand, it was, it is, as if Erica and Page were standing right here holding my hand, one in each hand. I can feel their hands though I'm holding this book in my left and this pen in my right, ghostly hands that touch me, touch my heart, touch everything deep inside me, and will as long as I live.

I know this is not real. I know they are not here. I know I cannot feel their hands.

I can cope with the big things. The places that remind me, the circumstances that could bring it all back, all the hatred and blackness. But not these tiny, unexpected things, things that should not remind me of anything.

I think, now that I think about it, that this little stone is something they would have picked up. Page probably. And presented it to me, here Mom, here's a present, here's something for you. They had so little.

Oh my dear god, my beautiful little daughters.

I have to stop this. I've squatted here long enough. It's ten years. They've been dead ten years. I'll put this back where I found it. A memorial to Erica and Page.

I felt dizzy when I got up just then. It's not normal to be squatting by the side of the road writing in a notebook, about a stone you picked up. I feel slightly fog-headed, a car going by and the people looking, I get these weak spells, I am after all not so young, sixty something or other. They would be teenagers now. My daughters. It's hard to see teenagers going by chatting away and laughing and screaming silly things, and thinking, they'd be there, they'd be chatting and screaming and sharing the latest dirt. I so wanted them to have a normal life. Be as stupid as teenagers. Full of life like teenagers. With so much to look forward to.

I had a vivid image, Noreen, this morning, some time between waking and sleeping. The way she looked the moment she died, the expression on her face. She didn't say anything, it wasn't like a movie. I used to wish I could take it all back, I can't, of course, I've stopped wishing. I use Marshall to fight it, when I see her, to distract me with something more exciting, to wash away the nightmares. I'm over sixty and I still get wet, thinking about a man who's been dead at least twenty five years, remembering how I was then, how he made me feel then. How he took away the deadness.

11:23 p.m. This has been a really strange day. I still haven't absorbed, I still can't write it yet, what I know, what I learned. It makes a huge difference, in everything. I can't write it, I can't absorb it.

I went to Dee's, like always. I love the walk through the trees, the road in has grown over now, the tree branches reach out and scratch the cars, especially Steve's pickup, which he hates, but that means it's better for walking, things close in more, the pine birds come closer and sometimes I can reach my finger out and one will light there, thinking I suppose it's a different kind of tree branch.

The house is like Dee. The upstairs windows are boarded and I worry about the stairs to the second floor, all I'd need is for Dee to fall and break her hip, so I've had Steve board up the steps too. I worry she'll tear them down and go up there anyway, but so far she hasn't. She's probably weaker than I realize. She sleeps in the downstairs room that used to be the sitting room and she can see the lake, so it isn't so bad. But it's dusty, it really isn't good for her. The lake is still the same, flat and marshy and mysterious out there beyond the scrappy islands and the white pine where they used to climb like a jungle gym.... No, I won't go there.

She was up, in her kitchen drinking tea. I worry she'll burn herself, I've told her, wait until I come, I'll make your breakfast as soon as I come, in the meantime sleep in. She can't. A lifetime of getting up. Five o'clock.

I'm used to the way Dee looks, I'm with her every day, but once in a while when I come in her kitchen like I did this morning I'm struck by how much she has shriveled up in the last ten years. She was sitting at the table with both hands around the tea cup she always uses now, getting stained, she was bending over, almost as if her shoulders and her back were shrinking together in a dried up ball. She walks bent over. That's sad. She was always old, but a tough old, she'd lug down her outboard motor and clunk around that beat up fishing boat of hers and rattle out to the marsh and go and go, twenty miles up the coast sometimes. The boat has been upside down, underneath the pine tree, for five years now, and still it looks better than she does.

There's a scorched spot in the ceiling above her stove where she almost burnt her place down and I only just stopped it, I think that was the luckiest entrance I ever made, I swear the flames were ten feet tall, a minute more and it would have been too late, I grabbed the frying pan and threw it out the door and I don't know how I made it that far, I almost set the place on fire myself. She begged me not to tell anyone, she felt so stupid she said, she knew better, you don't put a greasy pan on the stove and walk out.

She doesn't get it. Try to tell her she needs to sell the place and get out. I can't force her and I don't want to bring in anyone, like who, the cops, and make her leave. I owe her more than that.

But she's getting more confused. The first thing she said, as soon as I came in and she half looked up, then looked away as if she was mad about something, which she probably was though I'm not sure she really knows herself what it was, "Your girls never come and visit me any more."

I couldn't answer.

"Where are they?" she said. "Why don't they come and visit me any more? I know what's happening, you think I don't know what's happening. You think I've done something or other, I'm not sure what, I wouldn't know what, you won't let them visit me any more."

"They've gone to school." I don't know why I said that, it was the first thing I could think of and I barely got it out, when I could think at all.

"Oh," she said and I started talking about her breakfast and what she wanted and how she slept last night and she didn't notice, I don't think, how hoarse I was, I could barely talk.

Why did she say that? What triggered it? She knows what happened. It's like ten years never happened.

It's really hard to write about it here. It doesn't always help much, writing about it. It's not a magic bullet. Nothing is.

Her mind is going, poor Dee, I shouldn't hold it against her, I can't, she loved my daughters, she was unbelievably upset when it happened, she blamed herself, for years she kept saying if I'd only made them stay here it wouldn't have happened, and I kept reassuring her, you couldn't have stopped them no matter what. And that was hard because I'd thought the same myself, why didn't she try harder.

She doesn't have anyone, no relatives, no friends, nobody, just me. I have to get her out of there. If I don't, one day someone will come there and she'll be dead, she'll be burned up, she'll be starved to death, she'll be lying in a crumpled ball at the bottom of the steps bled to death. That can't happen.

And then I went to Monica's. I don't think I will ever quite get used to Monica, it is so strange, after all she did to try to get rid of us all, and now I'm looking after her. Me, of all people, care more about big fat Monica than anyone else. Her words. She doesn't call herself big and fat of course. More than anyone else. And she pays me. It's pathetic, really, someone who was so in charge of everyone, and now she depends on someone who was her worst enemy. Strange, life, how it turns out. And I actually kind of like her.

She's not only overweight, she's had a leg amputated, diabetes. She trundles around the house in a motorized wheelchair and out her front door on the ramp that Steve built and she really shouldn't even be here, but like me there was no way she was letting anyone drive her out, not that anyone wanted to in particular, they really didn't care, but after the collapse of Leslie's schemes people blamed her for the disappearance of all that money they were sure they'd be making and some of them had spent in anticipation and were really screwed and rather than blame themselves, blamed her. Someone had to take the fall and they couldn't blame me because obviously I'd paid a pretty high price, at least what I think was the reason, so she was the one they blamed. I think too she rubbed a lot of people the wrong way, she was capable of doing that. And I suppose she realized, but by the time she did, it was too late with everyone else, so she practiced the new nicer more, there's a word I want but can't really think of it now, more tolerant, but that's not quite the word, anyway she practiced the better Monica on me. I was the one she hired.

Steve arranged that, he suggested she hire me. I gather she thought he was completely off his rocker, to even suggest it, Melissa of all people, that person. Steve, though, is a calm guy, he lets people rave, and then comes back, calm, smooth, and brings people around. And he brought her around.

What was that word? This thing I've got, does that, the brain loses, memory, flexibility, and it never comes back. That's what's so awful. Never comes back. I feel like I'm sinking on a ship far out in the Pacific or some place and I have to shout, I have to shout everything I've ever been, that I've ever wanted to say, before everything I've ever been, is gone forever. And that's not the right thing to say either. I'm like the last person alive and everyone I've ever known and everything I've ever been is gone forever and I have to scratch messages on rocks and I know that what I'm writing may never be deciphered and in fact may just vanish before anyone sees it, or figures it out. Like those pictures on rocks where the people that used to portage through here painted, and who knows what they mean and who knows who they were, those people that drew them thousands and thousands of years ago. And they launched their canoes and vanished forever, out on the lake, like.... I haven't thought these things for years. This thing I've got, has brought it all back.

It's dark. The trees are, above me moving, making soft noises and there's sounds, animals softly padding by in the dark, mysterious lives out there living in the dark, and insects, mosquitoes, moths banging against the screen. Some big ones. Souls of dead people, battering against the screen, begging to get in, outside, screaming to get in.

I have to stop this.

Monica was waiting for me, but unlike Dee she was happy to see me, "Hi Melissa, what's it like out there today?" big smile, big Monica, I like her actually, which is strange, so much is strange.

She's rebuilt her cottage, she added a two storey porch out front, imitating the style of a hundred years ago, and a glass-surrounded extension out back where she grows small trees indoors and all kinds of tropical plants, bromeliads and orchids, and a big natural stone fireplace and a second floor sort of balcony looking down on the living room/den/family room, and four bedrooms up there. Her kitchen has a marble topped island and a brass hood over the stove like the reversed funnel above a medieval fireplace or the conical interior of a Frank Lloyd Wright house in Pennsylvania or the fire concentrating hood over Joan of Arc's stake the day she was roasted on a religious spit.

Monica's there alone and needs me to dust the place and sweep it up and do vacuuming and tend her plants and help her get around and make meals when she wants to be elaborate, she doesn't use three of the bedrooms or heat them in the winter and lives on the first floor, exactly like Dee but for different reasons, and she brings in professional cleaners once a month. She's big and whirs around in her wheelchair and is as upbeat as she always was, despite her amputation and all the medications she has to take and the problems she has just getting around in that barn.

She loves her kitchen. It's been modified to the height of her wheelchair, the floor is a big expanse of white tile and black marble counter tops and brass hanging pots on hooks that I have to get down for her, though that doesn't much bother her it's mostly for show anyway. People hate her. She's the only one who prospered out of that whole redevelopment fiasco. Fees for negotiating deals.

"I thought you were my son," she said and started following me around, I only had an hour and a half, Dee is taking more of my time all the time, I get tired more easily. "I heard the key and thought it was him," she said, "I must say I was happy it wasn't. I've been waiting for the little jerk to show up, getting mentally ready as it were. Could I get you a drink?"

The sound of that damn wheelchair was irritating, always coming up behind me and the hard part was, not letting her know how I felt, I need the money so I asked her for coffee so she'd leave and get out of my way so I could do my work and get out of there, I was bitchy and I don't know why, she buzzed off to get it, and was back in five minutes. While she waited for the water to boil she explained, and followed me around again, talking non-stop.

Half way through I had to suspend my work and help her do her toilet stuff, the part I've always hated, she's huge and her amputation looks grotesque and she can't take a shit very easily. She laughed while we maneuvered her on the seat and she would have followed me again after that, interrupting my work with her incessant chatter if her doorbell hadn't rung and she whirred off working the levers on that chair like she was a pilot on a 747 and then I heard her, "Oh my God." I thought as I heard that, the son must be here, but she sounded kind of happy and then she shouted, "Louise. Oh my God, Louise! Melissa! You won't believe who it is! Melissa!"

I put the dust mask on the top of my head and went to the hall where her big clanging grandfather clock strikes the quarter hours and there was Louise Johnson. She's been promoted. She was standing there in her uniform, not so slim as she used to be, Johnson the cop, smiling. "I hadn't expected to see you here," the bitch said.

"Melissa has been a tremendous help," Monica blurted. "I can't do without her, can I, Melissa? When did you get here, Louise?" and then they talked as if I wasn't there which suited me fine so I went back to my job and finally I could hear Johnson saying she had to go and Monica chirping how delighted she was to see her old friend back in town. But instead of going, there was Johnson in the door of the bedroom I was finishing off.

"Is there anything I can get you?" she asked.

What?

"I'm cleaning out the office," she said. "We've got some stuff on file you might want."

There was nothing she had that I wanted.

"Personal stuff," she said. "Like the note that woman left you."

I sat on the bed and stared at her.

"We'll probably be seeing each other from time to time," she went on. "I thought if there was anything I could get you."

Her eyes were blank shark eyes.

"We'll be seeing each other," she said and turned and left and I could hear Monica's merry voice saying good bye and closing the door, so I continued my work and behind me Monica whirred along coming toward me again.

"Can you believe it," she said, buzzing in the room. "She's in charge of the division now, I don't believe it," and she was launched again sitting in that chair in the middle of the room while I worked thinking, shut up, get out of here, leave me alone, "she just took over, it was so good to see her, she said she couldn't wait to come by here and say hello, I always liked her, what was she saying to you just then?"

I didn't respond, but Monica really didn't care what the cop had said to me, she talked and talked about herself and what she's worried about and all the things that go wrong every day and she doesn't know how it is she copes, it's amazing really. "Could I ask you a favor?" she said.

I brushed her nose with my duster as I passed by to my last room. "Sure."

"If you see my son's car out front when you go by in the next day or so, could you come in?"

"Sure," I said as she followed me down the hall.

"I've never been able to say no to the little jerk. I thought maybe if someone else was around I could do that."

The last was a sort of sitting room with huge plate glass windows with a view of the islands and the lake beyond. The sky was cloudless and the Sun made the trees black and the lake by contrast a vivid blue. I started with the window ledge and the divisions between the panes.

"You'd think I'd be able to handle my own son, wouldn't you. I know the little jerk. If I don't know the little jerk who does."

"You'd think," I agreed.

"I'd appreciate it if you would," she said. I was almost done the dusting and she told me not to bother vacuuming in here, it really didn't need it. "You've always been pretty tough," she said, "and I figure that if a person like you can deal with all the things you have, maybe you could help me out with my own little troubles. Don't you think?"

People constantly surprise me.

"Do you think you could?"

I said I guess I could.

"As I say, I'm begging you," she added, light heartedly though she obviously didn't feel that way because, when I left, she told me, "Make sure you come."

It was a strange day.

Steve had asked me to give him a hand and so I went to the cottage where he was doing some electrical work, to give him the hand he'd asked for, for which he pays me, finding the tools he needs, holding the other end of a piece of wood while he cuts it to shape, standing beside the ladder holding it steady, nothing he couldn't do himself, all of it make work to justify giving me something, which he puts on his bill.

Steve. The only one who cared, the only one who came, six months after they were killed, when I was closed up in my house not talking to anyone and he knocks on my door and asks, "Are you okay?" And since then, off and on, more on now than off, we've been friends, lovers, whatever. Sixty and seventy, not bad really.

Steve. I knew I had to tell him what I needed to tell him, but I couldn't find the right time. I convinced myself that it was too public, there in someone else's cottage, even though we were the only people around. The owners had asked him to fix up the place before they arrived the following week. And even when he drove me home and we were truly alone in the truck, I still couldn't tell him. I'm not so tough as Monica seems to think.

Half way there I saw a hydro truck backing out of what was left of the driveway at the house where Erica and Page were murdered. No one has lived there since, so what was a hydro truck doing in the driveway, the connection had been cut off years ago. I put my hand on Steve's arm and told him to stop, there was something going on at that house. Instead he turned the corner, pulled over to the side of the road, turned and faced me and said in his soft irritatingly calm voice that he'd known for a month now that someone has bought the place and they were planning to fix it up and moving in. He didn't know how to tell me so he hadn't said anything.

I wouldn't speak to him for the rest of the ride home and when he went out again to get some beer, I still wasn't talking. But as soon as he was gone I wanted him back and when he did return, I gave him a huge hug and told him that I have a brain tumor and three months to live.

We made love, to forget it, to try to escape the horror, he was so caring, my poor wonderful Steve, I tried to get excited and I couldn't and I finally thought of Marshall just as everything reached a climax. How sad. My poor wonderful Steve, whose girlfriend can only make love when she thinks of someone dead for twenty five years.

As I say, it was a strange day. I can't sleep, it's after midnight now and the whole night is still ahead, the time I hate the most, when I can't sleep. Everything I've tried to forget, everything I've tried to come to terms with, is back as if it only happened five seconds ago. All the nightmares of my life, all the things I've done, all the people I've hurt, all the horrible things I've done to people who didn't deserve it, I can see everything, I can hear everything, faces that have vanished, voices that are dead, kind-hearted and caring and doing whatever they can do to help the people they care about, trying to cope with life, like I can see them in front of me a living nightmare like I'm eighteen again before it all happened before it all started when I could have done something to stop it their voices, haunting me, like they're right here and I can see them and hear them and understand what they're feeling, their voices, I'm thinking too much, when I think that I'm hearing voices I know I'm thinking too much, I know I won't get to sleep now.

Noreen's Version

Shelley is bending over record bins, lifting up one CD after another, flicking them over in her right palm, reading the descriptions, if you can call them that, bored, bored, bored. Dropping them back with a sharp little crack, or putting a few of them aside in the growing pile of CDs she won't buy. While her mother stands here. Watching.

Friday. Shelley's bored. Shelly is bored because everything is boring. Her mother is boring. The cottage is boring. The whole world is boring. Shelley is twelve and everything is boring.

And that's why we're walking around this jerky little tourist town, at least that's what Shelley calls it, looking at blue jeans and T shirts and Harley Davidson jacket patches and horrific CDs. Shelley's looking at blue jeans and T shirts and Harley Davidson jacket patches and horrific CDs. Not me. I'm just here. Following along. Getting into arguments about cottages and parents and jerky little tourist towns.

She's spent the last half hour in this record shop, reading the cover of every CD they've got in here. Some of them shock me. They're meant to shock me. That's why she's doing it. At least it's air conditioned. They've got no place to sit down. I've been sitting down all week. I feel a little woozy.

I'd rather be back at the cottage. Sitting with a drink by the lake. It's taken me all week, just to get to this stage. All I want to do now is sit by the lake. With a drink.

She wants a tattoo.
Around her wrist.
I'm the dinosaur.
Just because they've got them on Fashion Television.

"You'll never get rid of it," she keeps picking CDs, ignoring what I'm saying, and people stroll by the window in the summer sunlight and my daughter is surrounded by light and she bends over the CD bin, she's slim, beautiful, young and invulnerable. She ignores what I'm saying but I'm a mother and I can't help myself. "You'll be ninety five drooling at the mouth. You'll still have that stupid tattoo. You'll wear long sleeves in the middle of the summer, you'll die of heat prostration, just to cover up your stupid tattoo."

She keeps selecting CDs, her blonde hair falls over her shoulder and interferes with her vision and she pushes it back. "Melissa has one," she says quietly.

I hadn't expected that answer, it shuts me up for a second or so. But I make a good recovery, at least what I think is a good recovery.

"I don't care what Melissa does." As soon as I hear what I've said, I know how ludicrous it sounds because I care a lot what Melissa does, and not in a good way.

I've never noticed just how much like my mother I sound. It's eerie. Twenty years ago she programmed the words and I open my mouth and they come spewing out.

"She showed me," my daughter says. "It looks good."

"When?" I demand.

She looks around the shop, to see if there's anybody standing here she knows. I'm embarrassing her.

"When?"

"Mom!"

"I want to know when you were talking to Melissa."

She throws down the CDs and walks out the door and I follow. "I want to know when you were talking to her!"

"You saw us!"

"When?"

She turns and confronts me in the middle of the sidewalk and people walk around us and a teenaged boy in long beige sloppy shorts looks back and shakes his head and turns to his buddy and they laugh.

"Why do you always have to do this?" she demands, her voice is full of angry tears. "You're awful, both of you. I hate you both."

She stands there confronting me. And I feel horrible. She's right, I hate myself, I know when she was talking to Melissa, last June, when I took her to the Registry. I have the feeling it's something else.

I should push this. I should demand to know when she's been talking to Melissa, what else Melissa has said to her. But I can't, not now, it's too public here, I can feel her humiliation, this is exactly what my mother did when I was her age, and I told myself right then, I will never do this to my daughter, never.

And now I have.

I'm everything I've always hated.

She is going to say something more and doesn't and turns and walks off and I follow and after about a block she slows down and allows me to catch up.

That's a good sign.

I hope.

We walk down a short hill to a liftbridge at the base of the street, to our right there's an Anglican church of dark weathered stone with a bell tower in English parish-church style, underneath a thick maple tree, beside a canal. On our left the canal opens out to a small lake, and on a level stretch of grass just below the bridge, beside the lake, is a large red and white gazebo.

"You used to hate it when Gramma Clark shouted at you," she reminds me as we cross the bridge. Outrage and betrayal fills her voice, she stalks beside me, so much emotion in a thin little blonde girl. I don't respond. "You told me."

"Maybe she had a reason," I suggest.

"You hated it. You said she didn't have a reason, you said she was mean and rotten."

I don't remember saying that. Maybe I did. Never complain about your mother to your daughter.

"Why do you want a tattoo?" I ask.

"What do you care!"

Near the gazebo is a wharf that looks from here like a wooden walkway painted white. It goes out across the level water from the edge of the lake, and another wharf section crosses the T at its far end, well out in the lake. An old wooden yacht is anchored on an arm of the T, and a father and his squat three-year-old boy are walking out to have a closer look. Shelley goes across the street when we've crossed the bridge and stands stiff and incommunicado, watching the father and son.

"I don't want you to do something you'll regret later," I tell her.

"Like you."

The sun dazzles off the water so strongly it hurts my eyes, I hold my hand up for a shade, the man and his son look black in the glare.

"I could pierce my nipples," she says. "Everybody does it." I don't respond. "You don't want me to do that." I have the sense to keep quiet. "Do you?" Silence from her mother. "It doesn't matter who does." Small thump and clatter from a car and a rental trailer piled with furniture, crossing the bridge. "I can't."

"Because I care about you."

"That's no excuse."

"Actually I thought it was a pretty good excuse."

"There's nothing in between, is there?" she says. "I'm all alone, or I'm a prisoner in a police camp, being spied on every second."

"Is that how we've treated you?" I don't mean to sound snide, it really worries me.

"Life is crap," she says and starts back toward the shops downtown. Don't say that, I want to say, it sounds terrible, I know better than to say it, she wants me to say it.

A green pickup truck with a large camping trailer moves slowly across the bridge, we feel the bridge giving way underneath the weight, it sinks like it's not going to come up again, and eases up as the trailer gets across. There's a line of cars half up the hill. Car exhaust. It makes me cough.

"I never know what I'm supposed to do," she says when I catch up. "Ever. I'm always trying to please people and I never can. Never. I'm such a jerk."

"No you're not," I object.

"I am. I'm a jerk."

She watches me eat a sandwich and I share my chips and she has a coke. "I wish you'd eat some more," I say.

"Thanks Mom." She smiles for the first time in an hour. "I'm watching my weight. You don't want me to get fat and stationary. Would you?"

"Absolutely not. One in the family's quite enough."

"You're not fat." I wish she wouldn't use that word, she could be more political in her choice of words. We're sitting on old falling-apart uncomfortable wooden chairs beside a cracked dusty window at a rickety table in an old house that's been made over to a restaurant, and it's noon and everybody's waiting to get in. "You shouldn't eat so much," she says. "It's not healthy. You have to get some exercise."

"I guess it's not easy, being a daughter."

"No."

"I don't regret marrying your father."

She doesn't respond, but I've answered the question she didn't ask, this whole thing has been hard on her, she has no idea where she is or where she stands, but then again, neither do I.

"I just wish he'd say what the problem is," I tell her. "It just seems to get worse all the time, he retreats inside his shell. I don't know what to do."

"Don't ask me," she says. She says it in despair, not defiance. "I don't know what he's thinking, Mom. I think I understand sometimes, and then I don't. And then I get uptight and say eff it, and then I feel guilty."

"Don't talk like that."

"Sorry."

"Do you think it's me?" I ask.

"No. I don't think it's you."

I shouldn't be having this conversation, I should be telling this to Bill, this is a betrayal. But who do I talk to if not my own daughter, who else will understand? "What is it?" I ask.

"Mom, I don't know." She resents the fact that at twelve-years-old she's expected to understand a forty-one-year-old man who has never grown up and a mother who's going through some sort of middle-age crisis. She resents me for putting it all on her. And me, I don't have anyone else to put it on. And neither of us understands.

"What was that guy phoning about?" she asks. "Stan or whatever."

"An investment. I told you that."

"I thought he'd be phoning every night. He sounded really insecure."

"You think so?"

"That's what he sounded like."

We've got a view down the street and can see half the lake and the bridge and the slope up the other side and the roofs of the cars moving off where the street splits left and right.

"I wish I could get him to go and see someone," giving her my thoughts out loud. Sometimes we click, she knows I'm talking about her father.

"Melissa says people have to solve their own problems."

Melissa again! "I don't think Melissa knows a damn thing about it."

"You know, Mom...," she begins, and then stops. I wait for her to finish her sentence. She doesn't.

I hold out my plate. There are about ten french fries left and she takes one of the longer ones and bites the end off. "Why don't you finish them?" I suggest. She shakes her head. I put the plate in front of her.

"I am so mad at him," she's back at her father again. "I tell myself I won't let him get to me, and then he does. Do you know why that is?" There's a tear at the corner of her left eye, partially formed and it wells over and trickles down her face. "He goes crazy. He just goes crazy."

I feel her anguish, it's so deep and it hurts so much, her whole world is coming apart, it's awful to be so young, you can hurt so much.

"He sits in that damn room at home," she says, "with the damn door shut. You try to be friendly and open the door and say Hi Daddy, are you okay, can I get you anything, and he just grunts. And you're supposed to think it's a huge big favor that he doesn't rip your head off. I'm sick of it. And then when I try to talk to him, all he does is yell at me."

She's eaten half the French fries.

"I know."

"How do you know?" she snaps. "You work half the night in the basement, excuse me for living." The tears are coming down both cheeks now and plopping on the plate and disappearing in the French fries. "I wish I had a normal family."

I could be really stupid and ask, "What is normal anyway?" but I don't, I keep quiet, I won't insult her.

"I feel like nothing I do is ever good enough," she says. "You're bad. Daddy's worse." The fries are gone.

"I'm sorry."

"I was lying around at that idiot camp you sent me to, listening to all those jerks talking about their families. I'm listening to them and all I can think is, how come I don't have a family like that. They get treated like human beings, somebody talks to them, and they're nothing but jerks. They aren't even special. They're nothing."

I can't say anything to any of this, it's too awful, I feel completely helpless. "Do you want something more to eat?" I ask.

"That's insulting. All you have to do is feed me. That's exactly what you think! Open your big mouth and eat and shut up!"

"That's not true."

"Don't leave me," she says.

It comes out of nowhere, out of somewhere deep and frightened, unrelated to anything we've been talking about, related to everything we've been talking about. I reach out and we sit with our hands clasped tightly together.

After a minute, she adds, "This means 'Yes'?"

Her flippant tone offends me and I release her hands and straighten up. There are so many layers to this little girl. I don't know where she's hiding.

"I am not going to leave you."

"I knew you wouldn't," she says.

I look around. It's noon and the restaurant is jammed and people are standing outside waiting and we've finished eating and nobody's looking over here, but they have to be hearing everything we say, she's made no effort to keep her voice down, she probably can't. I don't know these people, but they already know me, inside out.

"Let's go," I say, and she looks around and realizes what I'm thinking and follows me sheepishly to the cash register and we fight our way out the door past the waiting people.

"God I was humiliated," she says when we're free and walking down the street toward the car. "I am such a bigmouth! Such an idiot!"

"I'm glad you didn't say something else."

"Asshole, I'm an asshole."

"Please Shelley," I must sound desperate, two older ladies walking along the street look back at us, they probably think I use those awful words myself and that's why my daughter does.

"I am," Shelley says.

"I love you."

"I know."

"Do you want to go through some more shops?" I suggest.

"Let's get the eff out of here," she says.

"Shelley!"

"I don't care, that's what I feel like. That's an exact description of what I feel like."

"Keep it to yourself."

"That's the way it is, isn't it? Don't say anything. Just shut the eff up!"

"That sounds awful! Don't say that any more."

"I could say a lot worse."

"Please."

"Then listen!"

In a few years of course she will say a lot worse, she's still only twelve.

We're parked on a side street five blocks away and it's hot and I'm feeling faint and we stop and sit down on a bench under a scrawny ornamental tree that the town must have planted this spring. Its branches spray out like the metal skeleton of an umbrella, the shade is pathetic. "You need to get some exercise," she says.

"I should."

"Why did you marry him?"

"We were in love."

There's more to it than that, there always is, but the complete answer is too complicated, and I don't know what it is.

"Love sucks," she says.

"No."

"Love sucks," she insists.

Is she talking about me? I'm afraid to ask.

"I'm sorry," she goes on, "what I said at the restaurant."

I close my eyes. I think all this stress is getting to me.

"Are you okay?" she asks.

"I'm just tired."

"Your face is really red."

"All this sun."

"Do you want something to drink maybe? I'll get you a coke or something. You shouldn't be sitting here."

"I'll move in a minute."

"Are you okay, Mom?" She is really scared, which sort of surprises me. I open my eyes. The sun is glaring. She's right, I should get in, out of the sun. "I'll get you a drink," she says.

I'm just tired. I've been arguing with my daughter and my husband and I never get a rest and now I'm just running out of energy and motivation. I feel a little dizzy. What will they do if I'm not here?

Metallic cold on my forehead, it revives me. "How does that feel?" she asks. She's holding a can of coke on my forehead, she's smart, I am so proud of her. I smile and she smiles back, and kisses me, she really does.

"I'm just a little tired," I say. "We'll go to the car in a minute. I'll have a rest there."

"You should see a doctor."

"Really, I'm just tired."

"I'm sorry I caused you so much trouble, Mom." She probably means it, but I've heard this all before. "I can only be stupid once you know," she says. "I just thought I'd try it. I'm not an addict or anything. I just thought I'd try it. I promise. I won't do it again. I promise."

The sad thing is I'm sitting here feeling hideous and she's scared and she means it right now, but she won't stick to it.

"I think we should go to a family counselor," I say. "I don't think your father will go."

"Melissa doesn't think they do any good."

Melissa! Why does she haunt me, even when I'm hundreds of miles away feeling sick and hideous?

Monday, August 2

2:30 a.m. There's no point sleeping, I can't. I feel so strange, like I'm not me, like Melissa is some strange concept in some other, alternate universe, something in those stars up there at the other end of my telescope, shining with their own strange light. You'd think, with this thing inside my brain, I'd sleep and sleep, and maybe never wake up.

It's warm but the mosquitoes have mostly gone. I've got Deep Woods Off for the ones still around. Every two hours a new bit of sky rotates into place, one bit for every month. Now it's October. I'm using a red filter on my flashlight, so I won't spoil my night vision, so I can write this. Sitting by my telescope. Which I've lugged out to the side of the driveway. No cars are driving by, not even teenagers. I'm sitting on my fold-out camp chair, beside my Dobsonian telescope, the big light bucket.

When I look up I can see Cassiopeia, the Queen, her crooked crown sideways rising above the trees. I've seen this all before, but still it's awesome. Find the larger point of the W of Cassiopeia's crown, and it points straight at the Andromeda Galaxy, six lengths away. I can see it right now, a blur there, who needs a telescope.

But then my big light bucket shows marvels.

My God, it is bright, a huge blurred oval, and up there, a small circle, and down below, when I move the scope slightly, the smaller oval. Three galaxies, two small and the big one, Andromeda. Of which I can only see the middle, a bright blur and you wouldn't think it was much, but grasp it, this glow is one trillion stars, two to five times larger than our own galaxy, depending on who's counting. It spreads out so far its arms engulf that small circle up above it. You can't see the arms very well, even in the telescope, and the light out towards the ends where it gathers in that little galaxy, M32, is too faint to make out. Still, that enormous galaxy spreads, an immense island of stars, a vast marvel up above us. Not an island. A universe.

Slowly it's coming toward us. We are big, our galaxy, the Milky Way, 200 billion stars, something like that. But it, this awesome thing, is enormously larger. Five billion years from now, it will be here and then gradually, it and our galaxy will meld together until we are one humongous ellipse.

It's a lovely night. Everything here, these trees, these skies, everything on our puny little Earth, means nothing. Anything that happens here means nothing. And you'd think that would upset me. It doesn't. Everything here, is meaningless. All the rotten things that people do to each other, the murderers that kill little girls, the cops that harass their mother, the daughters that harass their father, the woman that tells me, you don't belong here – none of it is anything. That vast conglomeration of stars will be up there, billions of years, when every rotten thing that humans do to each other, will have blown away like sand, like rot. All these marvels, were up there long before these jerks were ever thought of, they will be up there long after these jerks have rotted away, like the rot that they are. It doesn't matter. Any of it.

I used to think I had mellowed. I haven't obviously. I should mellow. Good things have happened in my life. Between the bad. My beautiful daughters. This place, when we first came here, and the canoe trips we took, and the work I did, editing law books, finding rare flowers, loving people. Good things with Stan. Funny, how he seems so much better, now.

And these magnificent stars. Lyra, and the wonderful double pairs, and the Ring Nebula, a star blowing apart and so far away the explosion sits up there like an arrested cosmic smoke ring, and Agol the variable in Perseus, one night bright, another night dim, pulsing. It's all so huge, all so far above us, beyond us, making everything that has ever bothered us, bothered me, nothing.

It puts it all in perspective.

6:21 a.m. Gioblastoma multiforme sounds like a stupid explosion, a caricature of every Latin name in the scientific catalogue, some sick professor's joke. Gioblastoma multiforme is a brain tumor. Gioblastoma multiforme is my brain tumor. The symptoms include seizure, nausea and vomiting, headache, hemiparesis, whatever that is. The most common symptom is progressive memory, personality and/or neurological deficit as the tumor develops. In other words I go stupid and twisted and babbling.

I've got more than one, the doctor's not sure how many. It's more common in men, which doesn't console me a lot. This is one situation where I have a perfect right to ask, why me? I am not a man, hadn't you noticed? It tends to hit people over fifty, picks on Caucasians, Latinos and Asians, and can develop more easily if you've already got other things with strange names like neurofibromatosis. It might be genetic, so again why me, nobody back as far as I know in my line of human animals had anything like this stuff. Of course I don't know all that far back. Average survival without treatment is three months. No one knows what the average is with treatment. It could be three months too.

I don't know where I heard this story, I don't know when I heard this story. There was a peasant, somewhere in Europe, in the Middle Ages, say 1250. He was the lowest of the lowest, his life was rotten hard and one day he was staggering down a road somewhere or other with a huge bundle of sticks, half logs probably, his back was bent almost double, he could not stand straight any more, even when he wasn't carrying anything. His kids were sick, his wife was sick, his animals were sick, his crops were sick, he ached in every bony cell in his body and finally he flung down his bundle and said, "I am done, I am through, I am not walking another step. Death is better than this."

At once Death stood in front of him.

"You called?" Death asked.

"Yes," said the peasant. "Could you help me get this bundle back on my back?"

I'm like that peasant. There's no point pretending. I want the bundle back.

There are treatments, but everything I've read says, underneath all the upbeat optimistic language and all the upbeat prognosis, that the treatments are only palliative. They don't cure. So the question is, will they do more harm than good? I have to decide, and obviously I don't have much time.

8:32 p.m. Dee is not making this easy. I suppose I can understand, she's lived there most of her life and she's been strong and independent for years, at least she thinks so, and she loves her place, she loves the sound of the waves, the wind in the trees, the animals that poke around at her door and eat the snacks she throws out and the chipmunk that climbs in her hand and nibbles with its soft mouth in her palm and fills its cheeks with peanuts. At night she can hear them, squirrels and racoons scampering across the roof and the rain drumming, and even the cold when the weather turns sharp, she doesn't mind the cold she says, even though her hands are like ice when I come to make her breakfast in the morning and serve her the second cup of tea. She's already boiled dry the kettle at least seven times, that I know of, and I worry I won't get there soon enough in the morning and I'm always expecting to see curls of black smoke going up above the trees long before I get there, she will burn the place down, one of these days, the Canadian Tea Party.

"No, I am not leaving here," she said. "That's what you'd want. You can't wait for me to leave so you can get your hands on this place, everybody wants this place, well they are not getting it. I know what you're like, I know what you want. They tried to buy this place and I wouldn't let them and then they gave up."

At least she didn't ask about the girls.

It goes on and on. I've been trying, for at least the last year, to convince her she needs to leave and she's no more willing now than she was a year ago. And yet she complains that she can't manage any more, it's hard to get up, it's hard to sweep the place, she can barely bend over to feed the animals, she hasn't been out by the lake for the last month, it's too hot and she just can't bring herself to do it and she's noticed a whole bunch of shingles coming loose and she can't get up there to fix them and do I think she should sell the boat, what should she ask for it?

In a way, it would have been better if the deal with Leslie hadn't fallen through. I can't think about that. It is too connected – I can't think of that.

This is a typical conversation. It could have happened any time in the last year. Worried Melissa versus stubborn Dee.

"Look, Dee," I say, "I won't always be able to come here. I'm getting old."

"You're just a young chicken," she says. "Spry as ever." And she smiles.

"That's nice of you to say, Dee, but you have to face the facts, I'm not getting any younger and neither are you. Suppose I'm sick. Suppose I won't be able to come here for a week, two weeks, three weeks."

"I have friends. You're not the only fish in the sea."

"Who?"

"Wouldn't you just like to know that."

"Yes, I would. Who?"

"None of your business."

"You can't do what you used to do, Dee. You said so yourself. Didn't you say that?"

"I'm doing just fine."

"Dee, I have to buy everything you have here. You can't drive your car, you're too far away for delivery, I have to get all your food, everything, medication, you name it, I bring it. Suppose you get sick two minutes after I leave here today? Does anyone ever come here? Who would know? Suppose you get sick and can't get to the phone? Suppose you fall? Nobody would know until I came back tomorrow, and suppose I couldn't come back tomorrow. You could lie here for days and nobody would know. I worry about you, Dee. What if you bled to death?"

"You have a hyperactive imagination."

"And you are not being realistic."

"You don't have to be rude about it."

"Think about it, Dee. There is going to come a time when you just won't be able to manage, even if I do come every day. And I'm not very well myself, Dee. There's going to come a time, very soon, when I won't be able to come here."

"Nonsense."

"There's some nice places you can go to, Dee, places where you can be with people your own age and there's someone to look after you all the time. And I won't have to worry about you. And you won't have to either. You worry, Dee, I know you do. We both know you won't be able to stay here much longer."

"I am not listening."

"Think about it. Will you do that? For my sake."

"You would like that, wouldn't you."

It always comes back to that. She doesn't trust me.

Steve drove me there today, he didn't want to, he said I should stay home and rest but I insisted on it. When we got to Dee's, he asked if I wanted him to stay and help out, in fact he announced that he was staying and helping out, but I got out and closed the door and told him he was not, let me do this the way I want to, I said. So he leaned over and stared at me out the passenger side window with his big sad, doubtful eyes and said, okay, if that's the way you feel about it, call if there's a problem. He backed up, turned around and drove off and I could hear his truck brushing down the lane and I smiled, he loves that truck even though it's all dented and scratched and stalls and burns more oil and gas than it should and he drives me in here even though he hates to hear the trees doing more damage to his precious truck than it's had already, he must care about me, to sacrifice his baby like that.

When I opened the door with my key and walked in the hall and looked in the kitchen, she wasn't there. I called and she didn't answer. She was still in her bed and the blinds were all down, it was dark and I could hardly hear her when she answered after I said her name three or four times. I asked her how she was feeling and she said almost inaudibly she was all right, she guessed. I asked her if she was having any pain and she said no, she just didn't feel very strong. I put my hand on her forehead and asked her if my hand felt cool. She said yes. It didn't seem like she had a temperature but I went to her dresser and found the finger thermometer and clipped it on her right index. She just felt weak, she said, it was nothing really, she just needed a bit of rest. Her temperature was up slightly, but nothing serious and I asked her if she wanted some tea. She told me that would certainly be nice and I pulled the blinds, sat her up in the bed and propped a couple of pillows under her. When

I brought in the tea, she could hardly drink it. The only thing she was strong enough to do, was to insist that she was not going anyplace, she was just fine, if I thought I was going to talk her into something I had another think coming. Her stubbornness perked her up and after that she was a little better and eventually came to the kitchen, with my help, just to prove that she wasn't going anywhere, she was fine.

"Did I ever tell you we're a lot alike?" I said.

I tried a few more times to plant the idea, you need to leave here, Dee, I won't be around forever, you have to look after yourself. She wouldn't listen. I have to realize, if I push it too hard it will only get her back more up than it is already, not that I can imagine that. It's like there's some extra secret reason why she won't leave, as if there's a body buried here, or her childhood probably, or probably she thinks if she leaves here she dies. Which, sadly, is true, not right away of course but it is true, when she leaves she won't come back. There was a woman once who got it in her head that if she kept adding rooms to her house she'd never die. As long as there was something being built, she'd go on forever. And of course it didn't happen that way and the more she added, the more she had to and she couldn't afford to build decent additions, she was rich but not that rich and her house was on a hill and the additions started crashing down the hill and the neighbors complained, but she kept building until finally it all stopped.

I'm sure that Dee thinks that way. As long as I'm here, I'm okay.

I wish I could pretend that was true.

So I left her place no farther ahead than when I came. It would be awful if that happened, if I was gone and she died there, alone, when she didn't have to. Some things have to happen. That doesn't.

I want to keep active as long as I can and I knew where I was going next and I knew there was a path the girls and I used to take, it's quite lovely, there's views of the lake and interesting plants and trees and some quite rare wild flowers, and it took me straight to the house they were fixing up.

It should have been torn down. The cedars have completely hidden it and entirely grown over the driveway, except for a small section out by the road and this is where the hydro truck parked. There is a footpath where the rest of the driveway used to be and a clearing in front of the house itself. The roof had sagged in the middle and the entire house was leaning slightly, to the left. Half the shingles were off, but sheets of plywood that used to cover the windows had been taken off and were propped against the side of the house beside the openings they used to cover. The window glass was mainly intact, though a couple of panes were cracked and one was broken, about opposite where someone had made a hole in one of the sheets of plywood. The front door was open and the outside door with the screen still boarded over was hinged flat against the outside wall and nailed in place. The back windows had been uncovered as well so I could see something moving around inside the house, interrupting the light.

Why would anyone buy this place? Steve said they were planning to move in and he probably knew, he talks to all the guys who do work around here. He made it sound like they were fixing up the house, but it didn't figure, I was sure whoever got the place was planning to level everything, including all the trees, and start again, for sure once they'd seen the condition of the house they'd do that. If they were thinking of fixing it up, it had to be someone too young to know better, nobody in their right mind would touch the place. That had to be them moving around in there.

Him. Graham Laird. He was thin, about twenty eight I'd guess, a shaved head, a beard, an outgoing personality, a tattoo on his neck peeking above his green T shirt.

I was standing on the ground outside looking in the bottom of the front window to the left of the porch when he appeared out of nowhere, looking down at me. "Hi!" A big outgoing grin. I was startled and didn't say anything. "What do you think?" he asked. "Pretty run down, right."

I agreed.

"You wouldn't think it to look at it there was a murder in here."

I have no idea what the expression on my face was when he said that, I felt hideous.

He hadn't stopped grinning. "Pretty spooky, right."

It would be an understatement to say I was upset. I have never had a harder time keeping my self control, I needed to find out what his purpose was in buying this place. He had one, that was clear.

"Do you live around here?" he asked.

"I'm just here for the summer."

"All summer?"

"Pretty well."

"Do you know anything about this place?"

"Not really."

"Come on in," he said, "I'll show you around."

I had never been back in the house since I found their bodies and I don't know how I managed to walk up the steps and go across the porch and through the open door into the front entrance.

"It looks worse than it is," he said, appearing in the door of the front room on the right. "It's safe. I've tested the floors. Where do you come from?"

"Toronto."

"That covers a lot of sins." I should have laughed to reinforce the illusion that I was who I said I was. He pointed me to the room on the left where they were killed. "About thirty years, maybe more, before the murder I told you about, go on in," he pointed to the room, "an artist lived here, go on in, right here, don't be shy, a kind of late impressionist type, Group of Seven sort. You can see," and I stepped in the room where I found them lying in the centre of the floor, "all around the walls here, you can see the holes, here and here and here," he pointed to the holes speckling the walls where Shelley had displayed the pictures of Noreen, "where he used to hang his paintings when he had his exhibitions. He specialized in watercolor, you can see," he gestured toward the front of the house, "how the landscape would inspire him."

I was on the verge of throwing up.

"I have no idea what his name was." He smiled at himself. "I'll have to find out, won't I? I don't suppose you've heard."

I shook my head. I couldn't talk.

"He must have had a lot of showings, don't you think, look at all these holes. There's no way he could have had that many paintings. Not in one show. It doesn't figure. You can see where he's taken down some things and put up others. Some of these holes have been used two or three times, you can see how he stuck in new pins or whatever and didn't quite hit the first hole. They found the bodies in the next room."

He walked from the room toward the kitchen at the back of the house, "Right in here," he called, he was standing in the kitchen and calling back at me. I hadn't moved. "They were stabbed in here." I went in there. "The bodies were right over there." He pointed to the floor beside the back door, which was boarded up. "Have you heard about it?"

I shook my head.

"Two girls. Eleven and twelve. They were killed by some crazy woman. I'll be doing some research. Right there. You can still see a bit of blood or something, where the boards are darker. There was blood all over the place. They say the mother went crazy."

I couldn't respond.

"I guess you must think I'm the one that's crazy," he said.

I shook my head.

"So what do you think?" he asked. "You're not saying very much."

"About what?"

"Do you think anyone would be interested?"

I told him I wasn't feeling very well and got out of there and made it to the road before I had to sit down. Someone stopped and asked if I was all right but I told them I was fine, I only needed a bit of rest, I'd be all right. I have no idea who it was, I wasn't looking at them, I was looking away because I didn't want them to see that the right side of my face was twitching, I knew what this was, it was part of the tumor, you lose control of your body.

After a while the twitching stopped and I got up and made it home, I don't know how. As soon as he saw how I looked, Steve called the doctor, who increased my medication and Steve went out and got it. It seemed to work and I felt better, but not all that great. Steve insisted I stay in bed and that's what I've been doing.

What will I do about Graham Laird? My daughters are not a tourist attraction. As soon as I feel better I'll deal with it. But I'd rather just die.

Noreen's Version

Nine o'clock, I'm not thinking, I'm so tired I'm bringing in my briefcase instead of leaving it in the car but I'm too tired to turn around and take it back out and as soon as I get inside Shelley flies at me, I'm knocked backwards the briefcase smacks on the floor and my back slams against the door. She's shrieking incoherently I grab her wrists instinctively we slide down the door on the floor and she's shrieking and I'm terrified I'm thinking my God my God my daughter's gone berserk, we wind up twisting on the floor flailing for control I pin her I can't let go her strength is incredible and finally she's exhausted, I push her back and she sits splayed on the floor. Her one leg is out to the side and her other leg under her at a crazy angle and her hair is all down covering her face and she's roaring, bawling, cursing, roaring, "I hate you! I hate you! I hate you!" and my hair is all messed up and my good summer jacket is ripped all down one side she's ruined it and her eyes are wild and her face is wet and she's bit me. I'm just feeling it, now, on my right arm, it really hurts but she seems okay, except she's completely wild, my God, she's got drugs, her eyes are crazy, God knows who she thinks I am, she's having some kind of crazy drug induced nightmare.

We sit on the floor. I'm resting against the door and we're panting, totally exhausted.

"I hate you!" she roars again.

I reach out and try to push her hair off her face and she shrieks and tries to bite me and I grab her and push her over on the floor and hold her there and she screams, "Let me go! let me go! let me go!" and kicks me and I kneel on her legs, "I'm not letting you go, I'm not letting you go, stop it!" She tries to push up and bite at me and I hold her down. I'm still stronger than she is. The only thing I can do is hold her here, and when she calms down, I'll have to call an ambulance. A doctor. Somebody.

After maybe ten minutes, she does calm down but I won't let her up. She glares at me the whole time, she won't take her eyes off me, we're both wild now not sure who we are or where we are and finally, when she's calm, or seems calm, she says, "Did you enjoy it?" Where she's kicked me really hurts, I think I'll have to get a doctor. "Did you enjoy it?" she says again.

And she starts crying and doesn't stop and her wails get louder and louder like she's just lost everybody she's ever cared about or who ever cared about her and she totally breaks down, I let her up and she covers her face and sits against the wall and wails, roars, like the world has just come to an end and she's alone in a vast universe, she's the only thing alive in a dead and burned out universe, she falls aside and lies curled up on the floor, wailing, curled up around her pain like someone has yanked out her insides and she's dying, and I put my arms around her and she's too devastated to push me away and finally she wraps her arms around me and squeezes me as hard as she can and wails her heart out.

When she's done we're both emotional dishrags.

And that's when she reveals what Melissa told her, about me and Stan, that vulgar word. Is Melissa Hitler? Hitler said the bigger the lie the more people are likely to believe it. I'm leaning against the front door and before I can answer I can hear a car pull into the driveway and the engine turning off, and I can tell by the funny little clatter as it dies, it's the MG.

"Your father's here," I say.

Shelley stands up and wipes off the tears, her expression vanishes, her face is blank as metal. This is between me and her. It is none of his business. We will deal with it later.

Tuesday, August 3

9:45 a.m. I shouldn't lie here like this. If I don't make myself get up and do something, I start thinking, about everything that's happened in my life, all the awful things, the nightmares, the faces of my daughters, the faces of Noreen, Shelley, my father, Marshall.

I was sexually assaulted when I was seven years old and as soon as I told my mother she slapped me across the face and called me a liar. Called me a liar because I told her my father did it and she told him what I'd said and left us alone and he yanked down my pants and did it again and it really hurt this time and he told me if I ever dared tell anyone ever again he'd make damn sure I felt it next time, if I thought it hurt this time I didn't know what hurt was. Say anything and he'd rip out my tongue.

And I told her that time too, I was a defiant little bitch and she slapped my face so hard I cried for the rest of the day and I kept telling her, every time he did it or tried to do it. Finally she locked me in my room and told me if I didn't shut up I'd stay there forever. I'm proud though. I didn't take it and I wouldn't shut up. That amazes me. I wouldn't shut up.

And that's what stopped him. I feel good about that. I was a loud mouthed little bitch. Most kids that age shut up and let the bastards fuck them and grow up a real mess. Not me, I mean, I'm not so traumatized I can't function, I function pretty well I think. Except of course I've been angry all my life. I don't remember when I realized that, years ago for sure. It comes when I least expect it. Like over at Monica's. I control it though.

My childhood was a real ball. I wouldn't shut up and got punished. She made me clean the house every day and one time she hit me so hard, because she said I hadn't done something or other the way she said I was supposed to do it, I've forgotten what it was now, dusted the top of the fridge I think, she hit me so hard I limped for a week. I had a big black bruise all along the back of my leg and someone saw it and asked what had happened and she said I fell off a ladder I was too goddamn stupid not to, she said.

Sometimes the anger builds up so much I don't dare go anywhere. I keep out of everybody's way and they think I'm antisocial. After Erica and Page were murdered, I disappeared for six months. I can't think what I was like then, what I felt, I damn near went crazy. I'm surprised I didn't. I mean I must have had this guardian angel they used to say we all have, not that I believe it, but something saved me. Maybe that's what Steve is. A bald, beer-bellied guardian angel.

I've learned to be responsible. It hasn't been easy. Even yet, though, it surprises me, all this anger I've got built up inside me. Sometimes I explode over stupid things, things you wouldn't believe. I get angry over stupid things and then I want to hurt myself and sometimes I have to do that, to make it stop, all that hurting. It's awful. When they died, it surprises me, you'd think when I slashed myself over stupid things I'd slit my throat and be done with it, after something as horrible as that, but there was no way I was killing myself and letting all of them win because of what she did to my daughters. What they all did to my daughters. I had more respect for my daughters. For me. There was no way I was letting them forget.

I often think, how my father died and I never got to pay him back, I was still too young, and Shelley slit her throat, they say there was blood all over that office, she was always very dramatic and they knew I hadn't done it because the cops had me arrested on suspicion and I was locked up when she did it to herself, so they had to let me go.

They arrested me on suspicion of murdering my own daughters. I don't want to think about that. I had to deal with it, with the murder of my own daughters, in jail.

She was lucky she killed herself. I would have slaughtered her, if I'd had the chance, and they probably knew that. I suppose that's part of the reason they locked me up. Maybe. I never got the chance, she beat me to it.

When I get my moods, I make sure I'm alone. I can feel myself getting all knotted up and I don't think it's done me a whole lot of good, physically, over the years. It probably has nothing to do with what's going on now, but who knows, I'm not a doctor.

I think about that scumbag and I imagine what I'd do to him, cutting out his balls, chopping off his prick an inch at a time and grinding it up for meat while he shrieks and begs me to stop, and pulling out his guts and twisting them on red hot hooks the sort they hang steer carcasses on once they've slaughtered them and setting his guts on fire, like they did for treason in Henry the Eighth's time and ramming a white hot poker up his ass like someone did to some English king and listening to him roar and beg for mercy and standing back, smiling, smelling his anus sizzle. Even yet I imagine that. It makes me feel better. I wrote it out one time and came across it later and ripped it up and threw it away.

He died when I was fifteen, my father, drove his car at seventy-five miles an hour into the side of a train. As soon as she got the phone call, my mother turned with the receiver in her hand and glared at me, "I hope you're satisfied!" He was losing clients and his business was in trouble, apparently that was my fault too.

By then I was cute, she wasn't, she was fat and sloppy and jealous. I tried not to do that with my daughters, to make them feel rotten because they were cute and I wasn't. I wanted them to be beautiful, I dressed them up as much as I could, I was so looking forward to buying them things, dressing them for dances and weddings and graduations and everything I didn't have when I was their age, they would have been so beautiful, so magnificent. They're the only good thing that ever happened to me.

Anyway, I don't feel a whole lot of warm fuzzies about my childhood. I was so angry I'm sometimes amazed I didn't do more than I actually did, I'm amazed that anyone in the entire world is still alive, my anger was that intense. And the amazing thing is, I didn't realize how intense it really was, even then. Why did I let Marshall do what he did, that's what astounds me.

I used to believe. I was religious. That's what prison did. I knew my Bible. I was in prison for twenty five years it was the only thing that saved me. I used to read the Bible every day. I wrote out a reading schedule every day for three months and when I finished it, the first time, I put down the book, one of those small black books that, what's their name, the people that put them in motel rooms, the Gideons, the kind of Bible the Gideons give out – I put the book down and closed it and lay back and looked up at the ceiling of this hideous place I was locked in and thought, Jesus, I finished the whole goddamn thing. Ironic, right, to use words like that for something like that, as if he helped me. God knows, maybe he did. And then I went back and started over again, right from "In the beginning God created the heaven and the earth and the earth was without form and void and darkness was upon the face of the deep and God said let there be light and there was light" and so forth, I still love those words, I love the way they sound, so incredible. I don't know how many times I read that Bible through, cover to cover. I had lots of time. My favorite was Job, it fit, the guy lost everything and then got this rotten disease where his skin kept leaking pus and he had this potsherd thing he scraped himself with and he must have been a real mess to look at. And nobody had anything to do with him but three friends. I mean those are friends, that's the definition of real friends. I think of Steve. After six months or whatever it was and Erica and Page had been murdered and I was going through hell and I wasn't going out and I was buried in the house and close to going mad, it was Steve who came over and knocked on the door and asked if I was all right. Sometimes I think he looks like Stan, he sort of does, actually. The names kind of sound the same. Different guys though.

I tried everything. I almost went crazy. I read Job over and over, I pretty well have it memorized, and then one day it just hit me. I was screwed, as a kid right, and nobody wanted to have anything to do with me and locked me in my room when I wouldn't shut up and the bastard who did it, did it because he had the power, because he could. And it finally hit me one day, that's what <u>The Book of Job</u> says. When God answered Job, did he say I allowed the devil to do this to you? No. He just kept telling Job, I am God, I did this, I did that, and what can you do? Were you there when I created the world? And that's exactly what my pus-face father said, as far as you're concerned, I am God. And nobody said anything, and everybody asked me, what had I done to egg him on? I must have done something they said, it wouldn't have happened if I hadn't done something, he was just a man, a man doesn't have control he just thinks of one thing all the time so what did I expect, I led him on. At seven years old for godsake. At seven years old, it was my fault, I led him on. All I could think was, what do you mean, I led him on? Led him where? What did I know. I was seven.

When my daughters were killed, who got blamed? Me. If I hadn't done what I'd done, everybody said, or thought to themselves and didn't say out loud, my daughters would still be alive. I mean who believes me, right. I murder people. Just one, though, let's keep it straight. And Shelley made damn sure I made up for it. You kill my mother, I'll kill your kids. Two for one. That definitely made up for it.

So why am I still the bad guy? I've paid. I've more than paid. I did twenty five years, my whole sentence, I did my whole sentence for murder. Do you know anyone who serves their whole sentence any more? And after paying for it, I pay for it again, with them, their lives. They paid for it. My wonderful daughters.

So why am I still the bad guy? What have I done now?

Why did I think this? Why am I bringing it all up again? I was over this. Why am I reliving every nightmare in my life?

9:20 p.m. An interesting day after all. Soon after writing the stuff above, I heard a noise at the front door and someone unlocked it and came in. I assumed of course it was Steve and then a girl's voice I had never heard before said, "Melissa? Are you there?"

I don't want anybody to see any of this stuff I write stuff like this when I'm upset and I only had time to shut the laptop before a young woman came in my bedroom and said, "Hi." I was kind of resentful, to be honest, I don't enjoy dredging up that stuff, but I had just finished ranting and whatever satisfaction I get, I was still ranting on my laptop.

She was so thin I thought that if she turned sideways she'd disappear and god help me the first thing I thought was, I used to look like that. She had blondish/reddish hair bound up in a short ponytail high on the back of her head and jeans that were part of her skin but her face was beautiful, it broke my heart she was so beautiful. Not fashion plate beautiful, more classic I guess you'd say, her nose and her forehead and her mouth and her lips were in perfect proportion, not cold though, I don't know how to describe it exactly, some women look too perfect, she looked human, caring, kind of shy. But she knew she looked good, she carried herself that way, reasonably tall for a young woman, five nine or ten, straight up like she'd been balancing things on her head, but not pouty like models who think they're so perfect.

"I'm Drew," she said. I had no idea who Drew was. The odd thing is, this complete stranger walked in my house and I didn't tell her to get the hell out, I trusted her immediately. Amazing. How was that possible?

"Steve's my grandfather," she explained. Eighteen. A little older than Erica would have been, and I think that's what struck me, she doesn't look the same, but there was something that immediately reminded me, I felt a strange horrible chill go through me like a knife like I'd been surprised in some awful act and I almost cried out in pain.

She sat on the edge of the bed and smiled, a warm smile, shy, like she sort of is. She actually reached over and felt my forehead. Like her grandfather. That seems so strange. Like her grandfather. And she's the same age as Erica, would have been, more or less.

"Good," I said. "I'm fine," and I thought, dear god, don't take your hand away.

"You look pretty good," she said.

I took the laptop off my legs where I'd rested it and put it on the bed beside me. For a second my hand shook but I don't think she noticed.

"Do you want me to take that?" she asked and I handed it over. I would have handed over anything she asked, but I told her to put it on the table beside the bed, which she did and as she leaned over to place it there I stared at her perfect profile, I couldn't help it, she was completely relaxed, at peace almost, I thought. "Steve said you had a bad night."

"I'm just lazy," I said. "I'm enjoying myself." As soon as I said it, I knew that was a really bizarre remark and obviously not true. She smoothed down the blankets on each side of me and brushed her hand across my forehead again.

"I hope you don't mind that I walked in like this," she said. I have never met anyone I liked so instantly. My eyes are filling up when I write this, it was such a contrast and all I could think was all the good things that could have happened, what my life could have been and it all started at her age, I was her age when it all started and it was my fault, it was all my fault.

Her grandmother hates Steve and her mother hasn't had much to do with him but Drew has been in touch the last few years and they've gotten together from time to time she said, though not so often that me, her father's girlfriend, knew she existed. This time she's staying for a couple of weeks, maybe longer, she said, so maybe if I don't mind she said she'll come over from time to time and I told her, no problem, almost bawling that sounded so wonderful, I'm getting more emotionally unstable the more this thing goes on that I'm got inside my head. Her voice is incredibly soft, not quite musical I guess, but gentle. "How are you feeling, really," she asked.

"Tired," I admitted. She asked if I wanted anything to eat, and I asked for some toast and maybe coffee, juice, whatever she could find out there, and she patted my arm and got up and went to the kitchen.

She has no desire to be a nurse, she said, raising her voice so I could hear her from out there, she isn't suited. What she really wants, is to work in publishing, film, something like that, that's why she was looking forward to meeting me, I worked for a law publisher, didn't I.

"Not recently," I called.

I liked this, being served, I closed my eyes, I deserve this, I thought, I could lie here and be served all day, and almost at the same instant, thought about Monica, I wonder if her son has showed up? And then I thought of Dee, she really did need me.

"Steve said your friend is all right," Drew called from the kitchen. "He got her up and gave her some breakfast. She seemed to think he was somebody else. He didn't think she really knew who she was thinking of, exactly."

Drew appeared in the doorway with some toast and coffee in a mug and some orange juice on a tin beer tray with a woman in a long white frilly early twentieth-century dress that I bought at a dollar store a couple of years ago. "I wasn't sure we had orange juice," I said.

"You did." She set the tray down on the bed.

"Are you going to feed me?" I asked.

She smiled. "Only if you sit up."

"Are you some kind of guardian angel or something?" I asked as I sat up and she stuffed pillows at my back and fluffed them up and smoothed down my blankets.

"You don't know me, obviously." She smiled kind of privately, she found that amusing.

"We have to help her," I said.

"This first," said Drew and tilted the mug at my lips and I drank some coffee like a one year old child and I couldn't help thinking, Erica would have done this, Page probably too, in fact you never know, Page might have been better, she wasn't so cold. Sometimes I'll see something on TV that I know they would have liked and I'll call them, "Come and see this." I know they're not there, but it makes me feel better, to say that.

I insisted on getting up and Drew insisted that I take my medication first, she'd been reading all the bottles beside my bed while I ate the cereal. Once every three hours. Or once a day with food. Or whenever the pain gets too bad. And a couple of extra bottles just for the hell of it. She helped me get dressed even though I declared I would do it myself and she agreed to that, but then she helped me anyway, and I let her. "Did you ever think of writing your autobiography?" she asked.

My top was half over my head and as she pulled it down she emerged, looking down to make sure she pulled it far enough I suppose. "You're crazy," I said.

She fluffed my hair. She's taller. "You don't think you've had an interesting life?"

"Do you know?"

"Steve told me." How much, I wondered.

"I don't have enough time," I objected.

"You're writing a journal. Right?"

"No way."

She made a little noise that was a half flippant okay and shrugged her shoulders.

I'm torn. I want to destroy all my journals, all the evidence, but I don't want everything I've ever been to vanish as if I'd never existed. Whose idea was this, this autobiography thing? Obviously Steve told her about my journal, how else would she know. Once I'm gone, what does he plan to do with it?

"I could find a publisher, or something," she suggested.

It's good I don't have much time, I might get disillusioned and I like her too much to go through that. Everyone I've ever known has been like that, I think they're wonderful and then I get disillusioned, as soon as I learn what they're really like. I'd rather think of Drew the way she is right now, guaranteed she's got nasty schemes and secret places and does rotten things like everybody else, and I don't want to know about them, she'll act good as long as I'm around, probably, which isn't too long, after that who cares.

She drove me in Steve's truck, which she'd parked at the end of the driveway, which is why I didn't hear her drive up. When we got to the corner where the road ends and we turned right to go along the lakeshore road, I looked to the left. There were a couple of trucks in the driveway, I couldn't make out the names, a big lumber supply truck it looked like and a smaller pickup, pretty new and clean, professional looking. Graham was getting on with it. So will I.

"What have you decided?" Drew asked.

"About?"

"Steve said you were making up your mind about treatment."

"I haven't."

She didn't respond. I love her profile, I've never seen anything so perfect, everything exactly proportioned, exactly right. Her skin was a little coarse but she knew how to use cosmetics, just enough to disguise, not enough to bury. "Was your mother like that?"

"What?"

"Your skin is perfect."

"Yeah I guess."

"Does she comb your hair?"

"When I let her."

I told her to turn left into Dee's place. "I'm not crazy about chemo," I said, the truck bounded and threw us both upwards. "You'll want to slow down. Your grandfather hates this driveway. He'll want to know how much you've scratched the truck."

We were crossing the open marshy area where water filled up the potholes and approaching the section where the trees close in. "Scratch or walk," she said.

"I could do radiation. I'm not sure it makes much sense, really."

"What else is there?" The first branches screed along the doors on each side.

"Painkillers. Morphine. No matter what you do, it hurts, except for the painkillers. Chemo hurts a lot, it kills healthy cells, the ones I still need. None of it will give me very much time, no matter what I do."

"You have to," she said. We'd reached the worst section where Steve's face registers the agony his truck is going through. The scrawling was symphonic. "Anything that keeps you alive, right."

I didn't answer. It was my choice.

"Steve said you had a seizure."

"No big deal."

"It would be to me," she said as we reached the side porch at Dee's house and she stopped the truck. "Steve will just have to put up with it," she added, referring to the truck. There were bits of branches on the hood.

"Is this Erica?" Dee asked when we came in and she saw Drew. "Or Page, I'll bet it's Page, she was always the pretty one."

Wednesday, August 4

2:45 p.m. I slept all morning. Part of the afternoon too, I guess. I'm on my own today. I still don't feel all that great. Drew has gone off with Steve for some grandfather-granddaughter time, Steve in the passenger seat, chauffeured and looking smug.

"Don't you dare go anywhere today," Drew said as she put another cup of coffee on the kitchen table this morning, the keys were in her hand and her granddad at the porch door, waiting. "Drink that. Stay right here." I had to smile of course. "I mean it. You don't go anywhere. You save your strength."

I smiled and said all right, but thought, save my strength for what? It seems to me in fact that I'm better to use my strength while I've still got it. She's too young and healthy to understand, but too good to argue with. I did sleep though, and that was good.

Right now I'm sort of standing back looking at myself, amused at Melissa, this is not like her, to meekly go along with anyone, especially someone forty-four years younger than she is, than I am. Eighteen. I want to throw my arms around her and protect her from everything, especially herself. I was her age, when .... I'm so scared she'll find out. I really don't believe Steve has ever told her the awful thing I did when I was her age. I have so little time left to live I don't want this wonderful girl to think badly about me, I won't have time to prove I'm not the same person. I've spent all my life making up for that one act. There is no way I can defend it and no way I will ever make up for it. I can defend myself against the jerks, but not against a wonder like Drew.

Enough.

She promised she'll stop by and make sure Dee is all right, if there's a problem she won't go anywhere. If things are fine, she's going on with Steve for a tour of the area, the cliffs and the bays on the east side of the peninsula all the way up to the ferry, she thinks. She wants to see the flowerpots and maybe the underwater park.

Already Dee loves her, but still hasn't figured out if she's Erica or Page. "Did you ever have that heart operation?" Dee asked her.

"It got better," Drew said and combed Dee's hair and put some rouge on her cheeks and when we left, looked back at Dee's cottage and said, "She can't stay here."

"Maybe you can convince her," I suggested. "I can't." And maybe she can, Dee listens to this little eighteen-year-old girl the way she's never listened to me, and she's just met her. I'm kind of jealous.

So here I am, with my fourth cup of coffee, or fifth I can't be sure, and a cinnamon roll, and Sun dancing on the screens and delicious quiet air sifting in and the vague sound of waves washing on the lakeshore half a mile away, which maybe I'm just imagining.

According to my schedule, today I should have been going to Monica's, and maybe I will yet, I'm not dead yet. I have to take care of Graham. Some night I'll throw a Molotov Cocktail. He can't fix the place if it's burned to the ground. Soon though, I'll have to do it soon.

In the meantime I'll put down this laptop and enjoy myself, maybe go for a walk, not too far, enough to savor the white pines and the red squirrels and whatever else is out there. I have to deal with Graham. But not today. Today I am building up my strength, like I'm told.

8:40 p.m. And wound up instead getting out the car I haven't used for months and driving to Monica's.

There was a car in front of her house all right, like she'd said there might be, a big grey BMW. She must have heard me driving up, I didn't have to knock, she opened the door as I came across the porch. "Thank God you're here," she said and let me in. There were two men in the living room, a thin embarrassed looking balding man about fifty, or so, in a shabby grey-green suit who I found out later was a lawyer and a shorter somewhat overweight man with greying hair cut close, grey eyes, coarse features, Monica's son, Gavin.

"Who is this?" her son demanded.

"A friend," said Monica and drove straight to the centre of the living room, whirled her chair so her back was facing Gavin and asked me if I wanted anything to drink, coffee, juice, something stronger. "This is my son," she jerked her head back towards him.

"This is private business," Gavin told me.

"I want Melissa here," Monica snapped back, still facing me. "This is my house." She seemed to be in control here, so why did she need me?

191

"This is a private family matter, "Gavin said.

Monica turned her chair around and faced her son once more. "Two on two," she said.

I sat where she'd sort of indicated. "You have some kind of document," Monica said to the lawyer. "I want Melissa to see it."

The older man reached for a thin black leather document pouch he'd placed on the floor beside him.

"Get out," Gavin said, staring at me. "This is none of your business."

Monica buzzed over to the older man and held out her hand. "She works with lawyers."

"I said this is..."

"A private family business," Monica said, still holding out her hand to the lawyer. "We heard."

"I do not authorize this," the son told his lawyer. What was interesting was that Monica had not introduced her son by name. A financial adviser, I think she said.

"I can't sign anything if I can't have a look at it," Monica pointed out, still holding out her hand.

Gavin came over to her, turned her chair so that she was facing him and leaned down over her. "I want what's mine."

I stood up and walked across the room and stood beside him. "I think you had better stop this," I said, but he continued leaning over her, their faces were no more than a couple of feet from each other.

"I want what's mine," he said. Tears had started forming in her eyes. I had never seen Monica like that and never expected to.

I looked across mother and son to the lawyer. "Would you please advise your client that a document signed under duress will not stand up in court." It was obvious from his expression the lawyer wanted to be anywhere else but here.

"Bitch," said Gavin, stood up and walked away. The word was meant for all three of us. Monica swung the chair around, whirred off towards the downstairs bedroom and turned out of sight beyond the open door. Gavin went off after her and I followed.

"It's no use," the lawyer called. "She won't sign."

"Shut the fuck up," Gavin shouted and slammed the door behind him. I tried to open it and couldn't, he was holding it shut.

"Call 911," I shouted at the lawyer and Monica and anyone else who could hear, the door came free and Gavin stepped back as I strode by him to Monica.

I found her in the ensuite off her bedroom. "I told you he was a jerk," she said, her face all wet where she'd splashed it with water. "I really didn't think you were coming, he's been at me for hours, for hours, I really didn't think you were coming, thank god you were coming, I'm not going to cry now, I'm over that now, he was wearing me down the jerk, he's always been like this from the time he was a shitting little kid, he'd take all the strawberries." I washed her face off and dried it and got some toilet paper and she blew her nose and laughed at how ridiculous she said she must look and sound. "He wears me down," she said.

When we came back to the living room, Gavin and his lawyer were gone and Monica buzzed to the kitchen, upbeat, almost jovial. "I was holding out pretty well, I thought, until I started thinking how he looked when he was six months old and you'd think that would help me, thinking of him all tiny and helpless and shitting like that, but all I could think was all the crap I've gone through for his sake and this is what he was doing, this is how he was paying me back, but thank God, you showed up just about then, do you want coffee or what, I think I'll have something more in mine."

Alcohol is about the worst thing I can have now, so I just had coffee. "Anything I can do, you just name it," she said.

We sat in the living room by the fireplace not very relaxed, her especially, and I told her that once I had finished my coffee, as long as she was sure he would not be coming back, I thought I'd better get back home, I was feeling a little tired. But I was worried about her, she was gripping her mug like she wanted to break it and her face looked like she'd start twitching like me, like I do sometimes, and I asked her if she was feeling all right but she assured me she'd be fine, she had some tranquillizers and she'd maybe take twenty five or so.

"You don't mean that," I said. You never know about people. "Right?"

"You know me better than that, Melissa, I mean, can't I be a bitch when I want to be, I'm talking like you now. You know that surely. You've seen that. Even my son knows that. You heard him. I'm not going to kill myself. I'll kill him first."

I smiled.

"How dare him do that. Really, Melissa, how dare him do that, after everything I've done for him all his life. He almost killed me, when he was born he almost killed me, I had to take six months to recover, in the hospital goddammit, the little jerk almost killed me."

If she could be angry like that, then it seemed to me she was recovering, so I left.

It's a performance, like all the characters in my life are giving their last performance just before they freeze in place forever.

When I got home I slept and got up again about five thirty and had some soup and tea and made toast and felt not too bad, but not enough to want any more to eat. I called Monica. The phone rang several times and I was thinking she wasn't going to answer when she picked up and said hello, sounding drugged. "How are you feeling?" I asked.

"Melissa!" she perked up instantly, "how lovely of you to phone me, how are you feeling, you didn't look very good yourself when you left here, did you, how lovely of you to call, I'm fine."

"Nobody came back?"

"Not yet. I don't think he's done."

"Do you need anything?"

"I think I can handle it. If I can't I'll call. You'll be available?"

"Yes." I don't know why I said that, I knew damn well I wouldn't be, I couldn't be, obviously I still hadn't accepted what was happening to me.

"I don't think I'll need to. It's good to know I can, if I want. Call up the cavalry, as it were."

"You never said what it was all about," I pointed out.

"Why, he didn't tell you it was family business?"

"Pretty strongly."

"That's him."

"It's really none of my business."

"I have a couple of properties outside Toronto that his father left me, pretty big, with the understanding that when I go, he gets them. He wants me to sign them over right now, and I'm just stubborn enough not to. He should know that. How are you feeling?"

"Fine." Again, I wasn't facing it.

"As you can imagine with all the real estate going the way it is right now, they're worth a hell of a lot of money, and my little precious wants his candy right now. I didn't think he'd be so vicious, though. What surprises me about it all is that his lawyer would go along with it." I was reminded, of course, of how she tried to do the same to Dee, ten years ago. People are strange.

"You must come over and have a real drink," she said. "I owe you."

"I don't have very long to live," I said. The silence was immediate. "I have a brain tumor, a cancer. My doctor has told me that at most I have seven months, less if I don't start treatment right away."

Telling it to Monica made it absolutely real, absolutely final, for the first time, despite what I'd told myself and told Steve and told by implication to Drew. I guess it sort of made it official, for public consumption, as if now that I'd said it I'd have to carry through, I'd have to die now that I admitted it.

Drew came breezing in around eight, they had to get back here, she said, she wanted to get me something really good for dinner, as if I was waiting just for that, she had no idea there was so much to see, there's a huge slab that has broken off the escarpment say thirty kilometers from here on the other side of the peninsula and fallen straight down and buried itself in the debris at the foot of that steep hill and earth had filled in around it and it looks from a distance like a sort of cathedral with a pointy spire and you can walk up beside it and climb on top, it's thick through, maybe fifteen feet and it stands straight up and split in half as it fell, like vertically split, she's never seen anything like it and the view of the lake from there is stunning, blue and white where the waves come up far down there on the shore and the trees and the green and the grey of the escarpment, and a slab jutting out right above your head as you stand on that pointy spire and you think as you look up at it that a new enormous piece of the escarpment is coming down any second ready to crush you.

It was delightful to hear her talking, like life had suddenly been restored to the world. Steve got a beer from the fridge and sat in my ratty living room smiling at his granddaughter. "So what did you do?" she asked.

I told her.

She jumped up and came over and glared down, she was really angry. "You are outrageous! How dare you leave here and do that! I told you to stay here!"

I thought I had been telling her something sort of interesting, human beings being human. I smiled.

"Stop that!" she demanded. "It's not like you've got a lot of energy to give away or something! You are outrageous!"

"I guess I am."

"Don't you dare say that! Don't you dare take that attitude. You're important! I want you around!"

I didn't used to get choked up, that's not who I am, I am not sentimental, but I couldn't talk after that, I just stared at her and cried. She got down on the sofa and hugged me tight and said Steve cared and she cared and they didn't want me to go, I was too important to them both and that really broke me down. "We were talking about you today and I was saying how I wanted you to come and see all these things we saw. They were wonderful. I wanted you there to see them, it broke my heart you weren't, there's so much more to see, I want you to see them, I don't want you to go."

She feels sorry for her grandfather's girlfriend, the dying woman. If I was younger, and felt better, I'd resent it, I hated it when people felt sorry for me. Not now, I'll enjoy it while I can.

Thursday, August 5

4:02 a.m. That's what the time on my laptop says. I can't sleep. Why can't I sleep? I'm dying and I can't sleep. Steve is asleep in the bedroom, nothing wakes him, and Drew is camped out on the sofa in the living room. I had to tip toe by when I came out here, to the porch. I know they mean well, both of them, but I'd rather be alone, I'm used to it, and soon I'll be alone forever, in the meantime I want to be alone with my memories. My nightmares. Drew hates it when I say things like that, but she doesn't have to face it, I do. I've always faced the facts. I'll regret leaving her, even though I've just known her three days. The good things only last a little while.

The sky is getting light, Orion is still visible just above the trees, the belt is tangled in the branches, and the Pleiades are magnificent, a perfect blur. I wish I had binoculars but I couldn't root around and wake them. If I believed in gods like the Greeks did, I'd think I might join them up there when I die, beyond everything and everybody. Was it the Greeks? The Egyptians? Somebody. Becoming a star is only for bigshots, I suppose.

I wish I believed in anything.

I think of Noreen more now, in the last while particularly, since I learned what I have. I wish, so many things, I wish I could go back and change things. I did the unforgivable.

I can't think of that. I can't change it.

I still see her face, it's frozen there, the last moment she was alive.

5:26 a.m. Drew is standing right in front of me, she's been doing that for five minutes. She woke me up, and now she's smiling, she probably thinks I looked funny with my laptop on my lap fast asleep.

And typing away now.

I type, she smiles, I smile back.

She looks a little pissed, though, this smiling little girl, she thinks I shouldn't be up, I'll get a cold out here, it's damp, I'm not looking after myself, I should be inside in my bed, I have no right to do this, to not look after myself.

She isn't saying any of that, of course, but I know what she's thinking. She hasn't stopped smiling and of course I smile too, and keep typing.

I can type without looking at the keyboard. I want to see how long I can stare at this lovely girl while I'm typing, before she says something.

She's not, she's picking up a blanket and tucking it nice and warm around me, and my laptop, she's covered up my laptop, but I can still type and stare at her while banging on the keyboard underneath the blanket, typing by touch. I have to practice typing by touch, I'll go blind eventually.

Her mouth is lovely and small, she's wearing little blue shorty pyjamas, her hair is mussy, she is so thin, so fragile.

"Isn't that better?" she asks.

"Perfect."

Does she know who I am? What I've done? Does she know I will never be forgiven, that this person she is smiling at has done something beyond forgiveness? I don't think she does, I don't think Steve has told her. Her mother would never have let her come here, much less stay here if she knew the kind of company her grandfather has been keeping.

"What are you typing?"

"Nothing."

"I want to see. I want to know everything about you."

"Soon," I promise.

Soon. Soon I won't be able to say anything, it's the nature of the cancer that's tracked me down, it takes away everything, it takes away your eyes, it takes away your mouth, it takes away your brain.

"I saw your friend yesterday," she says. "She thinks I'm one of your daughters. We have to get her out of there." I nod. "What do you want for breakfast?"

6:20 a.m. I'm still on the porch with the blanket tucked around me and my laptop outside now, so it's easier to type. It took me maybe twenty minutes to retype what I did a while ago, to correct all the spelling mistakes and to figure out what I'd done, sometimes the words were so mashed together I couldn't make out what I'd done and had to guess.

Drew is inside making breakfast, just for me, breakfast out here, just the two of us. And I have to get ready for the day, psychologically, and the things I have to do yet. Dee first. She's still alive and I have a duty. Then Graham.

I am tired of Dee. It's one thing to be stubborn, it's another to be stupid. I will not leave her there to die alone, that is not an option.

So I'll go to the retirement homes and get their forms and somehow, talk Dee into signing them, so even if I'm not around, the process will be started and I'll just have to hope that whatever home has an opening it will do the right thing. I don't trust them, but I'll have to.

And here is Drew again, with the most marvelous breakfast.

"Will you put that damn thing away," she says, smiling to show she's still friendly, that she doesn't mean it the way it sounds.

It smells wonderful. Coffee, waffles, a cinnamon bun, orange juice, all arranged on a tray with a red sweet pea in a shot glass. They are delicate flowers with petals thin as paper, I know where she got it, growing on a bush just below the big white pine in a clear place where the sun can get at it. It will fade, they don't last long.

"Do you want me to put it on top of that damn thing?"

I'll close this up.

8:40 p.m. When I started this I tried to reproduce exactly what I said and other people said, but after a while I gave it up and wrote as much as I remembered, in the spirit as it were.

I phoned Monica just after seven this morning. I knew she'd be up and doing things, she's an early riser, and if I didn't call early she'd be gone somewhere. She's got a wheelchair-accessible van. It has a sort of elevator that mewls down and folds out a ramp for her to wheel her chair into and she hums herself up, chair and all, and buzzes to the front of the truck, it's a truck really though the dealer sold it as a car, she huffs herself from the chair to the driver's seat at the front of the thing. The seat turns sideways and she swivels herself forward, closes up the elevator and the side panel from the controls on her dashboard and drives off, using hand controls. She's pretty self reliant.

"Monica," I said when she answered. "Melissa."

"Oh my gosh! How are you, dear."

Fine, Monica, fine, no pity. "I have a favor I'd like to ask."

"Name it."

"You know Dee."

"Of course I know Deirdre! We're buddies from way back. What can I do for you?"

"You know I've been looking after her."

"Tell me something I don't know. I see you going by here every day. Well most days."

"She's not well, Monica, I mean sick. I never know when I get there in the morning if she'll still be alive, it's that bad. The trouble is I can't convince her she has to get out of there and I can't wrestle her to the ground and make her. I'm going to some retirement homes today to look them over, and I want you to look after her if you would for a couple of days."

"When?"

"Today."

"Oh gosh, Melissa, I don't know."

"You have to Monica, you're the only one I can ask. She trusts you. Like you say you've been a friend." Except of course when you tried to strong arm her into selling her place. "What I'd like you to do is go over there and take her to your place for a day or so, while I try to find a place for her to go to. She's easy to look after, she mostly sits around and sleeps. I need to find a place for her to go to and you're the only person I can ask."

"Are you strong enough?"

"I have to. I'm not having her die there, Monica. We have to pull together here. That's what neighbors do. That's what neighbors are for."

"Today?"

"This morning. About nine thirty or ten. I'll be over at her place and get her ready for you. Just for two days, until I can find some place. We can't leave her there alone, I've already done it too long and I'd feel terrible if something happened and I know you would too, like you say you've been a friend, you've known her longer than I have. As a favor, to me." We both knew it would be longer than two days, the homes are full and it might take a month, maybe two, maybe longer, before there's an opening. "I won't be long, Monica. We owe it to her. We can't have her die there."

"Nine thirty?"

"You're beautiful," and I hung up before she could talk her way out of it.

She was there at nine thirty.

"I don't know about this," said Dee. "What will the girls say?"

"I'm here," said Drew as we stood Dee up and guided her across the kitchen towards the sunlight. We could hear the elevator on Monica's truck descending.

"I can never tell. Which one are you?" Dee asked as she leaned on Drew, though Drew didn't answer. "You never tell me. Maybe you thought I didn't notice. I don't know what the big secret is supposed to be."

Once we got her to the porch, she was so weak we had to lift her down the steps. "Are you all right?" Monica called from inside the truck.

"Coming!" Dee called back. "What does she mean, are you all right?" she asked us. "What does she think, I can skip? She is such an old fool."

"There she is," Monica cried as we arrived at the elevator on the side of the truck and Drew guided Dee's feet onto the platform. "You'll have to steady her as I bring it up," Monica said. I got on beside Dee and there was no room for Drew, so she waited below as the elevator motor started to whirr. "Coming up!" Monica called cheerily.

"I don't know why I have to go to her place," Dee grumbled. "I never liked her."

Monica showed Dee the bedroom she could use and we got my old friend as settled as she was ever going to be. She didn't want to impose on Monica, she said, she'd rather come with Drew and me, wherever we were going, but I told her I was afraid that would be too tiring, she needed to get rested up so she could go back home all refreshed and take us on that boat cruise she keeps promising.

"I guess she doesn't know the boat's pulled up and turned upside down," Dee said, winking at Drew. "You and I know, don't we? I remember how you used to sit in the front of that boat and guide us through the channel, how many years ago was that now, before you got all grown up?"

I thanked Monica and told her as we left that I was sure we'd be back by three, it would depend on how quickly we could go through the homes and get back.

"Don't you worry," she said. "Deirdre and I will be just fine."

I asked Drew to drive. My eyes get tired, it's the August sun and the reflection from the lake and the sand is white and gives a lot of light. I hope she's happy to do it, I don't want to abuse her willingness but I do need her help.

"I'll be the navigator," I said as we pulled away from Monica's.

Terry Leeder

"No problem."

"This hasn't been much of a holiday for you."

"Whatever."

We could see a pickup in Graham's driveway as we reached the corner and turned east on the road into town.

"She really is confused," Drew said, I suppose to distract my attention.

"I wish she wouldn't say those things."

The first place was in town about twenty miles from Dee's. It looked like a collection of trailer homes nailed together, but it had a nice location, on a flat piece of land about a hundred yards from the lake looking across the water towards the escarpment. Dee would like this, it had a water view, something she's used to, it's close to her place, she's traveled back and forth to this town for, probably all her life, and I'm sure there are residents she remembers, or might remember, and for sure the staff knows her, a couple said they remember when they were kids and she was fifty or so and they used to see her drive to town in a funny little green Honda. There is no nurse on staff, though, she comes three times a week for the afternoon and I'd imagine she's so busy she hardly has time to give serious attention to anyone. The doctor visits once every two weeks, I was assured and is on call at any time. He practices in town and is just down the street, but does have his own patients outside of the home and will be away on occasion when he has to look after any patients that are hospitalized. The local hospital used to be open all the time but is now only operated on certain days, Mondays and Wednesdays for clinics. Patients must go to the closest full time hospital thirty miles away if they require more extensive care.

"Can they really look after her?" Drew asked when we drove away with a bunch of papers for Dee to sign. I suggested we stop for lunch before we went on to the next place, which was almost an hour away.

We pulled into the parking lot at a lovely little restaurant about five miles out of town, sitting on a slope looking down at the lake, and took a seat by the window. Drew ordered rainbow trout with fries and I asked for some kind of pita with ham.

"So what do you think that guy is up to?" she asked.

"The guy?"

"The guy who bought the cottage." I didn't answer. "Steve told me about it," she went on. "What do you think he's planning?" She tore apart a roll and gave me half.

"Some kind of tourist attraction. I guess."

She bit off a chunk of roll. "You're not going to let him do that?"

I shrugged.

"I think he's going to charge admission." She waited for my comment. "Is that what you want?" What are you up to, her expression said.

The next place was a three storey building with long halls and wings laid out in various directions. Every room had a name plate with flowers and the resident's first and last name with a nickname inserted in the middle, set off with quotations. "And what do her friends call Deirdre?" the assistant administrator asked as she took us along a hall on the second floor to an end room with windows at the corners and a view across a harbor with corners of houses and parts of roof peaks going up the hill on the other side. A church spire attempted to rise above the trees near the crest. "The person who lives here is off for some holidays, we don't have any openings right now but you never know, when it happens it usually happens very fast. We try to make our residents feel at home."

"How many nurses do you have?" Drew asked.

The problem was the cost, almost twice what it would cost Dee at the other place. On the other hand the dining rooms were well appointed, there was a large staff who seemed caring enough, the floors were carpeted and clean, there were lots a facilities for exercise and playing games and a well planned recreational program with regular excursions in the home's mini bus to points of interest and shopping malls and a casino a couple of hundred miles away. None of which would interest Dee. But there were six nurses on staff, one for each section of the home and a doctor who made regular visits once a week and had an office in the home with some basic medical supplies. I collected a second set of papers and as we drove away I felt more positive about the place, except for the cost. If Dee was accepted she'd have to sign over all her assets to the home.

"She's like a fish out of water," Monica said when we got back around four thirty, almost exactly when I'd told her we would. She sat us down in the living room, turned on the fireplace with a remote, and offered me a drink -- wine, rye and water, gin and tonic, vodka -- but I told her I can't, alcohol is probably the worst thing I could have.

"Vodka," Drew said, perky and eager, sitting on a cushion on the ledge of the fireplace.

"Like hell," Monica replied, wheeled off to the kitchen and brought back cokes for both of us, and rye and water for herself. "She's sleeping," she said, nodding toward the bedroom where she'd parked Dee, and took a drink. "She's worried about racoons, racoons are breaking in the house they've done terrible damage, she said, she's worried they'll chew through all the wires and burn the house down, trees and all. She's worried about forest fires, she'd feel terrible if she started a forest fire." She drank some more. "I told her she was being ridiculous. Other than that, we got along just fine."

"This won't take long," I promised.

"Nobody's kidding anybody, Melissa. She'll stay here as long as necessary. It's a pretty sad world if I can't help a neighbor. Even though she really doesn't like me. I'm used to people not liking me."

"Until they get to know you."

"I'll drink to that," she said, and did.

Friday, August 6

2:50 a.m. This is a pattern now. I wake up in the middle of the night and can't get back to sleep. Steve has his arm around my middle and I feel suffocated and have to work carefully to slide away and get out of bed. He snorts and makes mumbling sounds and I listen to his breathing, it's still deep and regular and I wait until he rolls over and starts to snore, very quietly. Did his snoring wake me up? It hasn't before. I can't see any stars, usually they make a lovely display through the trees at this time of night. A bright lonely star with some dim companions. I'm embarrassed that I can't identify which star in which constellation. I should know.

I've got things I have to decide. First, get Dee settled. She can't stay at Monica's. I've phoned all the possible homes, and today we go to see the last of the best, that is, the last of the ones who kind of suggested there may be an opening coming up. After that I'll keep bugging them, as long as I can.

Dee gives me money for groceries and such. She's got investments, and her house. All that will be turned over to the home to cover her expenses. She'll be as poor as I am.

Next -- what I've been putting off. What will I do about my cancer?

Horrible. My cancer. Like it's a possession I'm proud of. It scares me. Oh God it scares me.

Decision: take radiation. Not pleasant.

Chemotherapy. Awful.

Take medication so I don't feel a thing, just let it happen, and if it hurts too much, o.d. on pills.

Alternative treatments? Forget it, brain tumors don't screw around.

No good choices.

I have to decide on my will. What happens to this place, who gets what, all that stuff. Not that I have a lot.

I'll be dead in three months. How do I say goodbye? I'm glad the girls aren't here. That would have been awful.

I hate waking up in the middle of the night.

8:50 p.m. This morning, we took Steve to the cottage where he's working today and then Drew drove his truck to Monica's to drop off Dee's things, a couple of dresses, as much clean underwear as I could find, her medicines and so forth. Monica had Dee at the kitchen table eating breakfast.

As soon as we were sure everything was fine, Drew and I went off to look at another home, the farthest one yet, run by a husband and wife in a large old house on the side street in a little town forty miles from here. There is no water view, and the rooms are the sort of thing you'd expect in an old house, high ceilings, creaky floors, but the woman is a nurse and they have the most incredible chef. "The meals here are wonderful," one woman who looked about 85 told us. Everyone talks sensible and they play cards and carry on sensible conversations, she said. They all used to live here, in the town and the immediate vicinity. Ten or twelve women or thereabouts, sitting in the big front room all day watching traffic going by and talking about it. Except there is no traffic, and no conversation.

"A horrible place," Drew said as we left.

"It's better than leaving Deirdre where she is."

"I wouldn't put my worst enemy there!" she snapped.

We came back along the main highway that runs up the peninsula and Drew turned west about five miles south of town and wound up on the concession road that runs along the shore of the lake. I was tired and dozed and woke when the truck bounced in some especially deep potholes. The road is partly sand and the shore is marshy and twists and winds with very little view of the lake. I assumed she was thinking we'd be able to see the water and must have been disappointed.

Just before we reached the highway that turns off the road along the lakeshore to my place, she swung into Graham's driveway, between the cedars he's trimmed back since I was there the last time. I woke up smelling the tart odor of tree cuttings. She stopped the truck with its nose tight against the steps leading up to the front porch, and turned off the engine.

She turned and confronted me. "Are you just going to let him do this?" I was still dozy from sleep and she was out of the truck and walking up the steps and rapping on the front door before I said anything.

I rolled down the window. "I don't think this is a good idea," I told her.

"What is it, you're just going to let the little prick turn your daughters' murder into a tourist trap!"

I got out telling her I didn't want her to get involved in this, it was my business, I'd decide what I had to do about it, but she'd already tried the door, opened it and walked inside.

"You haven't done anything!" she said loudly as she walked along the hall toward the kitchen, all the time I'm trying to talk to her, to tell her this is not a good idea, let's get out of here, and thinking, she can't be connected with this, this is my fight, and I was hoping that Graham had left the place unlocked and was in town somewhere getting supplies or something so we could get out of here before anybody saw us and at that point, the back door opened. I could see out back, a tent pitched underneath a large white pine tree and a sleeping bag hung up and drying on one of the branches.

Graham stepped inside. "Can I help you?"

"Are you the owner?" Drew demanded.

"What are you doing here?" he asked, reasonably enough.

"Are you the owner?"

"Who wants to know?"

"Hello," I said. He looked beyond Drew and recognized me, and didn't seem pleased.

"I asked you a question," Drew demanded, really belligerently. By then she had reached the back door and was right in his face with her lips clamped shut and pursed defiantly.

"Get out of my house," he said, again reasonably enough, I thought. He must have been wondering what sort of wild person had invaded his place.

"Do you know who this is?" she demanded.

"I said get out of my house!" Now he was raising his voice. "Now!"

"This is the mother of the girls that were murdered here," she said, raising her voice as well. "How dare you!"

What could be said after that? There was a lot more shouting and I finally got Drew back through the house to the truck and as we got in, I could see him with his cell phone, calling 911, no question about that, reporting a couple of crazy persons. Drew almost T-boned a car that was passing by as we barged back out the driveway to the road. She wouldn't speak to me all the way home and slammed from the truck and walked to the house and walked up the steps and whammed shut the screen door on the porch.

For sure, I thought, I can't do anything now, if something happens to his cottage he'll charge her, because by then I won't be here, she'll be the only one left to charge. She really messed it up.

I had been awake since two o'clock and I was exhausted. But I knew it wasn't over, sweet Johnson would be on her way. I knew it would be Johnson, she'd been waiting for something like this, and I was sure Graham had recognized me, the strange woman who showed up at his cottage and reacted so oddly when he took her on a tour. He's probably found out who I was and Johnson would know immediately, as soon as he called and told her what had happened. She'd be out here personally, she wouldn't miss it.

I sat and waited and I'm pretty sure I fell asleep. I woke after a while, but no one had showed up so I got out of the truck and went into the house.

Drew was on the couch in the porch, listening to her iPod, and wiggled her fingers hello. I sat down beside her.

"Want to listen?" she said and placed tiny earphones in my ears. The sound was incredible, a full stereo effect from that tiny metal tablet. I am completely out of touch.

I asked her if she wanted some lunch. She insisted she'd get it.

"Sit there," I told her. "You've made enough trouble for one day." She grinned and I leaned over and kissed her and told her I wished my daughters could have known her, they'd love her. "What do you want for lunch?" I asked again and handed her back her earphones. There were tears coming down my face, I get emotional now, I don't seem to have much control any more, probably this thing I've got in my head.

She leaned her head on my shoulder, "Whatever," and that really got to me.

"Whatever we've still got," I said getting up briskly, if I'd stayed there any longer I'd have been an emotional wreck. "Can I get you anything to drink."

Whatever, she told me and I brought her some lemonade and made us ham sandwiches with lettuce tomatoes and mayo. We were sitting on the porch eating when the cop car pulled up in front of the house and parked on the road because the truck was blocking the end of the driveway. We watched as Johnson walked around the side of Steve's pickup and up the driveway.

"You stay here," I said. "I know how to deal with these people. I've had practice." When Johnson got close enough to hear me, I stood up. "Can I help you, officer?"

"Could you step outside, please," she asked. I opened the door and went down the steps. Johnson nodded at Drew and walked back towards the road. I followed and we stopped beside the cruiser. She took out a pad, and made a note of the time, tore off a sheet and handed it to me. A citation for trespass. "Who is the young lady?" she asked.

"A niece."

"She knows who you are?"

"She's a niece." I could hear the screen door clapping to.

"She's coming out here," Johnson said. "Could you stop her. I want to have a talk. I'll be here when you come back." I was surprised at how softly she said that, not judgmental, not like Johnson.

"What's this about?" Drew demanded when I met her beside her father's truck.

"Nothing. We're having a talk. Nobody's being arrested."

"I was the one that caused the trouble," she objected and called to Johnson, "She kept her mouth shut. She wasn't even there."

"Go back to the house," I asked and turned her around, "Please. I'll have a talk with her, everything's fine." As I escorted her back to the house I noticed a couple of new scrapes along the passenger side of Steve's truck.

"What did she give you?" Drew asked.

"A warning. It's nothing."

"That prick."

I smiled. "Didn't I tell you about your language?"

"He is."

"Learn to say it more elegantly. It's more effective." I took her to the door and waited as she went up the steps and back inside. She turned and stood on the other side of the screen, looking down at me. "Listen to your music," I said. "If you want to make yourself useful, make me some tea, I'll be back before you know it."

"I'll be out there if you're not," she shot back.

I returned to Johnson. She asked me if I'd mind sitting inside the cruiser and allowed me to go around to the passenger side and let myself in. "How's your niece?" she asked.

"Calmed down."

"Good," she said, softly. Her whole tone of voice was completely unlike anything I'd expected, she seemed genuinely concerned. "It's not worth getting herself upset about." I waited for her to continue, it was her party, not mine. "I understand you were over at Graham Laird's a while ago." I agreed that I was. "He seemed a little unreasonable, from what I could tell, what he told us didn't make much sense. I explained your connection with the place, and told him I could understand why you'd be upset. He came over to the division a few weeks ago and started asking about the murders and wanted anything we had on it. The officer he spoke to told him we don't share such things."

"What did he want to know?"

"Details." I made no comment. "It seemed to the officer that he had something very specific in mind, and when we heard a few weeks later that he'd bought the place and started to fix it up.... I understand your feelings."

"We did nothing."

"I pointed that out. I told him you had a right to your opinion, you've earned it." This I wasn't expecting. "He'll lay a charge of trespass if you go there again. Either of you."

"I'd like to know what he plans to do."

"So would we. We don't want any trouble over this. From either side." I nodded. "I can understand how you feel about it, and I told him that, and I suggested there will be other people who feel the same way, it's not something anybody wants to be reminded of. I told him I personally would not be happy, and neither would anyone else at the division, or the local council either."

"He keeps using the word tour," I pointed out.

"I don't think that's going to happen," she said, her voice quite gentle. "You can go now."

And I said something I never thought I'd say to Louise Johnson. "Thank you."

I slept most of the afternoon and when we picked Steve up about six, I told him he had a hot truck. Drew filled him in on what had happened today, with appropriate outrage.

"I wish you hadn't done that," he said to me.

"I made her," Drew cut in, "It was my idea. Why the hell does everybody blame Melissa? For godsake!"

"I think it's my influence," I told him. "She was sweet and innocent when she came here."

"Like hell I was," Drew said.

11:30 p.m. I'm tired but I can't sleep. Drew asked me to show her some stars so we got the scope out and I went through a few sights, the ones I could pick out. The Pleiades, Andromeda, which was hard to find, sometimes I hit it right away, and M13, the great globular cluster in Hercules, which I found at once, I aimed the scope dead on and there it was. She loved it when I pointed my Dobsonian at Cygnus and Sagittarius and showed her the absolutely stunning swarms of stars in the Milky Way, every one of them at least as massive and awesome as our own personal star and many that could swallow it whole. She finds it strange to call the Sun a star, she said, and I told her that some of those stars out there have planets and more are being discovered all the time.

"What happens when they find one like us?" she asked.

"That will be your problem."

"Don't say that! You're not allowed to say that."

"I have to face it."

"Go to hell," she said and went inside.

I had to put the scope away myself.

So here I am, at my laptop, and everyone's asleep. God I wish I could....

It gives me a chance to think about the day, I suppose.

I can't do anything to Graham's place now, even so much as break a window. He saw Drew there and the cops have a record. If the place burns down he'll lay charges and by the time the law gets its act together, I'll be gone and Drew will be the only one around to blame. You can count on it, Graham will push it as hard as he can.

None of that might happen, it probably won't happen, but I can't take the chance. As reasonable as Johnson was today, she could charge Drew as an accessory, especially if there's no one else around to blame. I can't let that happen, even for the sake of Erica and Page. What it comes down to, Graham's best guarantee that no one will damage his stupid place, is me.

Steve pointed out something else. The building is so dilapidated that the guy probably won't be able to fix it up and it doesn't look like he's got the money, he's sleeping out back in a tent and doing the work himself. The foundation is sinking and the wall on the west side is leaning. The contractor that he hired to prop it up has stopped work until he gets paid his deposit. What's likely going to happen, Steve figures, is that the guy will eventually give up and sell the place and somebody else will tear it down and build a big new cottage and everybody will be happy but Graham. That could be the reason he started talking tourists in the first place. He's short of money.

I'll never forgive him for violating my daughters' memory. I still feel like throwing a Molotov Cocktail, especially if he's inside.

I have a brightly-illuminated picture of him sizzling.

Saturday, August 7

9:15 a.m. Drew and I have been filling out forms for Dee, leaving out the financial information, which Dee will have to tell me about, if she can. I'll deal with that later. My eyes are bad, I'm typing this as much by feel as anything, though I can see better up close, sort of. Drew reads the questions, I dictate the answers, she fills them in. It's working pretty well. I have to deal with my own problems, my will, deciding on my treatment, dealing with Graham and his tourist schemes. Dee first.

So far, I haven't had headaches, though that's part of what goes on. I can feel a kind of tenseness and a sort of pressure with some incidental pain, it comes and goes like things that happen in the corner of your eye and are gone when you turn your head and look. My corners aren't so good any more, of course, but the comparison will have to do. Anyway I'm waiting for the headaches. I imagine they can get pretty bad.

I called Monica about seven and told her we'd be making out forms, would she mind if we got there a little later, I need them for Dee to sign off on and the sooner we get that done the better. "See if you can find out where her money is," I added.

"Why would I do that?" She sounded really suspicious. I can't blame her for that.

"I know. It does sound bad, doesn't it?"

"You want to believe that."

"It's a problem, Monica. The thing is, I need to know where her money is so we can find out how much she can afford. She's given me money from time to time for groceries and such, and her PIN number for one of her accounts, but I don't know what she's got and we need to know. The home needs to know. The alternative is for someone to agree to cover what she can't and I know I can't afford that and I'm sure you can't either."

"You've got that right."

"So see if you can't find out something, just by sort of talking to her."

"I would have thought you had, I mean you had more chances, right, being over there all the time."

"That was not what that was all about, Monica."

"So what chance do I have, if you couldn't? Assuming I wanted to."

"If we can't we can't."

"That's what it comes down to. Doesn't it?" She waited for me to say something, and I didn't, but I was pretty sure I knew what was on her mind. "So what happens now, Melissa? She can't stay here forever. I thought something had been arranged."

"I'm trying to do that."

"And when will that be done? She can't stay here forever, this is not a rest home or a charitable organization."

I could understand that, of course, but where did that leave me, or Dee for that matter? Who was it said, somebody, feel sorry for someone else and you'll wind up feeling sorry for yourself. I thought I was smarter than this. I thought I knew enough not to get involved.

Drew is in the kitchen clearing her throat, making noises so I won't forget we've got work to do out there and I'm holding her up.

The phone.

10:27 p.m. What a day.

The call was Monica. Soon after I phoned her, Dee complained that she felt really bad, she had terrible pains and her breathing was shallow and coming in gasps. "I've called the ambulance."

"Why did you do that?" I said. "I could get her there faster than they can. They have to come all the way out here and all the way back. I can be there twice as fast."

"I'm here all alone, Melissa, I'm in a wheelchair, I need help."

"I'll be over there in two minutes. I just wished you'd called me first."

"Trust me, I've been there, you drive her you'll sit in the emergency for hours, you send her in an ambulance she goes straight in and they take care of her pronto. Besides, they've got all sorts of stuff in that ambulance, you drive her yourself, she has an emergency half way there, you deliver a body. Trust me, been there, done that. "

"I'm on the way."

I told Drew to call Steve and have him pick her up at my place and get on over to Monica's fast, Dee's sick, Monica's called the ambulance.

Deirdre was pulling in air in gulps, her mouth was wide open her chest was pumping in and out and she was terribly frightened, her eyes were absolutely panicked. I sat on the bed and talked to her softly, everything is okay, the ambulance is on the way, we won't let anything happen to you, we're all here, I'm here, as soon as they get here they'll give you something so you'll feel a lot better, you'll feel a lot better, just be quiet, everything's fine, don't worry, save your energy, breathe easy and don't strain yourself. And I looked in her eyes and wondered, did she think anything I was saying made any sense at all, I'm telling her don't strain yourself, why the hell wouldn't she strain herself if the alternative was dying?

Steve and Drew arrived half an hour later, just before the ambulance.

"The neighbors will think it's me," Monica said as it pulled in her driveway. "They'll all be out applauding."

The attendants had Dee on a stretcher right away and within fifteen or twenty minutes she was off to the hospital. Even at that I was sure they were not being fast enough and I told Steve I'd follow the ambulance, there was no need for all of us to go, he and Drew should stay here and make sure Monica was okay. But Drew got in the car and shook her head when I told her it was okay, I'd be fine, there was no need for her to come with me. "You shouldn't be driving," she said, but at that point the ambulance pulled away and I started off behind it.

Actually I was glad she was there, I wasn't looking forward to hours and hours alone wondering how Dee was and getting bored waiting around and worrying about myself. I also got the impression that in a way the whole thing was a twisted sort of adventure for Drew.

Half way there she made me stop and we switched drivers. This happened soon after I almost missed a sharp right turn and we swerved towards the guard rail on the far side of the road and an instant after we got back on our side, a huge transport truck rushed by in the opposite direction.

The ambulance got to the hospital first and was already leaving the emergency entrance when we arrived. There were maybe thirty people in the waiting room, and no sign of Deirdre, so I lined up at the glassed-in reception desk behind six or seven other people, and when I finally got to the woman on the other side of the glass I'd say twenty minutes later, she kept me waiting while she looked down at a chart or whatever was on her desk and holding up her hand every time I asked about Dee. She had a thin head and blonde lightly bleached hair and thin fingers with short cream painted nails. I'd say she was thirty five.

"I need to know how my mother is," I said.

"In a minute," she replied still looking at her chart or whatever was so fascinating on the desk in front of her. "I won't be any faster if you keep pestering me."

"She was gasping for breath. I want to know if she's still alive."

"Name?"

I almost said Deirdre of the Sorrows, I've thought of her that way for so many years. "Deirdre," I couldn't think of her last name, Deirdre? Deirdre?

"You don't know your mother's name?" She kept looking at her paper, running her finger down the page.

"Ruddy. Her married name. Ruddy."

She reached for a phone without taking her eyes from the list or whatever it was she was running her finger down and fumbled until she found the receiver and lifted it up. "Deirdre," she spoke in the mouthpiece, and looked up at me.

"Ruddy," I said again. "I never liked her second husband."

"Ruddy," she told the telephone while she went back to her reading, "Deirdre Ruddy."

"What's the problem?" asked Drew on my blind side.

"Apparently they can't find her."

"Do you have some identification?" the woman on the other side of the glass inquired, looking at me for the second time as she put down the phone.

"She was just brought in," Drew said. "You haven't lost her already?"

The woman stared at her with expressionless eyes, I handed in my driver's license, the jerk looked at it and pointed to her left, "Through that door. Ask one of the nurses."

Dee was lying on a dolly in a line of other patients in a hall. Her vehicle with bed sheets had high rubber wheels and a tall stainless steel pole with a hook at the end where a plastic bag holding some sort of clear liquid was suspended and a tube came back down and was attached by a needle to her arm.

"How are you feeling?" I asked. She opened her mouth and said something, but I couldn't hear what. "Does it hurt?" She shook her head.

"Melissa almost wrecked us getting here," Drew said.

We waited two hours until an intern examined her, and she was transferred to a semi-private room farther down the hall. The intern was maybe twenty five, bright and young and serious, and took us to a space in the hall outside the door to Dee's room. "We'll have to do more tests and I can't say for sure, but it's possible she's had some kind of seizure, the heart most likely. We're sending her upstairs and she'll be in here at least a day, probably longer, at least until we're sure what's going on."

That's all he would tell me and an hour later she was transferred to a room on the sixth floor. By then she was sedated and the nurse in the green coveralls at the desk down the hall from her room assured me Dee was stable, she'd be sleeping for two or three hours at least, there was no point in our staying, we might as well go home and get some rest. She took down my phone number and name and relationship to the patient and I told her we were friends, she has no living relatives that we know of.

"We'll need to talk to a relative," she said.

Rather than argue, I told her we'd see what we could do and got the name of the doctor who would be looking after her. We ate in the hospital cafeteria and as we went to the parking lot I told Drew that I was totally exhausted, could she drive home.

"I would like that," she said, "I believe in living," and drove while I slept.

It was close to 8:30 when we got back. I woke when we turned west out of town and headed for my place. The Sun was flirting with the tops of the trees and lighting Drew's profile and her trim nose and the sweep of her hair. Her eyes were strained, she looked exhausted and I told her she should go home, take a hot shower and get something to eat, I wanted to go to Monica's to make sure she was all right. She pulled in my driveway and got out and walked to the porch, not looking back. I waited until she went up the steps, into the porch and I could see the door between the porch and the house opening and closing. I couldn't remember if I'd locked the place when we rushed out this morning, but suspected that I hadn't. Why hadn't I given her a key to the house, she'd left the car keys in the ignition? Surely she was okay, she should lock the door, surely she would.

I wasn't going anywhere until I made sure she was all right so I got out and went up to the porch, across to the front door, opened it and called in, "Drew." No answer. "Drew?" Still no answer. I stepped inside the door. "Drew?"

"Yes," muffled, from the back of the house in the direction of the bathroom.

"Lock the front door."

No answer.

"Did you hear?" speaking louder, "I said lock the front door."

"Okay!" She sounded exasperated though it was hard to tell, her voice was still muffled.

"Love you," I said, not too loudly, closed the door and walked back to the car. We still hadn't finished those forms. I wasn't sure why I was bothering, I'm not a relative, I'm not anything, I've got things I have to do for me, for people I care about, you'd think Monica was my mother or something.

Steve's truck was not in her driveway, but her son's big car was.

I tried the front door, it opened and I stepped inside. I could hear her son talking, angry and belligerent, and I walked down the hall and into the living room. He was sitting in the sofa facing the fireplace and she was sitting in her chair in the space between the fireplace and him. A long low coffee table was between them and lying on it a legal-looking document with foolscap-size pages.

"How is Deirdre?" Monica asked.

I told her what was happening while her son leaned forward and squared up the papers on the table and placed a pen beside the upper right corner like he was setting out a dinner.

"You've met Gavin," Monica said when I was done, looking at him. "He was explaining some documents he has there, something about a power of attorney, for property I think. He didn't offer to sign anything to look after my health, at least I don't think he did, did you Gavin?" He reached across the papers and took a drink, rye and water, and set the glass back on the table. "We've had a long discussion, ever since your friend Steve left, I think. About three hours, I think?" Gavin didn't answer. "It seems that long anyway. He's been talking a lot, haven't you Gavin. From the looks of it I think he's talked out. So what do you want," she turned to me, "liquor, beer, coke? Gavin's been drinking up my booze, haven't you Gavin, so why not Melissa."

"Coke."

"And for the love of harry sit down," she told me as she whirred off to the kitchen, saying as she went, "Gavin and I have been having a big discussion and I'd like you to join in too, the more the merrier. Ice? A bit of cherry juice? Something else?"

"Just coke," I said and sat on the ledge of the fireplace. "A small glass. I can't stay long."

"You must do that," she called from the kitchen. "Gavin has some fascinating suggestions, he seems to think it would be a good idea if I turned over everything I own, not my health of course, that would be too much work of course, but everything interesting, the house, the property in Toronto, our home in Nassau, you didn't know I had a home in Nassau, did you Melissa? My late husband. His son thinks I owe him everything and since he's getting it sooner or later, he wants it sooner, the sooner," she came back with my coke in her left hand, working the lever on her chair with her right hand, "the better," and she handed me my drink, backed up, spun the chair, faced her son and took out the fresh glass of rye and water she'd placed in the bottle holder on the chair for herself. "Have I summarized the situation pretty well, do you think?" She stared at Gavin. "I didn't mention the shouting, of course, Melissa was here the last time and she knows how that goes and I didn't want to bore her with all the petty details."

He looked straight at me. "I know who you are. My mother doesn't, but I do."

"I know a lot more about Melissa than you do," Monica said. "Right from the time she was eighteen. Not that she's told me directly, of course, word gets around and I'm a pretty damn good listener. I've been doing it for the past three hours."

"One," he grumbled.

"You've got some papers there," she said. "I want Melissa to have a look at them."

"You're crazy," he said.

"Maybe, but I wonder if I could look at those papers you've been going on about," she went on and held out her hand. "You keep talking about them. Maybe you could bring them over here for your poor old mother, I'm not so mobile as I used to be."

He didn't move.

"You've been going on about them for three hours," she said, still holding out her hand. "Maybe you'd be good enough to come over here and give them to your frail old mother. I'd like to have a look at them. Maybe Melissa could as well. I want Melissa to have a look at them."

"No."

"You think I'll just sign them?"

He stood up, walked over, handed them to her and then went around to her right side, leaned over and pointed to the top sheet. "If you look at this passage..."

"Gavin," she snapped, "I am literate, I can read the English language, I don't need lessons in grammar." He walked back to the sofa. "And don't sit down, I am a tired old woman and you've taken more of my time than is good for me. I'm hungry and I need a sleep, it's been a tiring day and I'll read this when I feel like it." He remained standing.

"You don't know who she is," he said. "I will not leave you alone with this person."

"Get out of my house, Gavin. Now."

"I am not leaving you here alone." They stared at each other for maybe ten seconds.

"If you don't leave right now," she said. "I won't sign anything. Ever." That did seem to make an impression and she softened her voice. "I'll read your papers, Gavin, I promise. When I feel like it. I want a rest now, I'm an old woman." He remained standing, staring at her. "And I'll choose my own company, thank you."

He picked up his briefcase and the laptop he'd brought with him and left the house.

Monica waited until he closed the outside door and she heard his car door slam.

"I must be going," I told her.

"You must be exhausted," she said. "You should have something stronger, it'll give you back your strength. It does that for me."

She took a big gulp of her rye and water and set the drink in the holder in her chair arm and listened as his car backed out the driveway.

"Could you put away that glass he's left on my good coffee table," she pointed at it and I went over and picked it up. She looked tired.

"My thought is," she went on, raising her voice so I could hear as I took the glass and the rest of my own drink to the kitchen, "I'll string him along. I'll tell him I've taken it to my lawyer and my lawyer advises me not to sign anything but, you know, maybe if he tells me what he has in mind, exactly, I'll listen. Maybe we can talk about something that's not so drastic. When my lawyer's here. When I have witnesses."

"Anything you want out here?" I asked.

"Yeah, bring the damn bottle." As I came back to the living room with the half empty rye bottle, she raised a remote she kept in a holster on her chair, aimed it at the fireplace, pushed a button and flame erupted between the metal logs. "Stay," she said, "have dinner, you must be starving. I'll order something."

I handed her the bottle. "I can't."

"He's my son, Melissa, I remember him when he was this long," she illustrated. "He's a squirmy little jerk, but he's my squirmy little jerk, I'd still like to see him from time to time. What I figure is, any attention is better than none at all."

"I don't think Dee will be back," I said. "I'll come over here tomorrow and get her things, I'm just too tired right now. I'm like you, I need something to eat."

"I'll get something for both of us. Who knows maybe I'll order it in. I am kind of tired."

"I have to get going, Drew's back at my place," and I promised her I'd be over tomorrow, if not me maybe Steve or Drew, someone would be here to collect Dee's things. "Thanks for all your help," I added and left and was so exhausted that when I got back in the truck, I sat for maybe five minutes with my eyes closed before I could bring myself to turn the key and drive home.

11:40 p.m. I don't know why I can't sleep. Steve has gone to bed. He's agreed to go over to Monica's and get Dee's things and then drop by her cottage and collect what he thinks she'll need in the next little while and get her stuff organized, or start to. She'll have to move, she won't be back.

Drew's asleep already.

I don't know, I don't know, I don't know anything, I don't know how much longer I'll be able to rely on that lovely little girl, I don't want to abuse her, she's been wonderful. She told me at supper she'll have to leave in a week or so.

I don't want her to leave, the news was devastating, but I told her I understood, what else could I say?

There's the papers we need to fill out and we'll have to go to Dee and get her to sign them, but when she'll be able to do that I really don't know, from the way she was today it won't be a while yet. I'll do what I can do. In one way her attack has made it easier, I won't have to talk her into leaving, she's in no shape to go back. We can never go back.

If I could just get some sleep.

Noreen's Version

The aisles are swarming, it's one ten, I have a closing in five minutes and the lawyer I'm supposed to meet is nowhere in sight, Linda puts a note on my desk, folded over. "It's your husband, he says it's urgent. It's about your daughter," she goes on to wherever she's going, nobody has any time for anything, I've never seen the Registry this busy, ever, there's constant calls on the intercom, a lot for Stan.

"Call home," she's written. Another lawyer at the intercom over by the door, "Stan Phillips. Paging Stan Phillips," he looks around furiously, he's slim and dark, a Mediterranean complexion I'd say, about thirty, they're all so thin and young any more. I can't see my lawyer anywhere, I'll likely be back by the time he shows up, he's running late, "I'll be back in five minutes," I scribble and leave the note on the desk. I can't even get down the aisle without shoving through talking people, or waiting-for-their-documents people, or showing-off-how-important-they-are people, the phone bank up ahead is totally occupied, at least twenty phones and they're all being used, I'm lucky, a freelancer has just hung up, I grab the receiver before someone else can get to it, I've left my purse at the desk, which was foolish, someone has left a quarter on the little shelf below the phone so I'm lucky that way, I'll have to keep an eye on my purse.

Bill answers as soon as it rings.

"I didn't want to call you."

"What's wrong?"

"Shelley's gone." So much for being lucky. All I asked was that he look after his own daughter for a couple of hours. It was too much to expect, obviously.

"I've been phoning all her friends. The ones I know about. Nobody knows who I'm talking about," I'm his mummy, he's giving me his excuses, "I've driven around, all the places she used to go. When I knew what was going on. I can't find her."

"When?" He doesn't understand. "How long has she been gone, Bill?"

"Two hours."

All right, so she's been gone two hours. Take a deep breath, wait for a second or so, so I can stop blaming him in my mind and he can hear it when I talk. So we can deal with the problem, calmly and rationally. Accusations are not going to help.

"How did it happen, Bill?"

"I was upstairs sleeping."

And? And?

"About three hours ago, I guess. Closer to three and a half, maybe."

"Yes?"

"I was exhausted. I was up late last night."

No excuses. "And?"

"I heard voices downstairs."

He waits for me to comment. What am I supposed to say?

"She had a boy in the house, Noreen, he was about thirteen I suppose, maybe twelve, he looked younger."

"You didn't recognize him?"

"I have no idea who her friends are now."

And whose fault is that, Bill?

"Sort of slight. Short."

"What were they doing, Bill?"

"What do you think!"

I don't want to, to be honest.

"They must have heard me coming, there was a lot of scrambling around, I saw him running out the door, I doubt if I'd be able to recognize him." He waits for me to say something. "He had brown hair, I think. I had the impression he was fairly short."

"What did she say?"

"She just stood there. Defiantly."

I can imagine what happened next.

"Did she tell you his name?"

"No."

"And she's not there now."

"No."

"How did that happen, Bill?" I'm crouching over the telephone, with my hand cupped around the receiver, there's hundreds of people coming in the front door and strung all around the outside of the Registry, in lines and clusters of lawyers and law clerks and freelancers waiting to register deeds and mortgages, the noise is extraordinary, nobody could possibly hear what I'm saying except maybe the people on the phones on each side of me, and they're so busy I doubt if they'd notice, but I'm still crouching, humiliated.

"I told her exactly what I thought. I didn't mince words."

"Yes."

"I had to."

"I'm not blaming you, Bill. Then what?"

"I went upstairs."

"Why?"

"I thought I'd made my point." I can imagine what he said, how he yelled and screamed, and how humiliated she must have felt, not that she didn't deserve it.

"And?"

"I heard the door slam. Fifteen, maybe twenty minutes later."

"Bill, why did you go upstairs?"

"I had to. I was so upset. I knew if I stayed down there I'd only make it worse. I wanted us to calm down. We were shouting at each other. I didn't think it was doing any good. I told her she wasn't moving until her mother came home and we had it out, once and for all."

And why wouldn't she want to stick around for that? "Yes?"

"I think we should go to that family counselor. You were right."

That's one thing. That's at least one thing.

"She's got some serious problems," he admits.

For the first time, he admits. Maybe, if we get through this crisis, maybe we can start dealing with my daughter's problems. Our problems. Maybe.

"What happened then?"

"I thought she was going off somewhere to cool off."

Oh Bill!

He says no more.

"When did you come back downstairs?"

"Ten minutes later. Maybe fifteen. She left a note on the kitchen table."

He stops. What was in the note, Bill?

"I guess I didn't worry about it, as much as I should have," he goes on. "I thought if she'd left a note."

He stops again.

"What did the note say?"

" 'I've gone to Melissa's.' -- Who's Melissa?"

"I would have told you that, Bill, if you'd been willing to talk about it."

"So now it's my fault."

"No, Bill, it's not your fault," I can't get into this, I have to find someone to look after my closings while I go off and confront Melissa and drag my daughter back home kicking and screaming since her father is not, no, I won't think that, we have to deal with this, accusations will not help anything, I'll leave that to my husband, it's already caused enough problems, this is too much, this is too much.

Saturday, August 14

4:00 p.m. I had a seizure early this morning. The right side of my face started to twitch and I put my hand on it to try to stop it but nothing was stopping it. Like the first one it lasted about half an hour, but then I was exhausted.

It's taken me five days to write this, in bits and pieces. I've put today's date at the top and the time it is right now.

Steve did some work at Dee's on Monday. The next day I drove over. It isn't far and I knew the road and could pretty well drive it blind and didn't give a damn if I stripped all the paint off the car against the trees as I drove in Dee's drive and did some serious damage in fact, a couple of big gouges. Drew arrived about an hour later in Steve's truck, two maybe, I was working and didn't notice.

She asked me was there anything she could do and I felt like hugging her and didn't, so I asked if she could get out the rest of Dee's clothes and go through them all and throw away what she thought was just too old and beat up, she won't have much room where she's going.

"Still upset about it?" Drew asked.

"I feel like I've betrayed her."

"She has to. There's no choice. She should have gone years ago."

"I should have told her years ago."

"You're feeling sorry for yourself," she said and went off to the bedroom and missed my smile.

"Kind of straighten up in there," I called. "I'm sort of getting things ready to sell."

"Who's doing that?" she shouted back.

"The public trustee. I'm assuming. As soon as he gets control. As soon as she's declared incompetent."

"Maybe it's a she."

"Maybe."

"The public trustee."

"Probably."

Dee talks more now, she asks us to get her some water, could we bring that blue dress with the flowers, when we can hear her she talks of getting out of this place and tells Drew it's horrible.

"Don't they take care of you?" Drew asked.

"No." She fumbled towards Drew and grasped her hand.

"You look better."

"I want," Dee said, and I leaned down to hear her, "get back," she breathed out.

"Your place looks nice," Drew said.

"The boat," Dee said, "gas for the boat." She gripped Drew's hand and gathered strength and said more than she has before, staring at Drew, "Could you bring gas for the boat ... next time you come?"

When we got up to leave, she wouldn't let go of Drew's hand. "I have to go," Drew told her.

"Page," said Deirdre.

"I had someone from the hospital call here," Monica phoned and told me on Tuesday. "I guess they got my name because that's where the ambulance came, they asked me if I'd known Deirdre a long time and of course I said I had and they wanted to know if she had any relatives. I haven't heard of any, have you? What will she do, I wonder, she really is a little waif in the storm, isn't she, I've never heard of any relatives. I'm sure she didn't marry, I've never heard a whisper of anything like that, she really is a strange little tyke, when you think of it."

"What did they ask?"

"Anything they could think of, who were you, what was your relation, how come you were the only one, what was your game and I told them the only game I knew of was Dee had been a friend of your daughters and had cared for them a lot and you'd been here for a long time and cleaned people's cottages and did other things around and maybe they should talk to Steve, so I guess they'll phone him too."

Steve has been wonderful this whole time. He's given me his granddaughter, sort of, I mean he's sent her over to help me out, he hasn't said what I'm really like and she still seems to treat me like a normal human being and he's spent two days at Dee's fixing up things, measuring furniture to calculate, on the basis of what we tell him about the rooms in the Georgian, what things can go in without crowding out Dee and yet giving her the feeling that at least some of her life is still alive and she's still somewhere she can live with and be maybe happy in. He's closed up the upstairs entirely and nailed down the windows, we can't be sure if the place will be sold or what might happen. He's cleaned up the yard and tried to make the property look reasonable, it's the land that will sell, not the cottage, whoever buys it will tear it down the next day, he said.

No one has called him.

She can't wait to get back, Dee says, every day we visit. We try to get in every day and see her and Drew's getting awfully tired of it all.

Wednesday she was better but confused and the hospital called later that day and said a place has opened. The question was, how had it all been arranged, though I had a pretty good idea, none of us were relatives.

The next morning Steve went to Dee's cottage to pick up everything we had decided she'd need in her new place while Drew and I drove to the hospital to accompany my friend on her move.

I stopped by the nursing station before we went in to see her and asked a young slightly corpulent woman in green coveralls with a white plastic name tag with blue printing, Nancy Trueman, "Was there a competency hearing?"

"I guess," she admitted. "We have a team in the hospital that arranges that."

"You needed the bed," I concluded.

"I have no information about that," she replied, turned away, unhooked a clip board hung on the partition beside the desk and flipped through some pages attached to the board.

The bed was cranked flat, Deirdre had a plastic tube in her nose, an oxygen bottle beside the bed, her face was sharp and pinched, she stared at the ceiling. A parallelogram of sunlight lay on the covers mounded above her feet.

"Hi Dee!" Drew said cheery and upbeat. I came on the other side of the bed and patted Dee's hand and she turned her head toward Drew's voice, said something, and Drew bent down and kissed her. "How are you feeling?"

"Page."

"We have a nice new place for you!" I thought Drew was a little too loud and bright and chirpy, though I appreciated her attempt to make the best of it. "It's all bright and sunny, Dee, and it's right by the water. You'll love it. And you're getting the hell out of here."

Dee smiled.

Drew pulled up a metal chair with a thin black cushioned seat and sat beside the bed and I remained standing on the other side, looking down at my friend and holding her hand. Dee turned and stared at me but did not react, no smile, no recognition. "Don't you think Melissa looks good today?" Drew asked. Dee turned her head back to the only person she wanted to react to. "Don't you think she looks good today?" Dee didn't respond. "Melissa."

"Who's Melissa?" Dee asked. Her voice was flat, hoarse, weak.

I rode in the ambulance that transported her to the home and assured her that everything was all right, the people at this new place would look after her, they were qualified and a doctor would be there and anything she needed she just had to ask and someone would be there at once, it was far better, she needed care and they could provide it twenty four seven, in other words day and night, I was so worried about her, she was too good to be left alone, especially since she wasn't able to look after herself any more and I wasn't well myself and I wouldn't be around very much longer to look after her and nobody else was able to do so.

"When am I going back?"

That was all she said the whole time we rode there. The ambulance rattled, the paramedic beside the driver looked around from time to time, "Everything all right back there?" and I said yes, and I lied, everything was not all right back here.

"There she is!" said the assistant manager when they rolled Dee in with the oxygen bottle attached and wheeled her to the elevator to take her to her room on the second floor. I stood on one side while the assistant manager went on about how they were all looking forward at the Georgian to welcome their new friend and get to know her, they had a nice snack all ready for her, she must be famished after that long ride over here, her room was all ready and as soon as her friends brought the things she needed she'd be all set.

"My friend is bringing them," I chipped in.

"Good. Wonderful. Everything is all ready for you dear. You'll just love it here, everybody does. We have cards, and animals, do you love animals, we have children who visit, there's a nursery school right here in the building, we all go down there sometimes just to see them play and enjoy their company. Gladys dear, you can't get on," she said as the doors opened and an old lost woman tried to step aboard and was nudged aside as the paramedics pushed Dee off and the doors closed.

We passed the nursing station where two young green-clad strangers sitting at a desk looked up from their paper work and crooned, "Hi Deirdre, good to have you," and waved and smiled and looked back at what they were doing. A young black cat sat on the counter and mewed as the gurney rolled by.

Drew came in to Dee's room with the cat purring in her arms while the paramedics lifted Dee off the gurney and settled her on her new bed. Steve arrived soon after and asked if he could get someone to help him bring things up. We arranged her stuff in the room, her old TV, a small table she's always had by her bed, a small bureau, her favorite lounge chair and another small chair that Steve had calculated was all that the room would hold. Drew set the cat down and she and I hung Dee's clothes in the closet the best we could. The closet was stuffed when we were done and the room laid out a little awkwardly. When the assistant manager came by and looked in, she said, "We'll have to take some things out, it's too crowded, my staff won't be able to get in here and do their job. We should take the cat out," and she went over and lifted the animal off the ledge where it was sleeping.

When we were done and said good bye and were going out the door, Dee suddenly sat up and shouted in horror, "Don't leave me here!"

I couldn't sleep that night and about one I couldn't stand it any more and got up and got dressed and Drew woke up from her sofa and said, "What are you doing?"

"I'm going to see my daughters."

"Steve," she shouted and he got up and came out in his shorts and mussy hair to find out what was going on.

"I'm going to see the graves," I explained to reassure Drew, she must have thought I was out of my mind, that I thought my daughters were still alive.

"Why?" she demanded.

I pushed away her hand.

"Steve!" she screamed. I headed for the door. "You can't see a damn thing! You'll kill yourself! Grampa!!!"

And at that point Steve came out dressed in whatever he could pull on and followed me down the porch steps.

"I'm driving," he announced.

I couldn't have done anything anyway, his truck was blocking my car.

"I'm coming," Drew shouted and within two minutes had climbed into the truck on one side of me and Steve was sitting in the driver's seat on the other. "It's two fucking o'clock in the morning," she said.

"I have to see them," I replied, quietly, and no one spoke after that though I got the impression that Steve thought I was enough to make anyone curse.

The cemetery is maybe five miles east on the road into town, beyond the combination causeway and bridge that crosses the marsh and river that drains Bark Lake. It's easily missed, the graveyard is set back from the road among tall balsam trees. A narrow two-track driveway goes in, up a steep sandy hill, curves among the graves and then turns back the way it came, out at an old iron and stone gate that was the original entrance before the graveyard was expanded. The east side of the cemetery is the oldest section, graves jammed together, thin stones leaning sideways, some snapped off, and a small military slab to commemorate a soldier who died in the First World War and is buried somewhere in France.

There is another way in from the road that you come to just before the cemetery. It runs along the west boundary of the graveyard and curves in at the back. This is how the hearses enter with their burdens, avoiding the steep incline at the front. As we passed the road our headlights flashed on a marble slab above a grave just inside the west boundary and I saw a white smear of paint zig zagged across the stone and two figures running toward the back of the cemetery. An instant later we were bounding up the slope on the narrow two-track drive heading toward the back where the old road makes its U toward the oldest section of the graveyard.

I saw their gravestone, which sits in a new section at the back part of the cemetery, underneath a line of pine trees. It was smeared with white paint. Before Drew was aware of it I had yanked open the door while the truck was still moving and hit the ground running. I could hear some kids' voices, boys, one yelling at the other to open the fucking door and the other swearing and then I was on the kid who was trying to open the door of a car that was parked on the road leading in from the back entrance. I don't know what happened to the other kid but I had the one by the throat and I had him in the ground squeezing the little bastard's life out of him as hard as I could I was kneeling on his chest he was pounding at my face and anything else he could reach his eyes were wide he was terrified he was gurgling and begging and hitting me as hard as he could and Drew was screaming at me and trying to pull me off and nothing would have stopped me except that somehow Steve pulled me away and I have a sense of him stretching the kid on the hood of the car and shouting at him if he didn't shut up and lay still he'd never have kids and the girls would have to go somewhere else for all their fun. I later found out he had jammed a wood chisel against the kid's crotch aiming at a pendant no man wants damaged.

The kid I almost killed was Ryan, seventeen years old he said. When he could talk, he told Steve the kid with him was Joshua but we never saw that one, he disappeared in the woods somewhere and we've never seen him since. When I went back to my daughter's gravestone and saw what they had done to it, Ryan was lucky that Steve was guarding him. They had defaced five other gravestones and would have probably done more damage if we hadn't showed up.

Until Drew told me, I had no idea he had bruised me up as bad as he did, especially around my right eye socket, the same place where Noreen hit me. Drew touched every bruise he had made and as she did, I could see fear in her eyes, as if she was just finding out what sort of person I really was.

Ryan and Joshua were the same kids she almost t-boned when she backed out of Graham's place and the car they drove was the same one that passed me when I was stopped at the side of the road looking at things that reminded me of my daughters.

Since then I've been sick. No police report, no trouble. I suppose Ryan doesn't want anyone to find out what he and Josh were up to when we caught them and probably doesn't know whose graves he defaced. He knows for sure I was mad.

I have no idea why I suddenly wanted to go see my daughters, in the middle of the night. Maybe I was going a little crazy, like Drew thought, maybe I sensed what was going on. Not so good for Ryan and Josh, for sure.

Monday, August 16

9:05 a.m. It took forever to write down that simple bit of information, the date and the time. This thing in my head is making it harder and harder to do anything. I'll set my mind to it, I'll work here as hard as I can and if I can't type it, I'll think it.

Drew left early this morning. She stayed at Steve's last night and he's driving her to her mother's place, so he's gone too, they'll be half way there by now. He wants some more time with his grand daughter, I'm sure, since I took most of it when she was here.

I wasn't feeling well. She woke me and got into bed and hugged me through the blankets, real hard, and said she loved me, she's sorry she hasn't been nice lately. "I'm coming back," she said, "you stay right here." Then, before I could get up and see her off, she was gone.

9:45 a.m. It's really quiet. I'm feeling a little better. I lay here thinking about her crazy suggestion, that I write my autobiography for godsake. It's one of those crazy ideas you can't help thinking about because it's so damn crazy. And I thought, you know I could do it, I've got this record of the last ten years and I can fill in the time before that.

It's one of those cool mornings with the sun out and I can hear a car going along the road once in a while, but far enough away that it doesn't bother me. There are some chickadees in the tree outside this window, they're making their strange little songs that sound like their name, chick-a-dee, chick-a-dee-dee-dee-dee. There's enough wind to move the branches of the tree and shadows play across the window. I used to love lying here early in the morning, before I had to get up to look after my daughters, just listening to the sounds of the birds and whatever else was out there, a red squirrel, and once a huge porcupine high up in the tree. Of course we didn't know what it was, what I heard was some kind of strange sort of rustling unlike anything I'd heard before, but when we came out later that morning we saw it, high up there. It threw some quills at us.

It still hurts, when I think of Erica and Page, but I also have lovely memories and the good memories are stronger now, I think, than the regrets.

11:28 a.m. I slept for maybe an hour and woke when the phone rang, exactly at eleven. Monica phones me every day at precisely eleven o'clock.

"You'll never believe what I just did," she said and we were off on a long conversation, the woman's lonely. "You know that guy that was over here the last time you were here. My son. Gavin. That one." I didn't respond, but that never matters with Monica, she was just catching her breath. "You remember that paper he wanted me to sign, that thing about my properties outside Toronto. The one I said I'd never sign. I just signed it. Not the power of attorney, I'm not ready for that yet, and not him when I do. Maybe this will buy him off. I can't believe it. I'm sitting here looking at this thing and I have to believe I've done it, I can see my signature on the damn thing, plain as day. So I must have done it, right."

"I thought you weren't going to."

"Tell me about it. Nobody's more surprised than I am. And nobody made me, either, I did it all by myself, all here, alone, no lawyer, nothing. Can you believe it."

I didn't answer.

"Are you there?"

"Yes."

"I had a friend once. If you can believe that. We were real close. We used to call each other every night, like clockwork, after supper. Some times we'd still be talking real late, eleven, twelve. I'd fall asleep and she'd go off and do things and come back and I'd still be asleep. When I'd wake up, we'd go on yakking."

"Uh huh."

"I felt sorry for him, Melissa. He kept coming here, wanting things. Like he couldn't get the thing himself, he had to come to mummy. So I thought, what the hell. I'm already regretting it."

"Yeah."

"Isn't that a fact. You've had kids. You know how it is. No matter what they are, they're still your kids, you have to help them out. That's what he's counting on, the little bastard." I didn't answer, I couldn't answer, not that it mattered to Monica. "What bugs me though, this isn't the last, he'll be back for more, he'll be back until there's nothing left to give and then he'll be gone for good. Until then, I'll never see the end of the little jerk. Why do we do it, right?"

"True."

"I dropped over to see Deirdre."

"How is she?"

"God, don't ever send me to a place like that. Please. I'll kill myself first. I mean it's all right, as good as you can get I guess, for a place like that. Just don't send me to a place like that. There's no privacy, there's no dignity. She keeps asking for her house, how is it, and her boat, and the damn raccoons, are the raccoons giving trouble, and when is she going back? She seems to think I had something to do with it."

"I wasn't leaving her where she was."

"I agree. But God!"

"I wasn't leaving her where she was."

"It's been sold. There's a truck over there right now, something demolition. Things go on." She paused, which was something for Monica. "Poor Dee."

It was the way she said it. "What else?" I asked.

"That's all, nothing."

"What else, Monica. There's something else."

"Nothing. It isn't important."

"There's something else, Monica."

"Nothing. You don't want to know."

"What else, Monica!"

She took a short breath. "She wanted to know when Page was coming over to visit her. Sorry Melissa, you said you wanted to know."

1:25 p.m. I'm no longer strong enough to burn Graham's house down and I'm not really sure I meant that anyway. I am tired, tired of it all. Steve says he's organizing his friends and getting up a petition to block the whole giving-a-tour-of-the-murder-scene scheme, and even Louise Johnson is on side. I'll write up something expressing a mother's outrage that anyone would make the place where my daughters were murdered into a tourist trap and I'll make it pretty strong and Steve will put it in as the final summary of his petition and maybe that'll clinch it. It will have to. Who knows, maybe Graham will think that what I did to Ryan I'll do to him some dark night when he's out there in his tent, word gets around. Or maybe I'll come back and haunt him and then there'll be two deaths and a third one, his, really horrible and mysterious, for a tourist trap. My poor daughters. I wish I could do more. I'll make what I write pretty strong, if I can and if I'm still around, and if there's some kind of meeting, I'll give a good speech, something full of outrage. It's time I got outraged. If I'm able to talk by then. Everything depends.

I'm tired. Drew is coming back, she's promised.

3:30 p.m. When I started this thing ten years ago, after Erica and Page died, I had a table top with a tower and a drive for floppy disks and stored all my stuff on 3.5 floppies. Then when I got a laptop I transferred my floppies to CDs, so now it's all on five CDs, with backups. I should put it all on a memory stick, I keep planning to do that and haven't got around to it.

For the last hour or so I've been looking at my journal, going backwards. And I found something else, something I'd completely forgotten about.

Nine years ago, when I could think about everything a little more rationally, I sat down and wrote out what you could only call a fantasy. It was a kind of strange attempt to flush out all the poisons, the rage I still felt. I still feel.

I was thinking, over and over, god how many times I lay awake here thinking -- that bitch cheated me. Shelley. I wanted her to suffer like I had, like she made me suffer, but she killed herself. They found her in the real estate office, covered in her own blood and blood all over. She slit her throat and then she walked around, bleeding over everything. It was grotesque.

She left a note. She loved leaving notes.

"Nobody can get me."

She got away with it.

So I imagined what would have happened if, instead of Shelley killing herself, I had caught up with her, somewhere private before anybody else knew what she'd done. I'm good at imagining things, I had to get it out, it was eating me up, and I enjoyed it, I have to say I enjoyed it, the thought, the imaginary scenario, what if I'd caught her, just what if? I always wanted to write novels.

I worked it all out. She'd be off on a boat with a married guy she was screwing with. Adam. I thought of her as Lilith. He's invited her on his boat for a day of sunbathing and other activities, on his big yacht, and she figures she'll talk him into running away and not coming back because nobody would think of checking boats, right, they'd all be out stopping traffic on the roads looking for murderers.

So she goes to the dock where Adam keeps his boat and tells him, "Let's go," and doesn't say anything about anything and off they go in his boat. But unfortunately for her, she's left her laptop at the scene of the crime and I find it there and look up her email and find all these messages back and forth, and directions to his boat, which he's given her hoping she'd come. So I take Dee's boat and chase them and catch up just when the guy's gone off somewhere, fishing, like a typical male, and she's out there alone.

It's a bizarre scenario. Completely implausible. I wrote it as if Shelley was thinking it, because I wanted to imagine how she'd feel when I caught her. I wanted to imagine her absolute terror, before I sliced her up.

I'm erasing it. I don't want Drew to see it. Hatred does me no good at all, it won't bring them back. It's sad we can't do that with every mistake we make in life, just erase them. I wish I'd told Erica why Shelley was haunting us, what I'd done. I was so afraid she'd hate me. I would have deserved it. What I did was inexcusable. I actually liked Noreen, in a strange way, I wanted to be like her, to succeed like her. The instant I murdered her we became one person, ever since, she and I have never parted. I've lived with what I've done ever since. If only my daughters hadn't, if only I'd told them, it would have been worth having them hate me for the rest of my life, as long as they...

11:45 p.m. Steve came back about an hour ago, pretty tired. We're not so young any more, we can't take these late nights like we used to. Except for me. This thing keeps waking me up. He's lying here beside me, snoring. I put my hand on him, once in a while, just to make sure he's there.

He doesn't talk much, Steve. More a guy who does things. He loves working with his hands, and he's pretty good, in more than one way. I don't think of Marshall so much.

He told me Drew sends her love.

"She knows what I did, doesn't she? She knows I killed someone, doesn't she?" I figured I might as well say it now, in a month or so it won't matter a damn.

He nodded.

"You told her?" I was hoping he had, and I was shocked he had. That makes no sense, does it.

"Not the details," he said.

"When?"

"A week ago, maybe."

"Why?"

"I thought she should know."

He was right, she should know. I'm glad I didn't know this, though, that she knew what I'd done. I've got good memories of Drew, that would have spoiled them, no matter what she thought, I wouldn't have felt the same, I wouldn't have been so relaxed, I wouldn't have enjoyed it so much. Everything now is good memories, or bad memories

"What did she say?" I asked.

"She probably deserved it."

"She?"

"That woman."

She must not think that. She must not think that, ever. "She didn't. Steve, she didn't deserve that. Tell Drew I said that. Noreen didn't deserve that. Drew mustn't think that, ever. She mustn't think that or say that, ever. I don't want her to think like me, I don't want her to be like me -- ever."

"She won't be," Steve said.

So now he's lying here and I'm thinking, why is he here? Pity, maybe, because he knew Erica and Page. Convenience, I'm the only one that will have him. I don't believe that, though. I really don't know why he's here. Maybe he doesn't either. No point thinking about it. It is what it is, don't look a gift horse....

12:30 a.m. I met an East Indian woman, Dr. Ishana Navine, at the hospital when we were visiting Deirdre. Her name is Hindu and is sometimes translated as "wish," sometimes as "sight," sometimes as "desire." The name has some connection with the goddess Durga, the supremely radiant goddess, who was created out of the desire of all the gods to defeat a demon named Mahishasur. Durga combines self sufficiency and power with fierce compassion and defeated Mahishasur, who terrorized earth, heaven and the nether worlds and could not be defeated by any other god, even the most powerful. And she beat him, laughing while she did it, this supremely radiant goddess.

This is the woman for me! I also have a demon who cannot be defeated by any other god.

As I say, we met at the nursing station in the hospital where Deirdre was staying and Dr. Navine recommended the place where Dee is now, promised she would put in a good word, and did so.

Afterwards, Drew and I were downstairs, standing in the lobby waiting out a fierce summer storm, and Ishana stepped off the elevator and joined us. While we talked about this and that, she reached up and touched my face and looked in my eyes.

"Tumor?" she said.

I nodded.

"I can tell by the eyes. You can tell a lot by the eyes, it's the first sign a woman is pregnant, long before the ultrasound."

I trust her. I want her to look after me and I'm sure she'll take me, especially when I say I want to fight this thing with everything she's got, radiation, pills, chemotherapy, I don't care how it hurts, I want as much as I can get, as much time as I can get. And she'll do it, death is her personal enemy, I can sense that. We'll be in this together. She'll do it laughing.

It won't be easy. Maybe I won't be aware, not much, but at least I'll have a chance that Drew will be back and I'll see her again. The end will be the same, but I can stand it.

I think about Erica and Page. The saddest part of all would have been, if they had never been born. Sometimes I think they are out there, in the next room, watching TV. I can't change things, I can't bring them back, but I'm glad that I had them as long as I did. They blessed my life, they made it worth living

There are stars and planets forming now, up there in the morning beyond our world, in constellations like Orion. Maybe, whoever is up there, will do better. I hope so.

We have been here, this talking life form of ours, for a mere million years. There is so much more to come, we will come apart and re-form, the carbon that makes us up, into something much better. I know that there is no reason for believing that, nothing in my life would justify it, not the things I have done or the things that have been done, or the hell that lives inside us all, but I believe it anyway and I will live just as long as I can. They think I'm crazy anyway.

Maybe peace is something a little crazy.

And in the meantime, I will fight.